*the*

# THRICE-GIFTED

*child*

SHADOW JOURNEY SERIES
BOOK TWO

*the*

# THRICE-GIFTED

*child*

SHADOW JOURNEY SERIES
BOOK TWO

## JO ALLEN ASH

Potter Street Books
Zionsville PA
2023

ISBN: 979-8-9870681-0-6

© 2022 – All rights reserved

Printed in the U.S.A.

Potter Street Books/Robin Maderich Publishing

Cover design by Robin Maderich

This book is also available in digital format.

# DEDICATION

*it is in darkness that*

*the light shines brightest*

# AUTHOR'S NOTE

Despite it's dark and terrifying attributes, there is a light in this story that lives in all of us. For this reason, I find myself happy to return to this particular world, to write again about Duncan and Grace, Carina and Mika, and, of course, the enigmatic child, Resa. They continue to grow on the pages as they do in my head. And, so no one gets bored, several more characters have made their way into these pages, each going through their own growth, their own changes.

Another book will follow this one, and still another after that. I hope you stick with us—me, and my young, troubled heroes—because your readership is so very much appreciated.

# ACKNOWLEDGEMENTS

I want to thank all those who read *The Shadows We Make* and expressed themselves so wonderfully in their reviews, their conversations with me and others.

I also wish to thank the various entities who assisted me with publicity with that book and this one. I've never been very adept at marketing or tooting my own horn.

I thank, also, the various bookstores who permitted, even encouraged me to put myself out there for book signings. I met members of the public whom I won't forget. My thanks to all of you, as well, for keeping me going.

I especially want to thank, though, those who believed in this book, *The Thrice-Gifted Child,* the second in the Shadow Journey Series. I'm hoping I haven't let you down.

*Grace*

Chapter One

When I was a child, I mean a very small child, I believed in the tales we were told. Not as if they were true, but as if they held a frightening yet somehow glorious, never-ending possibility of truths. Now, at sixteen, I knew the tales for what they really were: lies. Because the truth in them, the absolute truth in them, was so much worse than what we had been given to imagine.

Swearing, weapon in hand, I rose from the ground and stared through the darkness beneath the trees. I'd heard tales about The Wilds, too, and fully anticipated these truths might end up far graver than my mind could fathom. Yet to come here to this place had been imperative. With Stone Tiran's soldiers pursuing us, the best place to hide had to be the one they'd least expect. No one went into The Wilds. Not willingly. Not with any expectation they'd come back out. Besides, and maybe more importantly, knowledge existed in the stories associated with the Wildron. I only hoped we would survive to find it.

Years ago—centuries—mages broke from the tribes and sought refuge in The Wilds. They never returned to the world they'd known. But it was rumored mage lore lived on, passed on by word of mouth from generation to generation. I had need of this knowledge. Not to use it. As a warrior trained and blooded, my gifts were established. But with what I held trapped in the crystal hidden within the bag around my neck, I planned to learn something to save us all.

*Skelly,* I said, *I want to help you.*

*A little late for that,* he answered, his voice wisping through my brain.

My breath went out, slowly, as I took in the shadowed figures in the night. I adjusted my stance, berating myself for not having heard them coming. I should have. I always did. I'd become careless, useless to my companions. A warrior did not fail at her duty.

Yet, it appeared even the *conjure* was caught unaware. Alarmed, and therefore more dangerous than usual, the beast now crashed in my direction across the small clearing where we'd camped, stomping straight through the dying fire with his huge cloven hooves, scattering embers over my friends and startling them awake. Not Resa, though, I pleaded in silent desperation; please, not Resa, not profoundly gifted Resa. In her panic, Duncan's sister wouldn't differentiate between friend and foe.

The *conjure's* thickly-furred shoulder struck Duncan, who had risen beside me with makeshift spear in hand. Duncan hit the ground hard, his weapon clattering away. Prudently, he stayed put.

Chauncy—yes, I had given the brute a ridiculous name—thrust its head into the air above mine, hot breath shifting the curling strands broken free from my braid. I dashed them away with a forearm. The animal's corkscrew horn pointed into the air before us both like a bowsprit, nearly as long as I was tall.

"Be easy," I said. I had no idea if he'd recognize any authority behind the instruction. They were independent creatures, *conjures*, only rarely developing symbiotic relationships with such as me. The relationship required a lengthy process. We'd been together less than two days, a time measurement that meant nothing to a *conjure*. Even so, the creature had chosen to protect me in the first instant we met. Whether he did so by instinct or cognitive reasoning was probably something I'd never know, yet I found instinct the more disturbing choice. Instinct so rarely proved wrong. If he protected me by instinct, then danger was real.

Forcibly dismissing this thought, I studied the figures arrayed in a rough circle beneath the trees, counting the ones I could see without turning my head. I didn't want to appear weak or unnerved, refusing to glance around as if their numbers mattered. Far better to stand tall and unafraid. I could do so, because even disheveled and dirty and far too thin, I was and would always be a warrior of the Ser Irese. Nothing taking place in these past months could alter my heritage, my training, my determination.

Once called Olympian, The Wilds had been blasted and harvested by war and overgrown by vegetation through multiple generations. The people who inhabited the place had a reputation for being fierce, violent and intolerant, keeping to themselves. They didn't welcome strangers. They clearly didn't appear ready to welcome us.

In hooded cloaks colored like the night, some held raised, mechanized bows, extended, arrows nocked, while still more held weapons resembling the impulse used by Citadel guards, designed to release deadly energy pulses. I slowly bent my knees, lowering to the ground my *lathesa,* the weapon I'd constructed from fire-hardened wood to resemble the one I'd once owned, the one given to me by my mentor upon completion of my warrior's training, the one Stone Tiran had ordered taken away before sentencing me to death.

I straightened, hands up, palms out, grateful in the knowledge that in that last at least Tiran had failed. I still lived. So far.

"We mean no harm," I said. No one reacted. I repeated the words again, using the dialect often employed in the desert markets during haggling, a mixture combining common words from many tribes.

Someone snorted. "You were understood the first time."

I couldn't discern which mouth among the shadowed faces had spoken. I dropped my arms to my side, empty palms still facing out. Duncan scrambled to his feet behind me. I heard him but didn't look, hoping he had left his spear on the ground. The others hadn't moved since they'd bolted upright beneath flying ash. I risked a glance at Resa. She remained on the ground asleep with

Carina's hand on her back.

"We—my companions and I—did not mean to trespass." I tried to sound both confident and apologetic, although I felt anything but. Angered frustration coursed through me. I'd truly grown quite tired of persecution, of fear. As if sensing this, Duncan pressed his hand against my shoulder blade.

"Ignorance has never excused anyone," the same voice shot back. Arrogant, male. I'd almost picked him out, the speaker, but they stood too close together for me to be certain.

I could have taken him on without a problem, if necessary, but he was not alone and neither was I. Those I could see outnumbered us three to one. I had a responsibility to Duncan and Carina, to Mika and Duncan's sister. Everything that had happened in the past day was my fault. I'd thought I could do it alone, bargain, make an exchange: myself for Resa. I'd been wrong. In unguarded moments, I caught a look from Duncan, an expression, a tilt to his eyes, plainly saying he had not forgotten betrayal. Because it was betrayal. A betrayal of trust.

"I have no wish to be excused," I said to the speaker, "only to explain."

"We don't accept explanations, either."

"Okay, now he's just being a jackass," Duncan whispered. I jerked my head, shushed him. Like a child. He wouldn't like that either.

I straightened my shoulders, lifted my chin. "Very well," I said. "What, then, do you accept?"

This seemed to set the hooded fellow back a mental pace or two. Above my head, Chauncy growled, brandishing his fiendish-looking horn a bit from side to side. I heard a small whimper at ground level. Resa had started to waken, the gods help us.

"Carina," I said.

"I've got it." Her voice betrayed exhaustion, the tone weak, harried. I drew a deep breath, let it out. A possibility existed that things were about to go bad very quickly. I felt it in my weary bones, like an ache, like a rumbling in the ground beneath my feet, vibrating straight into my skull.

I glanced again at the *lathesa* I'd set down as a good faith gesture. Not too far away. I'd made sure of that. Mentally, I measured distances, contemplated how many I could take down before being overwhelmed. I wasn't worried so much about the bows as I was the impulse weapons, my friends in direct line of fire. I considered how swiftly I'd have to retrieve my own weapon from the ground and deploy it, pictured the spin in my hands, the strike, knowing there were too many arrayed against us. I tried very hard not to anticipate failure. To anticipate failure would mean failure, and I had to succeed. I would lose too much otherwise. All of them, friends I had never expected to find, could be killed.

Suddenly another voice spoke into the stillness left by my prior question.

"How do you come to be in command of the beast?"

I turned, frowned, attempted to locate the speaker.

"How do you come to be in command of the beast?" the voice asked again with remarkable patience considering how the questioning had been proceeding. A woman's tones, odd and coarse, as if she might be in need of hydration. How well I remembered that desperate lack. How well we all did.

I glanced up at the horn hovering in the air above me, thought about the razor-edged incisors positioned somewhere behind my head, the beast's huge size, his alarming countenance. People feared *conjures*, and with sound reason. I knew the stories. A *conjure* could remove a man's head with far less provocation than what Chauncy might be perceiving this very minute, with an array of weapons pointed in our direction. After all, he possessed that strange guardian determination. It might be best for all of us if I let them believe I did command him. Even so, I spoke the truth. Perhaps, I shouldn't have, but I couldn't snatch back the words once they'd exited my mouth. Besides, truth was supposed to be a warrior's keenest weapon.

"I do not command the *conjure*," I said.

"Am I to understand it protects you of its own accord?"

I hadn't asked for the animal's defense. Having it meant Chauncy constantly sensed a danger to me, if not to all of us. The fact it hadn't diminished remained a constant worry. Breg, the Ogdonian driver who had rescued us as we fled Tiran's temporary stronghold, had told me this. He'd recognized the *conjure's* change in allegiance.

Except it wasn't allegiance, not exactly. Not even loyalty, but more something resembling a forbearance for which I should be grateful.

"I have been told so, yes," I admitted.

I heard several whispered exclamations, sounding more like a rushing wind than voices. Yet, I heard words in that wind, cut short when the first speaker sliced the air with his hand in a cutting gesture.

"Who are you?" the woman asked. I saw her now, or the form of her, stepping away from the rest in her long, concealing cloak. "What are you called?"

Duncan's hand dropped from my shoulder, thumping against his borrowed clothes. I lifted my chin. Perhaps misplaced at this point, a prideful thrill shot through my veins. "I am Grace Irese, of the Ser Irese," I said, "and my companions are—"

"We do not care who the others are." The male again. Surly. Rude. Duncan tensed beside me.

"You should," I snapped, "because I do. Very much."

A hissing followed my statement, unpleasant in the extreme. It came from them, the Wildron, seeming to indicate their displeasure. I witnessed a sudden shift among them, as if they'd all moved a handspan to the left so quickly my eye barely caught it. I tensed, glancing to the weapon at my feet again. Although I possessed the capacity to wield the *lathesa* with great efficiency, too many stood against us. Still, I could protect my companions as much as possible until the end. I steeled myself, a heaviness in my heart I should not have allowed in. I knew better.

Abruptly, the woman raised her hand. The sibilant drone sputtered to a stop. The dark cloaks shimmered with violent motion and settled again. Intrigued, I studied them more closely, trying to ascertain how they managed the baffling movement. It definitely unnerved, which I figured might be the entire point to the display.

The female cleared her throat. I swung my gaze back in her direction, searching for the face beneath the hood. As if aware of my intent, she pushed the garment back. Duncan gasped. I managed to keep my reaction in check.

I had seen faces like hers before among my own people, aged, regal, fierce, battle-scarred. This woman's countenance possessed an oddly precise delineation between the ravages caused by fire and those by time, making it appear as though she wore half a mask like a disguise. I dragged my gaze away from the pale, ropelike scars mapping her flesh and met her eyes. She stared back, her own gaze shifting to linger overlong on the warrior's tattoo on my cheek. I would have thought the mark no more than a smudged shadow in the dark. Perhaps her strange blue eyes saw more clearly than most.

"Grace Irese, we have heard of you," she said.

"How?" Duncan demanded. I suppose he couldn't help it.

She ignored him, waiting on me to speak. "Why would you know my name here in this place?" I asked.

"Because Citadel was burned for you," the woman said. "Everyone knows that tale."

"That's a lie!" Again, Duncan. I wished he would shut up. He was going to be the one to get us killed if he didn't watch himself.

"He did not mean to say you lie," I apologized for him.

"I should hope not," the woman said in heavy warning.

I took a deep breath. "The story you've heard is untrue, however. Citadel was burned by Stone Tiran in war, to take control of government, not because I had refused him in pact. The implication otherwise is absurd."

"Oh," whispered Duncan, "good on you, diffusing the tension with that remark."

I curled my lip at him, not quite a growl.

The woman's face moved, only one side, the unburned side, twisting up, mouth opening. A sound barked into the air. It might have been laughter. I couldn't fathom such a thing, but at this point, anything could be possible. "I know this," she said. "Tales are often manufactured without regard to truths, but merely to suit a purpose."

I said nothing, reached back and grabbed Duncan's wrist, avoiding his fractured fingers, silently urging him not to speak out again. "Out of the frying pan, into the fire," he whispered anyway, for my ears alone. Duncan Oaks habitually quoted his grandmother, sharing the words as if spouting out astounding wisdom. I'd heard this particular phrase several times in recent days. In this instance the timeworn adage might happen to be dead on. His hand turned, bandaged fingers somehow managing to tighten around mine. Duncan Oaks, the boy who'd betrayed me in a way from which there should have been no coming back. And yet... Yes, and yet.

I squeezed and let go. Chauncy stomped his enormous cloven hoof behind me, his knee joint catching my thigh, causing me to lurch in an unintentional step forward. A half dozen weapons tightened their aim.

I raised my hands once more in supplication. "We are no threat. We are only five."

"You are not only five," said the mutilated warrior.

Sucking a startled breath in through my nose, my fingers shot to my throat, to the bag lying hidden beneath my tunic. The large crystal snug inside pushed against my sternum from the pressure. *If you let me out, I can explain what I am to her with a little show and tell,* Skelly's voice whispered into my mind. *She'll be impressed, I promise you.*

My hands dropped. Could the woman possibly know what I concealed, not only from her, but from my companions? I suppressed the ice-cold shiver making its way beneath my clothes, up my spine, across my arms. I had no means to control what Skelly Shane had become. When I'd called his manifestation down into the crystal back in Tiran's compound, I'd only accomplished it through some unexpected sympathetic reflex. If these people discovered what I carried, contained but uncontrolled, they wouldn't hesitate to attack. I couldn't blame them.

But my friends would not pay the price. I would see to that, no matter what I had to give up.

The woman made a small movement with her head, indicating the enormous horn still swaying above me. "You have the *conjure,*" she said.

Chauncy. I hadn't considered him. Relief made me weak-kneed. I tightened muscle, tendon, joints, to keep myself standing upright. "That is so," I agreed, "but we are still outnumbered. With all your weaponry, I doubt even the *conjure* stands a chance."

*You know what I can do, Grace. With me, you can cease your worry and save them all.*

I closed my eyes, squeezed them shut, forcing Skelly from my conscious thoughts. When I lifted my lids again, I saw the Wildron's weapons had all been lowered toward the ground. They were quite well unified, these Wildron. Precision marked their movements, their weapons at an exact level before them, their bodies all held in similar stance. Like well-practiced soldiers. I hadn't been aware anyone in The Wilds maintained a standing army. These warriors appeared to be rigorously trained. Why?

My gaze shifted at movement to one side. I'd been wrong about some of them. A group, including the male speaker, stood together. They did not possess the same symmetry as the rest. In fact, they appeared to be exchanging looks beneath their hoods. Perhaps noting my study, their attention suddenly snapped back to me.

"Why are you here, Grace of the Ser Irese?" the scarred warrior asked. "You bring outside strife to a place where we have permitted none for as long as only the eldest among us can remember. Those such as I am," she added, as if I hadn't caught the reference.

I bowed my head in respect for her age and position, the way I'd been taught, the way it had been drummed into me. Even if the teaching hadn't stuck, I recognized the necessity here and now. Offense would serve no purpose. "I understand. We did not mean to. I only—"

Duncan stepped past me. "We seek sanctuary."

I whipped around and gaped at him. Chauncy danced sideways at my abrupt movement. Mika let out an exclamation, likely shoved to the ground by an animal which showed no respect for personal space.

"Duncan," I whispered, reaching for his sleeve. He sidestepped away, straightening his spine beneath his soiled shirt. He tossed the dark hair from his eyes.

The ancient warrior turned toward him. "And who might you be?"

"I am...I am Duncan Oaks, of the...of the Oaks."

Something flickered in the woman's gaze, tightening the skin around her eyes. Amusement? Dismissal? When she spoke, her voice disclosed neither. "But you have no tribe, Duncan Oaks."

He tried to hold his stance, but his shoulders slumped. "No, m'am."

I wanted to hug him; me, the undemonstrative one. Hug him for all we'd been through together, for the moments when his actions had shone so brightly, for the times I wanted nothing more than to punch him in the nose.

"He has us," I stated. Though I spoke softly, my voice carried. She inclined her head in acknowledgment, continuing to address him.

"But you are brave."

"No, m'am," he said again. I imagined hugging him harder. Duncan, dear Duncan.

"I believe you are," the woman said. She spent a moment longer scrutinizing his face before turning to me. "You are wise to surround yourself by those who are loyal to you, Grace."

"These are my friends," I said, "not some strategic decision."

"Yet you met as total strangers only a short time ago."

My eyes narrowed. True, what she said, yet circumstances had bound us as fiercely as time. Maybe more so. "Wait," I said, as realization hit like a slap, a warning, "how do you know this?"

She pivoted her attention deliberately away, back to Duncan.

"So, you seek sanctuary, do you?"

Duncan jerked his gaze up, away from the ground at his feet where he'd possibly been considering his mistake in asking for sanctuary. I felt sure he possessed some notion sanctuary held universal meaning, that certain rules would be followed in that regard. That we'd be safe. No, we'd only be in their control.

"I do," he said, ignoring my gaze in his direction. "For all of us, not just me."

"Even the beast?" the woman asked, signifying Chauncy with a hand.

He hesitated. "Yes," I said, before a debate could ensue, "even for the beast."

She returned her focus to me. Scarred and aged, I could see she had once been formidable and beautiful; that she still was. "Sanctuary," she said.

"Are you certain?"

The figure I presumed had been doing all the talking earlier strode forward, tossing back the dark hood to reveal a face as unmarred as the other's was battered; definitely male, not any older than I, perhaps not yet my age. I doubted his smooth skin had yet known a razor's application. I had to remind myself that both my male companions hadn't much use for one either. The boy looked first to Duncan and then to me, lips twisting into a smirk.

"We also don't do sanctuary," he said.

Chapter Two

"Dandy," Duncan muttered. "He's a sweetheart."

Peripherally, I caught Duncan's movement, saw him bending toward his fallen spear. "Don't," I said.

He checked, straightened. "Why not?"

"If you touch it, Duncan, we're already dead. Leave our weapons where they lie and we might yet be able to work something out."

He nodded toward the unhooded boy. "With that guy?"

"No," I said, "with her."

The Wildron woman watched us. Although we spoke quietly, she appeared to be picking up on our conversation's gist. I considered what she'd said, her question: *sanctuary, are you sure*? The wording confirmed my concerns that sanctuary's provisions might contain some trap for us.

"How should I address you?" I asked, looking at her, not the male. He scowled. He didn't like being disregarded. As Duncan would likely say, oh well.

"I am called Nimue," she said. "I am Lyoness. And this—" she tipped her head sideways toward the boy, "is son of my daughter's son. Ren, he is called."

"Wren?" said Duncan. "Like the bird?"

This time, I did growl, a deep warning in my throat. I didn't know if the Wildron had knowledge of the tiny, skittish birds here, so far from Citadel's lovely gardens, gardens now burned to ash, but it seemed the Lyoness' great-grandson did. If not, he merely recognized the reckless taunt in Duncan's tone. Ren shifted his weight forward, onto the foot nearest us, his grip tightening on the bow he lifted. The old warrior raised a hand and he lowered the weapon with great reluctance.

"Ren," he snapped, glaring at Duncan, "like Renegade."

"Ren," Duncan echoed, "like Renegade. My pardon." He didn't sound in the least bit contrite. I wanted to kick him, knock him to the ground. It might come to that, if arrows started flying. As for Ren, he bore a chip on his shoulder worse than mine. I'd always been aware my attitude fell short, at least as far as my elders were concerned, and I hadn't much cared, but I witnessed now how annoying and hazardous it could be.

"Enough," Nimue said, her gravelly voice carrying. "Sanctuary, Grace, or no?"

"May I…may we have a moment?" I asked.

Nimue tilted her chin. "Your choices are limited, but yes. A moment." Ren mumbled something I couldn't hear to the person nearest him. Both heads turned toward the Lyoness, Ren's expression marked by several things I recognized: Concern, indecision. Fear?

Leaving Duncan where he stood, I ducked around Chauncy. Mika had, indeed, been knocked down by the *conjure*. He'd landed near Carina and Duncan's sister and sat beside them, brushing dirt from his clothes, his eyes on Carina.

Duncan scurried around behind Chauncy's rump, pausing beside us. "Well?"

I narrowed my eyes at him. "Is there any chance you could stop talking?"

"What? Why?"

"Nothing, never mind." I exhaled, turning away from him to study Carina. Her skin, nearly colorless already, looked paler still, almost translucent. The white hair tangled down her back seemed to have more substance than her flesh.

"Carina," I said. She glanced up at me, transmutable eyes a color I'd never seen them before, an odd and sickly green. Shadows like bruises curved beneath. I dropped to my knees. "Carina, you look terrible."

"I'm fine," she said.

"No. You're not." All her energy had been focused in keeping Resa calm or contained in a dreamless, slumbering state. She'd done the same for Duncan, for me, taking our pain, our altered, despairing, angered outlooks into herself. The toll had been obvious then, for something that had lasted only minutes. With Resa, she'd had to shut her down again and again since we'd rescued her. I feared permanent damage, perhaps to both. Carina would never give up her vigil, though, no matter the risk. I touched her hand. She released a shuddering, wearied breath.

"Speak," she said, "quickly."

I moved closer. "Duncan asked for sanctuary. If we don't accept, I can't be sure how much worse off we will be."

"I think you must accept it, but be wary. Seek what you need," she said, answering while she could. "Someone's mind may be blocking mine. I know nothing for certain."

I rose, nodded, glancing at Mika's naked emotion quickly shuttered, and away. I didn't believe anyone to be blocking her mind. Her strength, and therefore her gift, were failing. We had to figure out something else quickly. "Thanks, Carina. You'll be able to rest soon, I promise."

Mika raised a hand to his bald pate, running his palm across a bit of sprouting stubble. He'd at least had some familiarity with a razor, but no longer. The most rudimentary toiletries didn't exist for us anymore. He looked up at me.

"Mika?"

"Don't make promises you can't keep, Grace. I know you try, you always try, and you usually succeed, but a time will come when you won't. You know that."

"But—"

"No, Grace," he said, "accept it."

At his words, my face crumpled. I gulped a few times, trying to contain my irresponsible, tearful response. After a few moments, I managed to control myself and scoured my cheeks with my palms, smearing away the shaming tears. I dropped my fists to my side. Angered at myself more than anything Mika had said, I shook my head. "I won't accept any such thing. Carina will be fine. Resa will be fine. We'll all make it through this. Understand? All of us."

"Grace and her promises," Duncan said beside me.

Mika looked up at him, expression shifting in unspoken communication. "Grace and her promises," he echoed.

I swung my head, frowning at first one, then the other.

"So, we're agreed?" I said to both. "Sanctuary, and we'll deal with whatever comes from that?"

They nodded.

"Fine, then I'll go tell Nimue, shall I?"

I didn't wait for an answer but stalked back beneath Chauncy's head, calling out for the Lyoness. I stopped short. She wasn't there.

I checked the trees, the darker shadows beneath them, assuring she and the others had slipped away, leaving as silently as they'd come. Not all, though. Ren and about a dozen Wildron remained, all pointing their varied weapons at me.

I waved my hand. "Where have they gone?"

Ren looked at me as if I had no right to ask such a question. His eyebrows arched, oddly dark eyebrows with the hair on his head so...yellow. "The Lyoness said your answer would be yes. She said you had no choice. So, we are to escort you." He jerked his bow in Chauncy's direction. "Keep your beast in check or we will shoot it down."

I eyed him, his posture, his expression, a look

in his eye I could see clearly now he'd drawn closer. A good front, a false bravado. We all did it when afraid. Being afraid didn't make us cowards. If recognized and controlled, it made us smart. I didn't think he possessed the insight to fear me, to be honest, or my companions, or even the *conjure*. He probably didn't fear his great-grandmother, either. He hadn't enough natural respect to fear her. Besides, she'd gone. I didn't know what his problem was. I didn't think his fear would make him respond intelligently, though.

I listened, wondering if it might be something nearby beneath the trees spooking him. The forest around us did seem abnormally still. No wind, no sounds made by creatures other than ourselves, although this might have been due to Chauncy's presence. I heard no telltale noise in the distance as the contingent moved away. I should have heard something, because they couldn't have gone far. It had only been a few minutes. Indeed, I ought to have heard them, seen them, when they first surrounded us. I'd not been asleep, after all. I'd been standing watch.

I remembered how Skelly Shane had walked in silence, always appearing without warning. He'd thought it made him somehow potent, invincible. Stealth certainly hadn't saved him. It was darned unnerving, though.

"We'll get the wagon loaded," I said.

He jerked his bow. "No. No wagon. The trails will not accommodate."

I swore, loud enough Ren heard me. Duncan was always on me about my mouth, although he had little room to talk.

"Nice," said Ren, his tone not exactly reading sarcasm.

I paid no heed to his comment. "We have two among us who won't be able to walk far," I said.

"Won't the beast carry them? You control it."

"You weren't listening. I do not. Besides, have you ever heard a *conjure* to permit such an affront?"

He lifted his head and shrugged. "We'll leave the weak ones behind, then."

I reached out, shoved my fingers into Chauncy's thick coat. "No," I said to Ren, "we will not."

Thus challenged, he hesitated, glancing at those nearest him again. I heard a footstep, glanced over my shoulder to find Duncan there, looking grim, solid, strangely daunting. Duncan Oaks, who didn't recognize his own courage. I'd rather him at my back, Carina and Mika, too, than any number of these Wildron warriors.

"I'll carry Resa," Duncan said. "No problem." The last he directed at Ren, holding his gaze, as challenging as I had been. Only this time, Ren bristled like an old warrior's chin.

"Let's pack everything up," I directed Duncan, stepping between them. "Ren, we'll need some time. We have supplies still in the wagon to be redistributed among us for transport." The Ogdonians had been generous. Breg had provided the *conjure* and the wagon along with blankets, water and food, before kicking us from their territory and setting off with several others to fabricate a trail to mislead Tiran's soldiers. For the

Ogdonians' sakes as well as ours, I wasn't about to leave any supplies behind. "We'll be happy to share, if needed," I added as I prepared to duck again beneath Chauncy's head.

"Wait."

I looked back. Ren's features twisted in silent debate. "Fine. Take the wagon." He blew a breath out past his lips, no doubt irritated with himself for his own capitulation.

"Thank you," I said.

"We will reach a point where you'll have to abandon it. Understood?"

"Understood." I turned, bent, scooped my *lathesa* from the ground and moved on. Let him try to take my weapon from me.

Duncan followed me over. Most provisions had not been removed from the cart bed. The few items lying about on the ground were quickly restored to their places. I kicked dirt over the dead fire, knocking the ashy remnants about until the last ember expired. Duncan lifted his sister from the ground. She woke, saw his face and smiled, the first I'd seen from her. He carried her to the wagon, a light weight, undersized for twelve. Still, she had Carina beat, in height at least. I studied Resa a moment clinging to her brother in his arms, wondering if it had ever occurred to him his sister's heritage was not his. At least not on both sides. In my head, I'd questioned her parentage when I first saw her image on the prison's library monitor. I hadn't asked Duncan though. I wouldn't.

Mika followed with Carina, helping her inside. I heard him telling her to rest. I thought she could actually have a respite, as Resa seemed content with her brother for now, unafraid, watching his fingers as he signed to her.

Only one more thing remained to be done. I strode to the wagon's front, slipped my *lathesa* under the bench seat and drew out Chauncy's halter. The tiny bells—meant to soothe the *conjure* as well as warn one and all the beast approached—sang in the night air with a delicate sweetness. More bells lined the traces lying slack along the ground. I looked to Chauncy, who looked back, showing me a choleric eye.

"Really?" I chided. "Now is not the time." I held the halter up in both hands.

Following a brief standoff, Chauncy sauntered over, settled his horn on my shoulder and slid the serrated edges over bone, rather painfully, until his head came close to mine. I refused to acknowledge his incisors' proximity to my face, calmly fitting the jingling halter around his head and fastening the buckles, my eyes not far from his. He possessed a white ring around the nearest, ruining the symmetry as well as the full horrifying effect otherwise to be found in his fearsome countenance.

Moving away, I speculated again on Ren's reasons for being afraid. We might all know the cause soon enough. Whatever frightened the arrogant Ren would likely be a danger to me and my friends, too. One more reason to keep my eyes open and my weapon near to hand.

Chauncy followed me around the cart and stood with remarkable patience while I completed his attachment into the conveyance's apparatus. After checking to make sure everyone else had settled into the wagon bed, I climbed into the seat, turning to let Ren know we were ready. I noted right away he was down three cohorts.

"Where did the others go?" I demanded.

"Gone," he said.

"Gone? Where?"

He compressed his lips, declining to reply.

Gone. Vanished was more like it. I frowned into the nighttime shadows beneath the trees, searching for movement, but the dark cloaks and whatever clandestine craft these people possessed kept them hidden. At a signal from Ren to move out, Chauncy jerked the wagon forward and followed him, not taking orders from Ren, but assessing the situation and acting in accordance. He as easily could have refused to budge or bolted, if the situation warranted. I took some comfort in the fact he'd chosen compliance. It had to be a good sign, or at least not a bad one.

We made our way along the rutted track, the reins hanging limp from my hands, as Breg had instructed me. He'd said there would be no need to use them, and he'd been right. The *conjure* appeared to glean direction in some other manner. Berg had called it "mind-tea infusion." My own mind set at the time had been too dour to react, but I suddenly found the term quite funny.

"What are you laughing at?" Ren demanded.

"Nothing," I said.

Glowering, he ordered several Wildron to drop back to take up positions behind the wagon, weapons at the ready. Duncan, with Resa thankfully drowsing at his shoulder, fixed his gaze in a fierce glare on Ren's yellow head. Sensing my eyes on him, Duncan glanced over to me and adjusted his features into a humorous display of displeasure, like a comical snarl. Ren rubbed me wrong, he really did, but for Duncan it seemed personal somehow, which made no sense. The two were acting like captive *lyawars* in a confined space, reflecting an animosity that could end up a huge problem.

I turned back to Ren. "Where are we going?"

I thought he might not answer. He certainly took his time doing so. "To the City of All Dwellers," he said. "I'm sure you've never heard of it."

"I have not," I said, trying to be less abrasive. "Is it anywhere near the former capital? Birthright, I think it was once called, before it's destruction."

A look shot my way, then returned to the darkness ahead. "It *is* the former capital," he said. "I see they teach you something of history where you're from."

My jaw clenched. I forced it to loosen. "Yes," I said, "we are all well-educated where I'm from. It surprises me you'd believe otherwise. Is there really anything in the City of All Dwellers? I'd heard this whole province remains one huge forest of ruin."

Duncan snorted behind me, recognizing my annoyance at Ren's disdain. I heard a soft chuckle from Mika, too. Ren glanced back at them both before addressing my question, lips stiff.

"Yes, there is. You won't be laughing, I promise you."

I exhaled, closed my eyes, thinking of my

brothers. I'd been very young when they were about the age of Ren and Duncan and Mika, but I realized with sudden clarity why my mother expended so much energy reprimanding them.

*　　*　　*

We traveled deeper into the wooded Wilds for many hours without the need to abandon the wagon. Once Carina awakened, she sat close again to Resa, distracting her by untangling and plaiting multiple braids into Resa's long black hair. Resa seemed not to notice anything strange in the guard accompanying us. She barely looked at them.

Around midday, Duncan and Mika portioned out food. I suggested tactfully, and with the hope such an offer might tender a little less animosity, that they offer some to our Wildron companions. Ren and several others accepted. The rest turned it down with silent head-shaking or a waving hand. Ren's acquiescence and quiet gratitude surprised me, although not as much as the refusal from the rest. They hadn't eaten anything on the march. Apparently, they possessed far more stamina than I credited them with.

Curious, I studied them closely again, from their lightweight garments to the way they carried themselves. Frowning, I noticed one thing further. A few more had abandoned their ranks. I lurched upright from the wagon bench and stood. Chauncy took exception and jerked between the shafts, almost tumbling me over.

Regaining my footing, I checked the forest to all sides, then counted the Wildron number again.

Satisfied I'd not make a mistake, I swung toward Ren. "Where are they?"

"Who?" he growled, reverting to his usual surly self.

I indicated the remaining Wildron. Counting Ren, they were now seven. "More of you are gone."

He glanced around, then to the trail, before looking back around again. "Yeah," he said. "So?" At some point, he'd picked up a leafy bough from the ground and was using it to wave away swarming insects as he walked. He avoided my eye. His nonchalance didn't fool me.

"Had you any idea they'd gone?"

He didn't respond. I frowned. How could he not know? He must have sent them on ahead. I studied the seven Wildron left, measuring our chances to take advantage of their lessening numbers. Very possibly, we were heading into a trap the vanished members had gone on to prepare. I couldn't understand why. We had accompanied them willingly.

In truth, none of them had made any claims as to their place in society. They all might easily be nothing more than bandits, intent on taking our possessions and supplies at some vantage point ahead. Yet why wait? Such robbery could have been more easily accomplished when we were outnumbered by so many.

I assessed those who remained, noting only three among them held impulses. Those three would have to be disarmed first. Space existed between them to permit me the necessary action, yet small enough to hinder theirs. Both impulse and arrow required distance for effectiveness and had no place in hand-to-hand combat. If necessary, I could handle all seven by myself.

Still, I hoped it would not come to that. I had to trust that if not sanctuary at least some situation we could work with existed in the City of All Dwellers. We needed a place to rest, regain strength, figure out what to do next, find, I hoped, an answer to my many questions. We'd made impossible escapes before and we'd do so again if we had to.

It occurred to me that leaving her great-grandson to bring us safely in might be a test devised by the Lyoness. Among the desert tribes, warriors were given such trials during training. Perhaps this was why his companions kept drifting away, to increase the difficulty. Ren's concern about failure in this task could explain the trepidation I'd sensed…or not. I knew next to nothing about the Wildron as a people, about their customs, their beliefs. The little knowledge I claimed to have, had been based in stories, not fact.

I couldn't keep second guessing myself. What I knew with certainty was that if we left The Wilds now, we couldn't run fast enough to escape Tiran's soldiers, his turncoat warriors, the Citadel guards. As long as no one expected us to seek refuge in The Wilds, we might yet be safe.

I sat back down, observing for a moment the metronomic movement made by Chauncy's single horn as he plodded along the narrowing track. Soon we would have to abandon the wagon. The conveyance had nearly rubbed against the trees at certain points already. Once necessary for all to travel on foot, I supposed we could rig a blanket between two branches, load the supplies into it and drag the contraption along behind. Well, I could drag it. Duncan and Mika would likely have their hands full with Resa and Carina.

I sighed, lowering my head into my hand. The other hand pressed against the bag hidden beneath my tunic.

*Cheer up, buttercup, you're not alone. You got me.*

My spine snapped straight, head lurching up, both hands slapping down onto my thighs.

"You all right?"

Ren. Looking up at me, fingers curled against the wagon's side, he seemed to display real concern. I couldn't figure him out. I didn't want to, not on any personal level. I especially didn't want his sympathy. Suddenly, the conveyance rocked. Duncan clambered over the seat and plopped down next to me.

"Of course, she is," he said.

With a muttered invective, Ren stalked away. Realizing how close he was to Chauncy's head, he veered to the side, circling back to walk beside a Wildron who'd chosen to share our food. In fact, he or she—the flowing cloak prevented loose identification—still gnawed a hunk of bread.

"Seriously," Duncan said, "are you okay?"

Exhaustion dragged at my limbs. "Tired."

"Is that all?"

"Isn't it enough?"

"I didn't mean that. I didn't know if something else might be wrong. I'm not surprised you're tired.

We've all been going flat out since we escaped the facility."

We had been, not only fleeing and fighting and hiding, but also evading death. One of us hadn't managed the last. Again, almost of its own accord, my hand stole up toward the concealed crystal. I forced it back down to my lap.

Duncan's fingers skipped across the bench and settled onto mine. "It'll be all right."

I pulled my hand from his. I didn't need him weakening me further. "I know it will, Duncan. I just don't know when."

He nodded, eyes returning to the path running through the trees. Unlike Emerald, where almost no sunlight made it to the planet's surface, here shining shafts cut through the tree canopy at regular intervals. Miniscule wings shimmered in the light. Birds about as big around as my fist blew through the midge clouds, plump and greedy, snapping up what they could in their tiny, pointed blue beaks.

"Do you see that?" Duncan asked quietly. He'd lifted his hand to point, his right hand, broken fingers still bound in grubby bandages. Mika had promised to re-bind them. There hadn't been time.

I followed his pointing, glimpsing something odd through the trees. Like pigments dribbled down wet parchment, something appeared to be forming deeper in the forest, revealing itself bit by bit through gnarled trunks. I blinked to clear my vision, narrowing my lids for focus. I couldn't quite make it out, even though my eyesight usually outstripped Duncan's. For the past hour, the path had been climbing, accompanied by a rumbling bouncing off the large rocks on either side. Since the Wildron hadn't been reacting to the sound, I'd dismissed it as some natural echo made by the wagon's progress through the trees. I knew better now. It came from whatever Duncan had pointed out, thrumming in the air as we rounded a bend at the top of the rise. The vibrations pounded in my chest cavity.

"What is it?" I asked.

Duncan grinned, leaned close. "Never seen a waterfall, desert girl?"

My cheeks heated. I couldn't say why. "Actually, I haven't. Doesn't look much like water to me. Where are all those colors coming from?"

"The sun," Mika answered, from the wagon bed behind us. "Light refraction through the water droplets. I suspect there might be some phosphorescence going on, too, from plant matter?" He addressed his question to Ren, still trudging along on the wagon's left.

"Yes," Ren said, "and some element in the stones."

Mika had changed since our escape from the facility. We all had, but Mika especially seemed different, as if he'd given himself permission to be...*more.*

"Very well," I said. "I get it now. This is a—"

"A waterfall," said Ren, as if I needed reminding.

Waterfall seemed too simple a name for something so thunderous and colorful, so beautiful and powerful and, yes, frightening. I had no desire to get any closer to it and yet, I couldn't stop looking. After several seconds I addressed Ren again with another question.

He didn't answer. I spun on the seat, searching for him. He and the only three Wildron now left to him gaped openmouthed at the wagon's back end. Duncan swore and leaped over the seat with his arms outstretched.

Resa's power had broken free.

Chapter Three

Anything not strapped down in the wagon whipped in expanding circles through the air, glancing off trees, objects tumbling away into the near distance. Mika and Carina, too, flopping and spinning, attempting futilely to protect each other. Duncan struggled to maintain his balance, to push toward his sister while keeping his feet on the boards beneath him. I could see them slipping, see him lifting into the air to be borne away in the vicious whirlwind. As Carina had once done, I launched myself past him and right into the maelstrom, aiming—unlike Carina—without gentleness. I had no alternative. I could be flung away, too, so very easily.

The air sucked from my lungs upon collision with the cyclone force. Momentum carried my body forward, through the perimeter. Resa's newly braided hair cracked like whips against my face, my eyes, the arms I tried to close around her. My fist latched onto her shirt and I pulled her in. An instant later, we were tumbling from the wagon and crashing onto the hard, root-encrusted track.

Everything airborne slammed to the ground, Carina and Mika included. I heard Carina cry out, followed by words, and then she appeared beside us, blood smeared in a vivid lash across a too-white countenance. Fingers wide, reaching, she made contact. Resa's feebly thrashing form went still.

I pushed up from the ground, dragging a forearm across my face. Stinging tears streamed from eyes battered by Resa's braids. For a moment, I couldn't fully open them, relying on sound. After the ringing in my ears from the deafening clatter subsided, I heard only the rumbling forest.

Fighting to my feet, I looked to Chauncy first, his huge, blurred body remarkably calm in the traces. I spun next to Ren and his three companions, who still stood stunned and immobile. Next, Duncan, crouched beside Carina and his sister. Nearby, Mika wrestled himself into an upright position.

"Is everyone all right?" he asked.

No one answered. They all still breathed, though. I'd take that. On the ground beside Resa, Duncan lifted his head, looked straight at me. His eyes said something to me his mouth didn't.

"Duncan," I whispered, "I tried not hurt her. I was as careful as I could be."

"I know," he said, one beat too long in coming.

"I had no choice."

"I know."

He turned away. His head might know, but his heart clearly didn't. After going through the last episode with Resa together, he had to remember how hard the battle had been to stop her, to save her. We hadn't exactly come away unscathed. Except for Mika, we'd all carried noticeable new injuries. After being battered against the trees, Mika surely had plenty now of his own. I watched Duncan's tender ministrations, Carina's concentration beside him, willing Resa to calm.

"She isn't hurt, right?" I asked.

Duncan drew several deep breaths, finally sitting back on his heels. "She's okay," he said. "You… it's okay. You did what you had to. I know that. I really do. Thank you."

So oddly formal, that thanks. My lips twisted. I nodded. Crossing my arms, shoving my fisted hands beneath my biceps, I pivoted away. I would never hurt Duncan's sister, not by design. I'd done my best to protect her from the ground with my own body. She'd needed to be stopped before maiming or killing Mika and Carina, before the storm grew and took us all out. Duncan knew that. He couldn't have gotten through to her in time. He was already losing ground when I dove in.

Stomping around the wagon to the bench up front, I paused, head down, blowing air past my lips, listening to Ren and his companions in low discussion about what they'd just witnessed. Ren pushed for some action on their part, the specifics inaudible. I bit my lip, reached beneath the bench and yanked out my *lathesa.*

Spinning the weapon in my hands, I made the air whistle, disarming Ren and the warrior nearest his right in the same movement. Before they could recover, I'd taken out the next and, ready to use further tactics, was moving on to the last. He threw his metal bow to the ground without a fight. I swung about on my heel, facing Ren. His gaze was fixed on the weapon in my hands.

"Will you teach us that?"

I stared, startled and disbelieving. "What did you say?"

"Could you teach us that?"

Once, not that long ago, I'd begun instructing Duncan and the rest. The lessons had been short-lived. Circumstances had changed and we'd had to stop. "Why?" I asked.

One of the others bumped him in the arm with an elbow, as if to tell him to shut up. Ren's gaze dropped to the ground, to the weapons lying useless near my feet. He looked back up at me. The shock at being tactically disarmed had subsided. His expression hardened.

"We've heard stories about the desert warriors, about their skills."

"And you've heard stories about me, too, apparently. Or so your great-grandmother says."

He nodded. "We have," he said. "It's true. There's…talk."

I waited, meeting his eyes dead on. No one among them moved. They seemed to be waiting, too. "And you're not going to tell me what that talk is, are you."

"No."

Duncan appeared, moved past and around me, picking up the mechanized bows. He stopped at my side, clutching them all in his arms. "Anything else you wanted to ask?" he said.

"Yeah," said Ren, the word almost a snarl.

"What's up with the girl? Where's she from? How'd she do that?"

"The girl's name is Resa," said Duncan. "Resa is my sister."

"And?" said Ren.

"And nothing," I interrupted. "Why don't you tell me why you weren't as surprised by what you witnessed as you might have been? Are there tales about her, too?"

"Yes," he said. "There are tales of the thrice-gifted child."

The weapons jerked in Duncan's arms. I laid a hand on his elbow. I'd told Duncan what the guard had called her when we rescued Resa from the compound. This was now the second time she'd had been referred to in that fashion. My eyes narrowed. "What might those tales be?"

"We don't have time," Ren answered. "We need to get moving."

Duncan rattled the bows again, deliberately. "I don't think you're giving the orders anymore, do you?"

Ren scowled, lurched forward, stopped himself.

"We're still going with you," I said. "That hasn't changed. But you are outnumbered now. You've seen what I can do. You've seen what Resa can do, as well, but that has no bearing on what I am telling you. We are not your captives. We come with you willingly. Understood?"

Ren gave a short, begrudging nod.

"And before we move on, I have a question."

"Ask it, then."

"Where have the others gone? It is they who

have permitted you to be outnumbered." I was more than curious. Leaving Ren at a calculated disadvantage seemed less a test than desertion. I really needed to understand the reason for it.

He eyed the *lathesa* clasped loosely in my fist. A muscle in his cheek twitched. He turned to the others with him, looking a question at them one by one. The nearest lifted a hand, shoving back fabric to reveal a girl's face, around Ren's age, short-cropped flame-red hair, eyes a shade as silver as polished steel.

"Tell her, Ren."

He inhaled, deeply, causing a creak beneath his cloak. I realized he must wear something thicker than cloth beneath the garment. Leather, perhaps, as protection.

"Yes," said Duncan, "tell her, Ren."

I almost stomped on his foot. Came quite close, my own raised above his, heel downward, before good sense took over. We didn't want to be exposing dissent among the ranks.

"Please," I said. "I'd appreciate it."

Ren released a sigh, a loud expulsion only a decibel shy of rude. He shook his head, tossing his rather long hair away from his face. "Fine." He snorted another breath through his nose while shooting a sharp glance at the redhead. "Fine," he said again. "You want the truth?"

"Yes," I said.

"There are no others. There never were."

*     *     *

I couldn't help my reaction. Neither could Duncan, who blurted a few choice words.

"Ren," I said, "I don't understand. Are you saying there were only the four of you, even in the beginning, when we were surrounded?"

He nodded.

"What about the woman? The Lyoness? Your great-grandmother? I spoke with her. How is that possible?"

"They are the replicants," the redhead answered in Ren's stead.

"The replicants?" I echoed blankly.

"Yes. They are us, but not us. Holographic images. It was all we could muster."

I narrowed my eyes at her. Ren stared at the ground. To either side of me, Mika and Duncan kept silent. "Meaning?" I asked.

"Meaning we needed something more than the four of us for this."

"What is 'this'? You're not being very clear."

She waved her hand in a broad, encompassing gesture. "To take you," she said. "You, and your companions. You would not have accompanied us had we been but four."

"Hannah," Ren hissed in warning.

"I don't care," she said. "I will speak."

Beside me, Duncan snorted. He darted a hand to his mouth when Ren's gaze shifted his way. Hannah stepped forward.

"We wanted to reach you before anyone else did," she said.

"But the Lyoness—"

"She wasn't meant to be there," Hannah said.

"There could be trouble."

"Hannah." Ren again. His eyes were wide. Great-grandmother or not, he really did fear Nimue. "Enough."

"No," I said. "I want to hear more. What kind of trouble? Are we not still welcome in the city? It was the Lyoness who granted sanctuary."

"Of course, she did," said a companion who had, until then, been silent. Ren sliced his hand downward through the air, as if for silence.

Hannah ignored the signal. "Your coming was foretold."

"Well, crap," muttered Duncan behind his fingers, "I didn't expect that."

A tingling danced across my skin at her words. Carina possessed awareness of others' thoughts and sometimes precognitive knowledge, but the latter could often be sporadic and unclear. It would take more than a mystic's abilities to make a prediction specific enough to warrant these four setting out to find us, and actually doing so. More likely, Hannah lied to cover up the truth, and it was only a matter of their communications still being in working order and word of recent events having been received in that way. In which case, we were in more danger than I'd realized. "You must tell me," I said. "Does Stone Tiran know where we are? Did you intercept a communication?"

Hannah's nose wrinkled in disgust. "Him? The

new and false Revered? He knows nothing or your whereabouts. Not yet, anyway."

"Then how did you know where to find us?" Duncan asked. "Whether our coming was foretold or not, locating us required something a bit more precise, wouldn't you say?"

Hannah's facial muscles stiffened at his sarcasm. "There is one we call the Far-Seer. She knew." Nearby, Ren made another cutting movement with his hand, cautioning her once more. She continued to ignore him, her silver-gray eyes on mine. The prickling chill grew stronger. I raised a hand to my nape, smoothed the hairs down, slid my fingers around to my throat, unintentionally brushing the bag concealed beneath my tunic with my forearm.

*Let me out! Now!*

I gasped at the energy, staggering back as though physically struck. My hand dropped to my side. Duncan looked a question at me I pretended not to see.

"Who sent you? Did she?" I asked. "And why?"

"There are legends. There have always been legends. But now they are becoming truths. And no one sent us. We took it upon ourselves to come for you."

"Why?"

She glanced at Ren's furious face before

looking back at mine. She bit her lip, not answering. How often I'd been called stubborn I did not care to count. But stubbornness was not obstinance. Stubbornness had purpose. My stubborn nature had saved lives. It had saved my own. Her reticence could cost us, in so many ways.

"Hannah?" I prompted.

"Just come with us. Please."

"To the City of All Dwellers."

Again, she looked to Ren. When she turned back to me, her head moved in a slow nod.

Mika stepped forward. "Before we go anywhere with you, I'd like to know more about these replicants," he said.

"So would I," Duncan agreed.

"Why are they gone now?" Mika asked. "Do they have limitations? What is their purpose? For you, I mean. Your people."

Ren and Hannah exchanged another quick glance.

"That is a long telling. We really need to get undercover before nightfall," said Ren, looking over his shoulder toward the lowering sun.

"Understood," I said, "but answer me this. Does each one represent someone who actually exists somewhere?"

Hannah nodded.

"And Nimue?" I said. "The Lyoness? How was she able to speak with us. I noticed the others were all silent."

"Hers is a different manifestation. A stronger one. One that doesn't fade the way ours did. She wasn't meant to be here," Hannah repeated.

"Enough," Ren said. "We should go. We still have a long journey ahead." He shot a keen look at Hannah, who clearly understood. She nodded.

Feet shuffled in the humus soil. Not Carina, who paced more lightly than a cat. Resa. She trailed up to her brother's side, slipped her hand into his, Carina no more than an arm's length behind. Ren and the two unidentified Wildron moved their fingers in a way similar to what Ilyisa had done, back at the compound. A sign against enchantment. I wanted to scold them, but I kept my mouth shut, watching Hannah. She offered no such sign, eyeing Resa with interest.

"Should we be worried," she asked me, "about the little one?"

"Resa," Duncan said again, holding his sister's fingers. "Her name is Resa. And not as long as we're together." He slid a sidelong look at me. "All of us."

I allowed myself a small smile. Duncan Oaks was a resolute friend and a dedicated brother. I had a feeling he hadn't always been so, but I didn't care. I saw him as what he'd become.

"The wagon will need to be left behind now," Ren said. "We can help to carry your supplies. You must set the *conjure* free. He cannot travel beneath the falls."

"Beneath the falls?" Duncan echoed, shaken. "How?" My gaze went to the plummeting, flashing torrent, pondering the same thing, and not happily.

"A passage exists," Ren said in brief explanation. He led the other two Wildron to the wagon. Tossing his great, shaggy head, Chauncy glared back at them, his long teeth gleaming in the sunlight. I hurried over.

I'd known at some point Chauncy would be given his freedom. Breg, his former driver-companion, had made me promise when our partnership ceased the beast would be set free in The Wilds, where others of its kind roamed. I hadn't expected it to be this soon. Grasping the shaggy red-brown coat on his neck, I curled the coarse hair beneath my fingers, regret and anxiety seeping out in the touch.

After a moment, I released him and carefully unbuckled and removed his halter with a plan to stow it and the harness in my pack, on the chance we might again need it. Not for Chauncy, of course, but we often ran into circumstances where the strangest things came in handy. We couldn't afford to cast aside anything.

I patted Chauncy again, several times, like one would a dog, stroking his back, his neck, before I unfastened the girth straps and lowered the wagon's wooden shafts to the ground. I stepped back. I cleared my throat.

"You're free."

Giant, cloven hooves stomped on the forest

floor. He glared at me.

"Go," I said.

He stood unmoving. I backed away. In the minutes I'd taken to complete my task, the wagon had been emptied. I spotted my makeshift pack lying at Duncan's feet and strode swiftly to his side, where I shoved the straps and harness inside. I straightened. Duncan's eyes widened. A long, deadly shadow fell across us both, Chauncy's serrated corkscrew horn coming swiftly into my line of vision, heading like an axe for my shoulder. I flinched but did not move. There wasn't time.

The horn touched down like a finger, delicate and gentle, leaving fabric and flesh intact. I spun with the horn still in place, hardly feeling the sharp edges, and rushed beneath it, throwing my arms around Chauncy's neck. The *conjure* made a noise in his throat I'd never heard before, almost like mourning.

"You may yet meet again," Carina said in a quiet voice.

I didn't argue, yet I understood any circumstance for our paths to cross did not exist. The wilderness was vast and our road was not his. He might even return to Breg, given the opportunity. But not to me.

Besides, what did it matter? The creature and I did not possess the connection fostered by long-term association. We were, like people in similar situations, only strangers. Still, I stood for several minutes longer, breathing in the distinctly unpleasant odor from his hide, patting him and rumbling in rhythm with his voicings until at last he lifted his head, horn pointed skyward. Releasing him, I turned, as we all did, weighed down by our burdens, and walked away.

A dozen strides on, I swore. I didn't look back though. Duncan jolted me with his elbow.

"It'll be okay."

He was always saying that. I wondered how he could be so sure.

Chapter Four

I didn't like Ren. I couldn't say why precisely, except he was arrogant and impatient and possessed a pretty boy's entitlement, to boot. Yeah, well, obviously I *could* say why. Not out loud, though. Grace seemed on a short fuse. I couldn't be sure she'd tolerate it. But my head kept right on going, mounting up reason after reason for dislike as I glanced at him striding along on Grace's far side. As if he had some right to be there. As if he suddenly thought he was one of us. As if I couldn't, mightn't, oughtn't reach out and punch him square in the jaw.

Picturing Grace's reaction to the last, I shoved the satisfaction the image brought far away, because Grace really was, and had been, in a strange, dark mood since we fled the compound. I tried asking her why, yesterday. If she'd been a *conjure*, she would have taken my head clean off. Not that she'd said anything. She hadn't. It was the look she gave me—made my guts quiver. Made me get up and resituate myself on the opposite side of the flames where Mika had been taking a turn cooking a meal.

A real meal. Nice and hot. We hadn't had one of those since…I couldn't remember when. Back at the facility, I guess, although a meal from a prep-unit, warm or not, could never quite be the same.

In response, my stomach growled. Loudly. Without a word, or even looking at me, Grace reached into the deep pocket in her trousers and pulled something out, shoving it into my hand. I glanced down at the object in my fingers. Dried fruit. I grunted my thanks, shoved the tangy sliver gratefully into my mouth. What would I, what would any of us, do without Grace?

She'd say the same about us. I knew she would.

And she was probably right. We, Grace, Carina, Mika, me, made quite an effective team. Lucky for us. Things could have gone so much worse. They still could. Different world, different problems, but yeah, they still could. Horribly wrong. Like they had for Skelly.

I shut my eyes a moment, trying to block out memory, but the dark behind my lids only made the image stronger. I swallowed the fruit in a hurry, nearly choking on it, and began a little deep breathing the way Grace had taught us once upon a time. In through the nose, out through the mouth, concentrate on oxygen's intake, the exhale, the mechanics involved in quality, quantifiable air flow.

Grace heard me doing it, despite the roaring falls close at hand. No surprise. "You okay?" she asked, still without looking at me.

"Yeah," I said. "Skelly."

"What?" Her eyes were definitely on me now. She stumbled on the uneven track.

"I was thinking about him, about Shane," I said, frowning at her, pausing while she readjusted the pack on her shoulders. Resa and Carina went on, hand in hand, Mika following after a quick glance at Grace and me. The two reticent Wilders or whatever they called themselves flanked them. Joy-Li, a narrow girl with hair like Ren's, and Hugo, dark-skinned and broadly built. They didn't have much to say, those two. Ren and Hannah waited, watching us.

"Ready?" I asked, when Grace appeared to have gotten herself in order.

"Yes." She started off again at a brisk pace. I hustled after.

Soon, any conversation became close to futile with the falls practically filling our vision. Ren stopped us at a point where the path turned in an abrupt descent toward the river below. He and the others no longer carried their weapons nocked and at the ready. The arrows had been stowed and the bowstrings loosened. Grace had insisted, before she would return them.

I stepped up beside Resa, lifting her onto my hip. She was small, yes, but not that small. Her knee rammed the supplies in my pack. She made a face, yet no other reaction, not from the crack, not from disconnection with Carina. Could have been dangerous, poised here at the brink. Heck, Resa's power was dangerous no matter where it released.

"We go down from here," Ren instructed, directing his words to Grace and no one else. His eyes avoided mine, dodged Resa's altogether. I couldn't blame him, as much as I hated to admit it.

He pointed to the waterfall. "See that ledge? We pass into the mountain along there and make our way through to the other side."

"Into the mountain?" Mika asked. I heard the anxiety in his voice. I hoped Ren and his buddies hadn't.

Hannah answered him. "It's no big deal."

I'd used those exact words with him only a few days ago. I realized now how dismissive they sounded.

"No big deal? I doubt that. Some of us—like me," I lied, "aren't all that fond of cramped spaces. And exactly how do we see where we're going when we're underground?"

Ren sent me a look I couldn't quite read. I pretended I didn't see it, staring at Hannah instead. Her short red hair stuck out in all directions, resembling an ill-used brush. Made me think of one I'd handled often, worn to nubs scrubbing floors to help out Gran. Gran. I realized I actually missed her. Like I was five or something.

"Will this work for you?" Hannah said.

Ren rounded on her, his mouth opening, jerking forward as if to stop her. He didn't get the chance. The rest of us? We backed away quick. My heart zipped into my throat.

I don't know how she did it. I don't think anyone saw the actual act. One moment her hand lifted and the next, there it was, a flame-ball hovering above her palm. Even in the daylight forest it shone bright—in the darkness underground the light would be blinding. Grace alone went closer, leaving Ren at a distance, his face twisted in fury.

"How?" Grace asked. "How are you doing that?"

Hannah closed her fist, extinguishing the flame. "I learned it." She glanced at Ren. "Not everyone can. You have to possess the right bloodline."

Grace took another step forward, frowning first at Hannah's hand, then her face. "I imagine that's true," she said. Something weird moved through her expression, some mixture of fear and awe. At times they amounted to the same thing, really, but I wondered at it anyway. "Mage blood?" she asked.

Ren hissed, like a serpent, like a kettle, like he was about to lose his mind. He rushed her. She put an arm out in a move so swift I hardly caught it, and toppled him to the ground.

"Stay there," Grace said, her *lathesa* now pointed at his chest, her eyes on Hannah, waiting. "Hannah and I are talking."

Ren did, stayed on the ground, his gaze on the *lathesa's* wicked, sharp end, and then on Hannah's face, pleading silently.

Hannah paid him no heed. To be honest, I would have told him to shut up myself. I wanted to hear this. At a light touch, fabric brushing my arm, I glanced down. Carina had drifted up beside me, for Resa's sake, her eyes wide and nearly colorless.

"Yes," Hannah said, "mage blood. Diluted. Those of us who still possess it are nothing compared to what the originals once were."

Ren made a strangled noise, fists clenching on the packed dirt.

"Or so the tales say," she added, glancing at

him.

"I've heard them, too," Grace said. "The tales. We were raised on so many. I always had my own version in my head of the stories told to us as children, all of them, but recently…I've come to view them differently."

"With good reason," I muttered. Beside me, Carina concurred. The horrors on Emerald had surpassed any shared, scary bedtime stories. Not that I'd heard all that many. Gran believed in using her words to impart practical knowledge, not to frighten the wits out of me. She did that in other ways, when necessary. Still, the kids I'd occasionally interact with had been more than happy to pass grim tales along on a dark night.

Ren scooted out from beneath Grace's weapon and stood. Grace let him go, lightly grounding the crystal tip in the soil.

"You can't say any more, Hannah," he said.

Hannah shifted around to face him. "I think it's time to say exactly everything."

Ren shook his head in tiny, rapid movements. Frankly, he looked terrified. The other two, Hugo, Joy-Li, observed the goings-on in silence, hoods pulled up close around their faces still. Hannah and Ren maintained their stand-off until Grace spoke again.

"Later, then. We should keep moving, yes? Ren, you know the way. We'll follow."

Everyone complied as if Grace suddenly gave the orders to be obeyed. With the tension diffused, Grace returned to my side. Hannah's lengthy, sidelong glance at Grace ended when she increased her pace to walk beside Ren.

"What's going on?" I whispered.

"I'm not sure," Grace answered, just as quietly. "Keep an eye on them all, though."

Carina, having overheard, slipped away to let Mika know what Grace had said. "That flame-thing," I went on, "that was pretty awesome. And frightening."

"And unexpected," Grace said. "I hoped I might find knowledge, here, but I hadn't envisioned anything else."

I knew Grace hadn't wanted to go into The Wilds at all, but she'd said she thought she might be able to learn something from the people here. What, I had no clue. Something like this? "Is it a bad thing or a good thing, what we've just seen?"

"It could be either."

I said nothing, trying to remember where I'd stashed my spear. It should have come to me straightaway, but Grace's statement sent a buzzing through my brain for a minute or two as I imagined the damage Hannah could inflict with that flame-ball of hers. I kept telling myself it provided light, not heat, but I didn't know for sure. I doubted Grace did, either.

Grace released a long, slow breath at my side. Although she couldn't hear it, Resa turned her head, dark eyes observing her without alarm. "About two hundred years ago," Grace said, "a group of tribal mages formed together and broke with the desert peoples. They went into The Wilds and never came out again. It was reported, with much conjecture over time, that they were killed. I'm thinking they weren't."

"So, what are you saying?"

"It's not what I'm saying. It's what Hannah said. She and others like her are descendants. I expect we'll be finding out soon how much power they've retained."

"Crap. Double crap." I adjusted my grip on Resa, taking the first deep step down the precipitous path to the falls.

To be honest, I'd never experienced anything like this waterfall. Fountains, sure, and tumbling watercourses in the Citadel gardens and elsewhere. The waterfall, however, dropped from a hundred feet above our heads and churned into the river another forty feet below. The water sounded like a living, breathing monster—a many-hued monster, because from this vantage point, the shimmering colors in the water were even more impressive. As we descended, I tensed, fully expecting an explosive reaction from my sister, and made myself ready. So did Carina, who stayed no more than inches from her. Instead, once the path leveled off, Resa dropped from my arms to the ground, walking at my side unconcerned, even in the cold spray showering us all. She signed to me she could feel the sounds making me flinch, and telling me not to be afraid. Resa, telling me not to be afraid. Our communications before she'd been sent away to the Sisterhood had been rare and often frustrating. But sometimes they were special. Like this. And yet nothing like this. It couldn't last. I knew it couldn't.

The fact she spent so long interacting with me now was new. Normally, frustration set in way too quickly. She'd been doing well with the Sisterhood. Calm, their messages said. Self-aware. Happy. Thriving. All the encouraging words. Gran had been delighted each time a dispatch arrived from the Sisters. Relieved. Me, too. When I was around. By the time I stowed away on the interspace flight down from Riley to try my hand at conning the citizens of Citadel, I'd convinced myself Resa would be safe forever.

That might have been true, until I met Stone Tiran. Until I balked at his offer. Until he sent his soldiers to snatch Resa away from the Sisterhood to assure my cooperation. I blamed him for what had happened to my sister since, but I couldn't blame only him. My hands were dirty, too.

Slowly, my gaze slid from Resa to Grace. Grace, the girl in the glass box. I thought of her as my betrayal, but she wasn't the first. The first had been Resa.

Guilt torqued my guts into a writhing knot. Grace had forgiven me, when I hadn't ever expected forgiveness from her. I didn't deserve it. I could never forgive myself for what had happened to Resa.

Ren shouted suddenly. The water-roar muffled

his words but I guessed his meaning from his gesturing arm. We'd arrived at the point where the rocky trail went underground. Everyone started talking at once. The four of us had questions, the four of them were spewing out the gods knew what. Resa alone remained unmoved, silent as always— nothing changed that—staring at the dark opening.

Finally, we all stopped speaking. We weren't getting anywhere shouting into the waterfall's roar, after all. I figured Ren, as much as I begrudged him any respect, should be the one to listen to right now. I waved my hand and we moved closer to hear him. He acknowledged my effort with a brief, perhaps grateful nod. I still wanted to smack him.

"You five," he said loudly, pointing at us, "need to stay close. It's not hard to lose your way in here."

"So, why are we going underground?" Mika drawled. "You never actually said."

Ren narrowed his eyes. "What's your name?"

"Mika."

"Well, *Mika*, we go this way because I say we go this way."

Grace stirred, lips clamped, her eyes on Ren.

"And he says we go this way, because you wouldn't want to be caught out anywhere above once night falls. None of us would." Startled, I looked to Joy-Li. These were possibly the first full sentences I'd heard from her.

"Why's that?" Mika asked, still argumentative. I had a feeling Ren got under his skin the same way he did mine, and it showed in the questions to Joy-Li. I'd never known him to be aggressive. "What goes on 'above'?"

"It's the Perimeter. Anyone who steps inside it dies."

"Only at night?" Carina piped up. "You said, once night falls."

"All the time," said Joy-Li. "At night it's worse, though. At night, the hunt is more indiscriminate."

I couldn't stop the shiver that went tromping along my spinal cord. I remembered, we all remembered, the hunters on the Emerald. Grotesque, horrifying creatures, including those humanoid beasts whose mind-control had been a predatory tactic tough to beat. Beside me, Grace uttered a quick, soft prayer. I'd only heard her do so once before.

"Grace?"

"I'm fine," she said to me, before addressing Joy-Li. "What are these hunters?"

"Men, for the most part. At least that's what we're told. Brutish, violent, maybe even a little mad."

"And the other hunters? You said 'for the most part'."

Joy-Li shrugged. "The usual. The forest is filled with creatures."

Ren cut the conversation short. "Sometimes the Kanon wander beyond their boundaries. However, they don't like the confinement underground so we'll be safe there. Let's go. In another hour or so, it'll be night."

They'd come upon us in the dark, Ren and the others, but maybe they'd traveled in daylight to get to our campsite, waiting for night only so they could surround us undetected with the replicants. Or maybe they lied now, and this was a trap. I hated not being sure. Feeling vulnerable. Wanting to lash out. I took a deep breath.

"Grace," I said again.

She gave me a short glance, a smaller nod, pushed back tangled, curly strands from her face. Her tattoo, her warrior's indigo blue tattoo, stood out in the golden sunlight across her cheekbone. "Let's go," she said, echoing Ren's words.

We did. Of course, we did. We'd follow her anywhere.

Chapter Five

I narrowed my eyes at the flame swirling above Hannah's palm. Outside, in the sunlight, the many colors in it hadn't been visible. It resembled now the colors in and above the water. Coincidence? Probably not. I sure as heck couldn't figure out what was going on with the whole mage thing. Grace had talked a bit about them, about their mysterious, outcast role in her tribal society, but she'd avoided referencing the scary particulars. Like blazing balls of light. Like controlling those blazing balls of light. Like conjuring them up from nothing.

I had a feeling we should be more worried than Grace let on.

Hannah moved her hand, causing the light to sparkle along the damp, craggy walls. "This way," Ren said. Once again, Joy-Li and Hugo dropped back to walk behind us. I could hear them talking, minimally worded sentences back and forth in undertones. Had we been in the forest I probably wouldn't have heard them at all. The stone made things echo. Their voices, our footsteps, the pinging drip of water somewhere. Other noises I couldn't identify, whispering up from smaller tunnels to either side. Cave-dwelling animals, I figured. I hoped, anyway, and that they were all quite tiny.

"How far?" I asked. My voice blasted around us. "Sorry," I whispered.

Hannah glanced at me. "Some few hours. We'll stop halfway to rest."

"And eat," Grace said. "We have plenty to share."

Hannah nodded at her. "Thank you."

At the fore, Ren let out a loud snort, not even trying to keep his disdain under control. I found myself wishing something would fall on him. Not anything that would hurt, necessarily. A slimy clod of mud would suffice.

Carina giggled, stifled behind a hand. I glanced down at her. Her eyes flickered in the light from Hannah's flames. She looked from me to Ren and back again. Right. Sometimes she knew exactly what we were thinking, and not just those wispy glimpses. Resa possessed the same gift, except she never heard me in her head, never sensed me, only others far away.

Today, though, she'd recognized the noise from the falls had been bothering me quite clearly, and had responded to it in understanding. My breath rushed out.

I stared hard at the back of Resa's dark head, at the multiple braids Carina had made for her swinging back and forth as she walked in front of me. Stared and called her name inside my mind. Once, twice, a dozen times. She didn't react, didn't slow her pace, didn't look around at me.

Yeah, I'd probably read more into our earlier interaction than existed. I used to do that a lot. Back when we lived under the same roof, when I'd hoped things could be different, when I tried to make them better. I'd been an optimistic young sod.

I reached out, tapped her shoulder. She turned. Immediately she dropped back, put her hand in mine. She seemed so much younger than her age in so many ways, yet when she looked at me, really looked at me, I knew better. I wouldn't have wanted to be in her head, wouldn't have wanted to see all she had seen. I figured she felt a hundred years old inside.

My focus suddenly went to Hannah. She'd gotten the flame ball to bounce between one hand and the other. A show-off move, something I would have expected from Ren if he had the gift, which he obviously didn't. He wasn't happy about it either. His scowl looked about to turn his pretty-boy face inside out.

"Don't your arms get tired, carrying that thing for hours?" I asked. Not because I wanted to know. The movement from the light, across the wet stone, in front of my eyes, was disorienting. I meant to distract her enough to stop.

She did, holding the ball in the air equidistant between her two hands. "I could make you carry it," she said.

Like a threat. At least, I took it that way. Apparently, so did Grace.

"But you won't," Grace said.

"Of course not. If my arms get tired," said

Hannah, grinning rather malevolently at me, "I can put it on my head, like this."

She positioned the eddying, circular flames a couple inches above her spiky red hair. Cocky, as if showing us, showing everyone, she was in control. I wondered if that meant she wasn't, that she pretended mastery over her gift. I shifted Resa to my other side, away from Hannah and her dancing light trick.

Behind us Hugh and Joy-Li stopped talking. Ren came to an abrupt halt. He spun to face Hannah.

"That's enough," he said.

Hannah's expression changed, became mutinous, stubborn and set. I traded a glance with Grace. We'd had our moments, Grace and I, the four of us even, but this looked like something about to erupt. The tunnel's natural dimensions could never afford us enough room to get the heck out of the way.

Grace lifted her hand to her shirt below her throat the way she sometimes did now, a kind of nervous tic, worrying in itself. Grace didn't do things like that. Grace was strong and focused and yeah, sometimes afraid, but never to the point that frightened me. I was about to open my mouth, to say something, when she abruptly slammed her hand down to her thigh, the noise her palm made against fabric and the skin beneath echoing through the cave.

All eyes turned her way, even Hannah's, even Ren's. Intentional or not, the distraction worked.

"I don't understand this," Grace said. "I've

been trying to figure it out, but I don't get it. We, my friends and I, are alive today because we stand together. Always."

*Not quite true, Grace*, I thought, but didn't say so. It didn't make a difference anymore. It really didn't. The realization caused a weight to shift in me, the anger I'd been carrying around inside from Grace's irresponsible, unshared plan back there at the compound releasing its hold. I'd been determined at some point Grace and I would talk about what she'd done. I understood now if we never did, it wouldn't matter.

"But you four," Grace continued. "You're not exactly strangers, but definitely four people who don't like each other very much and don't know each other all that well. That's the picture I'm getting, anyway. Am I wrong?"

They didn't say anything. Hannah and Ren's eyes shifted around in sullen avoidance. Nearly perched on Hannah's hair now, the flame started to dim.

Ren's head jerked up. "See to that. We can't lose the light right now."

Wordlessly, Hannah complied, bringing the flame-ball back down to hover over her hand. I eyeballed her hair. No smoke. Perhaps the flames held no heat after all.

We started walking again. Hugo's voice drifted up to me, barely heard. "This is crap. Why don't we use the cylinder lights, like we did before? I still have mine in my pocket. I—"

"Quiet," Joy-Li hissed, no doubt catching the fact my head had turned to hear him better.

"Something's up. Just shut it."

So, they had some form of artificial lighting with them. I thought I might understand why they weren't using it. Relying solely on Hannah's ability put the four of us at a disadvantage. Ren hadn't wanted her to do it, though. I caught that much in their exchange outside the cave. I'd assumed Ren led them, but now I wasn't so certain his leadership went unchallenged.

I wandered closer to Grace, whispering. "Grace—"

"I heard," she said.

"This is my fault. I should never have piped up about sanctuary. If we'd known how few there were we could have—"

"Not your fault. And nothing we can do about the rest of it. Not yet anyway." She uttered the last in a voice so hushed I almost missed it.

She walked with her *lathesa* casually slung over her shoulder, as if she had no plan for its use. I saw the way she held her hand on the weapon, though, the way she'd shown me a time or two. She never really allowed herself to relax, not completely, but I could tell this wasn't only her warrior's readiness. She anticipated trouble.

I reached back pretending to adjust my pack, taking note with my fingertips where my spear had been crammed. I wouldn't take it out, though—not if I didn't have to. If it came to a fight, I'd use my fists, even the broken one. When we'd defended ourselves on the prison moon, it had been against creatures as far from human as a body could get. We'd been fortunate since then not to have to battle with people. Well, most of us, anyway. Grace had been the exception. Mika, Carina and I? We'd done a lot of running. A lot. My legs still ached from it.

As time passed, battling our way out seemed to lessen as the next step in the agenda. Hugo and Joy-Li's muttering quieted down, Ren kept to the fore with an occasional look back, and Hannah had lost her enthusiasm for intimidation. We didn't stop until hours after night had doubtless settled in outside the dank network of tunnel-like caves.

"Will you really share your food with us?" Ren asked. "I'm thinking we should eat and then sleep."

"Did you not come prepared for this journey?" I muttered. He heard.

"No," he answered honestly enough. "We left in a hurry. We wanted to intercept you before someone else did."

"I get that. Who? Who is this someone else?"

He didn't answer me. Instead, he glanced at Hannah and away. Hugo and Joy-Li came forward, sat down on the rough stone and dirt surface. They each pulled a packet from a cloak pocket and set it onto the floor. Joy-Li reached forward and opened them, revealing some green, leafy substance inside. "We have this, if you'd like. Tastes a bit like grass, but it's also kind of sweet. Good for energy."

"Maybe save that for the morning, then," Grace said. She went around gathering food and water from the packs everyone had shirked from their shoulders. Carina joined her. In short order, they'd set a selection out in the space between us all. I noted the offerings didn't include everything we'd been given by the Ogdonians. Grace held a great deal back, not taking chances we'd go hungry again.

Good idea, Grace. If we have to make a hasty departure, we'll need it.

Hannah placed the orb into a natural niche in the stone. A deep shadow stretched over much of the wall and the tunnel behind and before us. She sat near to the flame-ball, physical proximity probably keeping the thing active. Either that, or she expected we might try to steal it.

We started out consuming our meal in silence, too hungry for talk. About halfway through, Mika followed up on the question I'd had. He paused with some strange-looking vegetable to his mouth. I hadn't worked up the appetite to try one yet. Except when in dire straits, vegetables had never been my choice entrée. Right now, not dire enough.

"Who did you think was coming for us?" he asked.

"No one," said Ren. Carina stared at him, searching for the answer in his mind. After a few seconds she looked away, flustered by defeat.

"It was more a precaution," Ren added. I didn't believe him. No one did, not even his own. I spotted the looks they gave each other. I could read a face. Early training with the Grif-Drifs had pounded that into me. This group wasn't hiding anything, weren't even trying, not in the keeping-secret-feelings way. Everything stood out there in the open, with one thing plain. No trust among them. I didn't like that. Not at all.

When our meal concluded, the remainder got packed away. Grace brushed her hands together, palm over palm. "Okay," she said, "who takes the first watch?"

I wondered if there'd ever come a time when Grace wouldn't have to ask that question. It felt like we'd always been in this position, that we always would be. The Idiot-Four, however, frowned at her as if she'd sprouted a fungal growth in the middle of her face.

"Who needs to watch?" Hannah asked. "We're safe here. We should all get some sleep."

Ding. Call me paranoid, but a tiny alarm bell went off in my head at her response. "I'll go first," I said. Ren's left eyebrow shot up.

"Not alone. I'll take the watch with you."

The looks shot his way now, less gross fungal than what-the-heck-are-you-doing. Yet I understood his reasoning. If this was an us against them scenario, you couldn't have the enemy guarding both sides. After all, who knew what mayhem we might cause while they slept. But I didn't think they'd actually planned to be sleeping. Not all, anyway. Something about this stank like a ruse. With one from each side keeping watch, it became a stalemate.

"Deal," I said.

Hannah frowned. "You're going to be keeping watch in the dark. The total dark. That flame goes down with me."

"You go ahead and do that," I said. "I'll take the device Hugo's carrying around in his pocket, though. We'll be fine." I held out my hand.

Hugo snarled something under his breath. A swear word, by the tone, but nothing I recognized. Joy-Li gave him a withering look. Not waiting for him, she reached into her cloak and handed me the device she carried. I took the metallic object with a brief thank you. I expected Ren carried his own.

"Do you know how to work that?" Ren. Observing me with a little twist to his mouth.

I rolled the cylinder in my hand, studying the buttons on the side. At one end the cylinder had a deep hollow. I supposed any light came from there. I pushed a button with my thumb. A beam shot out, making a perfect circle on the wall opposite.

"Good guess," Ren mumbled.

Gods, this guy needed to grow up. I pushed the other button, which I expected would turn it off. It didn't. The beam got way brighter and larger. Hands flew up, shielding eyes.

"The other one," Joy-Li said from behind her fingers. "The first one you pressed. It's for both off and on."

"Thanks."

Silence settled again when the illumination blinked out, a more strained silence, all eyes on me. Resa's too, looking at the device in my hand, then back up to my face.

*All good,* I signed. *Time to sleep.*

Everyone grabbed what they planned to sleep in or on or around. Except me, of course, and Ren. Resa curled up close to Carina and Mika rather than me, out of recent habit. I suspected she also recognized Carina could keep her demons at bay. Either way, I breathed a little easier seeing her there. Grace bunked down about halfway between them and me. We'd gotten used to sleeping close together, like a pack, like puppies, for comfort and protection. She kept her *lathesa* at her side, one hand curled loosely around it. I doubted she'd sleep soundly. I don't think she ever did.

Ren took up a position directly opposite me, his back against the curved stone wall. Hannah, true to her threat, made the flame-ball vanish. We briefly plunged into a blackness so absolute it snatched the breath from my lungs. Ren flicked on his illumination gadget, stuffing it under his cloak's edge to reduce the glare. I did likewise, rolling the borrowed device beneath a fold in my trousers. We held no weapons. My fairly useless spear remained in my pack, Ren's arrows and dismantled bow in their carrier. I let out a deep breath and heard Ren do the same. Our eyes met. We nodded at each other.

Truce. Worked for me.

I leaned my head back, wincing as my skull contacted cold hard stone. I could have used a pillow, but I hadn't had one of those since my time spent in a cell. A pillow would have been too comfy, anyway. I needed to stay alert. Not because I worried about any move Ren and his quasi-friends might make. I kept thinking about the Kanon hunting in the woods above. The crazy brutes casually mentioned by Joy-Li. Maybe too casually. Yet that could be Joy-Li's way, to toss things out as if they didn't matter. It did give her a tiny gloss of courage. Still, I couldn't help speculating whether these Kanon posed a threat, especially if they decided to track us down here. We only had Ren's word for it they didn't come underground. Actually, his words had been more along the lines of 'they don't *like* coming underground.' Big difference. Major difference. Potentially hazardous difference.

I shifted my butt around on the hard ground, reconsidering the wisdom of leaving my spear packed up. I wondered if Hannah might be able to conjure more alarming things than a heatless flame ball. Not for use against us, naturally. But something like that could come in handy.

My gaze shifted in her direction. I found the dim light reflecting in her open eyes. Staring back at me, she gave me a long, slow wink. I looked away. She laughed.

I thought I'd liked her, back when she was crossing Ren in the forest. With each minute since, not so much.

*     *     *

I'd started to hope the night would pass uneventfully, that in a reasonable amount of time I'd turn over watch to Grace, leave the rest to sleep. Ren clearly was. Asleep, I mean. Before the estimated first hour ended, he'd slumped to his right, slid down to the floor. Soon after, small snores erupted from his open mouth. Part of me, the really exhausted part, had been tempted to follow suit. The part schooled in caution overruled.

Good thing. At first, I thought I imagined the sounds I heard, fabricated by an overtired brain. A thumping, not with any particular beat. Not like footsteps, or someone pounding out a rhythm. But they did have…something. A thump, and a shuffle, maybe two more thumps, followed by silence. Then two thumps, a quieter shuffle, several more thumps.

Fully alert, I listened harder. Yeah, not imagining. Something scraped the walls in a soft slither, followed by more thumps, headed this way. Silence again. I jumped up. The little light-thingie rolled over the stone, illumination wobbling across the cave's slumbering occupants. Only, not everything was asleep. I wasn't. The thing moving closer wasn't. And not Grace. Not anymore.

I hadn't even heard her get up before she appeared beside me, pushed me back behind her and away. "Wake everyone," she whispered. "Grab what you can. Get out of here."

In the still rolling light, her shadow danced over the walls, the weapon in her hands parallel to the floor. The crystals at each end glinted. Not the same as before, I told myself. Reflection only, please.

"I'm not leaving you," I said.

"I'm not asking you to. But I need you ready. We're probably going to have to run, so get everyone prepared, will you?"

I obeyed, alerting first our party and then theirs. The cloaked four were already waking by the time I reached them.

"What's going on?" Ren asked in testy tones.

"Something's coming," I said. "We need to go now."

He scrambled up, his gaze shooting straight to Grace. "What does she think she's doing?" he asked.

"Giving us time." This, from Mika. Somehow, he always seemed to recognize a selfless act.

"Grab everything and start moving," I said. "If

we have to drop the packs, we will, but it would be great if our supplies don't get left behind."

The ensuing scramble echoed loudly. The thumping, shuffling, scraping was louder still, out of sight and closer. I hurried over to Grace where she stood with her warrior's stance, strong and strangely elegant. She looked more like a dancer than Carina did right then. A dancer with lethal skills.

Ren scurried up to my other side. He glanced around me at Grace. "Can she—"

"You've seen her in action," I interrupted him. "Do you doubt it?"

Ren turned, tossed the light in his hand. He probably meant it for one of his own, but Mika caught it. Mika lifted my wide-eyed sister into his arms at the same instant Carina touched her. Resa slumped down onto his shoulder.

"Go!" Grace said. "Now!"

"I'm staying," I said. Me, the weaponless fool.

"Me, too," said Ren, equally empty-handed. We did have our hands though, and our feet, and my borrowed light cylinder finally at a stop on the floor. That might be good for something.

Grace swore.

Swore and darted away into the dark.

Chapter Six

*Grace,* I shouted silently, *it's not your job to save us.*

Clearly, though, it was. To her, it was.

Ren and I raced after her. I heard her cry out, beyond sight, beyond my reach, and then again. Not fear. Not pain. A name.

Chauncy.

The huge and supposedly impartial *conjure* had followed her right down into the ground. I grabbed Ren's arm, jerking him to a halt. The last thing any of us needed was a skewered pretty boy. I wouldn't have missed him much, but the end result would have been messy, in more ways than I cared to think about.

Ren shook me off, eyes flashing.

"Wait," I said. "Give them a minute."

He released a thunderous and petulant sigh. At least it seemed that way to me. I supposed it could have been a perception thing on my part. On occasion, I did manage to be honest with myself and forced myself to give him the benefit of the doubt.

Grace appeared around the bend in the tunnel,

Chauncy at her back. The beast's eyes shone like the embers in last night's fire. Reflecting the light in my hand, I knew, but the effect was unnervingly sinister. Even the dimwit recognized it and took a few hasty steps backward.

Grace's face twisted in a crooked smile. "I think we're stuck with him."

I'd witnessed many of Grace's changing moods, but happy Grace was the one I liked most. Small things made her happy, in a series of events that had little time or means for happy moments. Chauncy was a rather big thing. A stinking, dangerous, hulk of a thing with Grace's heart plastered across every square inch of its filthy hide.

The others drifted back in our direction, muttering or exclaiming, depending on *conjure* preference. They hung back, wisely not crowding in.

"Since we're all awake," said Grace, "maybe we should just continue on?"

Ren grunted agreement, signaling to his three companions. I doubted we'd be comfortable trying to sleep with Chauncy hovering above us anyway. There'd been little enough room before his arrival.

Grace walked behind us. If she hadn't, Chauncy would have crushed us all. Within the hour, lack of sleep began to drag at my shoulders. Ren, too, although he'd gotten more than I had, sleeping on watch. I hadn't expected him to stay awake, not really. He seemed a bit negligent, that guy. A lot of bluster and even more arrogance, but essentially useless.

Maybe not quite useless. He had taken a stand

beside Grace back there. I wouldn't dismiss that, no matter how much he bugged me. I kind of hated myself for being so…principled. Principled, said the guy who'd joined the Grif-Drifs at the age of ten.

If I'd spoken those words out loud, Grace would have punched me in the arm. She did, whenever she decided I was being an idiot. I recognized the affection behind the gesture, but occasionally it hurt. It wasn't as though she was stronger than she looked. She was just, sometimes, and quite by accident I told myself, stronger than me.

"How much longer before we're back above ground?" I asked. I spoke to Ren. I should have called him by name because he didn't even glance back. Neither did Hannah, who'd abandoned her theatrics with the flame-ball for some reason, nor did the other two. I looked at Mika, beside me now. He'd turned my slumbering sister over to me. Carina walked at his back, scooting forward every now and then when Chauncy's huge horn got too close. Mika shrugged, rolled his eyes. In the illumination from the light cylinders held by the Wildron—yes, Grace had corrected me in this—his flesh seemed pale, a little moist. He needed sleep even more than we did. I wondered if he'd taken his meds. Here, walled by stone, a seizure held the potential for more damage than usual.

"Mika," I whispered from my mouth's corner, not wanting to alert the Wildron to his condition, because who knew how they would view it. "Have you taken your—"

"Yeah," he said.

"Did you bring enough?" I don't know why this thought only struck me now. He and Carina had left the facility with more haste than Grace and I, and although I knew he'd brought a medication supply, I had no idea how much. We certainly wouldn't be able to get more anytime soon. If at all.

"He's good," Carina answered for him, "for a while."

I nodded, returning my attention to the dark tunnel ahead, filled with the dancing lights from the cylinders, wondering again about Mika's condition.

"Yes," Carina said, reading my thoughts. "The lights are troubling him."

We had to hasten our pace, then, return to the world above where hopefully the sun would soon be rising. "Ren," I said, calling him by name despite the bad taste it left in my mouth, "how far?"

"Not much more," he said, deigning to respond.

I turned my head. "Mika?"

Mika nodded. "I'll be okay."

I let out a breath, stepping up closer behind Hugo and Joy-Li, trying to nudge them forward into a quicker pace. "Watch it," Hugo growled when I snagged his cloak with my knee. I grunted and dropped back.

"Maybe you could ride on…you know," I said to Mika, jerking my head toward Grace and Chauncy behind us. "Then you could close your eyes or something."

Mika snorted. "Uh, no. There's not enough room anyway. Do you see how close its shoulders are to the ceiling? It can't even lift its head."

I'd seen, marveling at the fact Chauncy had

managed to make his way in total blackness without getting stuck somewhere. I marveled even more at why. Grace. He'd come for Grace. Grace had spoken about the *conjures'* relationships with humans. The knowledge the creature had switched allegiance in such a manner and on such short notice both awed and unnerved me. As long as he didn't bite me, though, I was darned grateful.

Grace was pleased to have him returned despite the problems she was having keeping him from stomping right over us. Odd, that, because I'd been pretty darned sure she'd possessed some reservation about his presence. I didn't know why. She didn't talk about things the way she had before we'd rescued my sister. The feeling something had happened to her in Tiran's compound surged again to the fore, something she held close and wouldn't discuss. I'd get it out of her, though, as soon as I could. Or I'd cheat, and ask Carina. Carina always knew. Or almost always knew. Lately, caring for my sister, she wasn't quite on her game.

My gaze slid to where Mika and Carina walked side by side now, not speaking, no need to speak. I'd called them Gran and Pop once, because they reminded me of them, quietly dedicated. Carina had smiled in appreciation. Mika had looked like he couldn't decide whether he wanted to laugh or smack me.

Passing Resa to Mika, I dropped back a little more, squeezing myself opposite Grace with Chauncy's huge, shaggy, scary head between us.

"Grace," I said, "you'd tell me if something bad was going on with you, right?"

"Sure, I would," she said, not looking at me. My eyes narrowed.

"You're a really poor liar."

"So I've been told."

Yeah, I thought, by me. Annoyed and sucking in a breath, whiffing Chauncy's odorous hide, I slipped up front again, past Mika and Carina, past Joy-Li and Hugo. I found myself striding alongside Hannah, Ren a scarce two feet in front of me. I had to slow my pace to keep from tripping on his heels. After a minute, I stepped around him, too.

"Where do you think you're going?" he demanded.

"I need to stretch my legs."

"Yeah. Gotcha. Right." For some reason, he thought my words an invitation to join me. Apparently, he hadn't noticed the surly expression puckering my face. Lifting his hand, he flashed the light along the tunnel ahead. "Seriously, you could break a leg. I don't want to have to carry you out."

"Like you could," I muttered.

"We could try it and find out."

"Boys…" This, from Hannah. Normally, it would have been Grace speaking up, but at a glance back I could see she hadn't even looked in our direction, just went right on walking next to that lumbering beast, a hand at her throat. Something was definitely wrong. Ren's head turned, his eyes finding Grace, too. He studied her for a second or two before shifting his attention to someone nearer. Mika, or maybe Carina, or even Resa. I couldn't tell. Not until he pivoted to face front and I glimpsed his expression.

"What's up with that sister of yours?" he asked in a casual tone, as if he hadn't had the living crap scared out of him, as if his face didn't tell all.

"What do you mean?" I asked, playing dumb, just to make him fess up to his fears.

He shrugged. "You know."

"I don't," I said. Gods, I was enjoying this.

"She can't hear, can she?"

Oh. I shook my head. "Not the way we do."

"She doesn't speak either."

"Not using her mouth for conversation, no. In case you hadn't noticed, she does communicate quite well in other ways."

"The finger-hand thing? Yeah, I saw that." He paused, staring at the ground while we strode side by side. His ludicrous yellow hair hung forward over his eyes, his body language making me think less concentration, more an attempt to appear indifferent so I wouldn't shut him down, refuse to answer. "You were talking to each other."

I nodded, confused by the conversation, by his asking and my bothering to answer him. He addressed his curiosity's core a moment later.

"And the other?"

"Other?" I echoed. His brow lowered.

"You know what I'm talking about. Tossing everything around with her mind. That's what she was doing, right? Is that her power, her gift?"

"Gift. Curse. Depends on your viewpoint."

He bobbed his head several times in short, agitated movements, then let a long breath out through his nostrils. "Is she…is she mage?"

I went still inside. Kind of cold, and shocked

when really, I should have questioned such a thing myself the first time Grace spoke about mages to me. Somehow, we—Gran and I, the doctors—had never considered origins, only the manifestation. I'd never even heard of desert mages at the time, and probably wouldn't have associated the tales with my sister if I had. After all, these and other powers were not unknown. Gifts, less powerful gifts from what I'd been told, appeared randomly among many populations. We only wanted Resa to be helped. We wanted to be helped, too, because neither Gran nor I had any idea what to do to keep the three of us safe, together. But to be mage, the way I believed Ren to mean it now, meant a tribal bloodline, deeper than the water-downed version Hannah shared. Resa's gifts were frighteningly strong. I thought about my mother and Gran, the only power we possessed in common a will to survive. I knew nothing about Resa's father, except that he was not mine.

Slowly, I pivoted my upper body to look back. Resa, with her black hair, so much darker than my own, than our mother's, and her skin a ruddy bronze like Grace's. Both of them half-bloods. I could see it now. Why hadn't I done so, sooner?

I raised my eyes to where Grace strode beside Chauncy. I wondered how much of our conversation she might have overheard. Her gaze met mine, unblinking, not even curious.

Suddenly, I understood. Grace *knew*. She had always known.

*       *       *

I spun back around. Maybe not known, but at least suspected. Definitely recognized the possibility of Resa's mixed blood, probably from her first sight of my sister's image on the monitor. And once she'd witnessed Resa's power in the compound's subterranean confines, well, it hadn't been a great leap to reach the mage connection.

I felt…not betrayed, exactly. Left out. Cheated? Scared. Yes, oddly scared, because why would Grace keep this secret? Granted, there hadn't been much time for confidences in our flight into the Wilds and later, while we settled in to rest, regain our strength, she'd been, well, preoccupied. With this? Or something more? Just how much trouble were we in?

I decided not to answer Ren's question, and hoped he wouldn't repeat it. Instead, I asked my own. "Why did you come looking for us? You never really said."

He didn't answer.

"With an army, no less," I went on. "A fake army, yeah, but the intent at intimidation wasn't lost on me, on any of us."

His head jerked up. He tossed his stupid hair from his eyes. "Shut up."

I tensed. "Look, *Ren*, I don't—"

"Shut up," he said again, raising his hand. Not toward me. In signal to the rest. Hannah and the other two jerked to a halt. Mika, with Resa in his arms, was a bit slower to react. He stumbled into Joy-Li, who steadied him. Chauncy continued forward as if he'd walk right over them all, but at the last moment he stopped. Grace ducked beneath his chin. Her eyes met mine again as she raised the weapon in her grasp. I pivoted to the tunnel ahead, staring hard and listening.

"Crap," I said beneath my breath.

Ren doused the light in his hand, the cylinders still held by his pals casting our shadows out long before us. Turning his head, he spoke over his shoulder to them.

"They're coming."

My breath rushed out. "Who?" It had to be the Kanons, the ones they'd been worrying about, the hunters from above. I shirked my pack from my shoulders, shoved my hand inside for my spear. An *impulse* would have been a big help, like those the replicants appeared to carry. Our four cave-mates had only their bows, and they were unstrung, stowed away. When I looked around for Mika and my sister, hoping they and Carina could squeeze behind the *conjure*, I saw not a single Wildron had made a move to ready their weapons. I stepped up right next to Ren, spear in hand.

"Who is it?" I asked again. "Who's coming? Because it's not the Kanons at all, is it."

"No," he said. "I'm pretty sure it's the Lyoness."

"Your great-gran?"

He shot me a look, a narrow-eyed, I-think-I-hate-your-guts type look, before turning his eyes away to a point in the distance where a vague illumination had begun to grow. "Don't count on any cozy family reunion. Believe me."

A pitying twinge made me ask why.

"It doesn't matter."

"Did you do something to piss her off?"

"Always," he said.

"Got it." Boy did I get it.

Accompanied by grunts and various exclamations, Grace made her way to my side, Chauncy on her heels, shunting everyone else to the rear. We stood in the shadow created by the *conjure's* bulk, the long horn scraping the ceiling above our heads. Glints from the handheld lights behind shimmered along the ground between Chauncy's feet.

"What now?" Grace asked. "What can we expect? You'd said the fact Nimue had appeared at the campsite could be trouble."

"The Lyoness," corrected Ren. "And I didn't say that. Hannah did."

"So, it's not true? The trouble," I clarified, watching the strange, yellow glow grow larger, nearer, the shadows within it recalling something I would have preferred not. I could tell Grace experienced the same unease. She shifted her weight, her stance, her grip on the *lathesa*. I eyed my spear's negligible length. By design, it was meant to be as long as me, not the length of my arm. I'd constructed it on the fly. I'd hoped one day we might spend enough time not running for me to make another. I hoped more for a day I'd never have to.

"No," Ren said, "I'm pretty sure it's true."

Grace made a noise in her throat. She glanced at me, then slipped past to stand between me and Ren. "Replicants?" she asked.

"What?"

"Are they replicants we're seeing, or real warriors?"

Ren shook his head. "I'd say real. Replicants don't cast shadows."

Grace swore, picking several harsh but eloquent invectives from her extensive vocabulary. Beside her, Ren's mouth stretched into a grin. Seeing his amusement, I frowned. My hand tightened on the spear's shaft.

In silence, we waited for the light to reveal the people within it. Cloaked and hooded and crowded together made it difficult to gauge their number. Grace stood with shoulders relaxed, feet unevenly apart, knees loose, her weapon parallel to the floor. Grace in her relaxed, but no less imposing, warrior's stance. Ren gave her a long onceover before shifting his gaze to mine. My eyebrows arched and I nodded.

"Yeah," I said.

We could hear them now. Whispering cloth. Light footsteps. An occasional word. Chauncy's horn tapped the stone overhead. The rhythmic noise echoed toward them. Not behind us though, almost like he aimed it. More likely, the reverberating sound got dampened in his thick hide.

While still at a small distance, a group broke away from the rest, gliding eerily in our direction. If not for the slap of soles on stone, they would have seemed to float. A figure in front carried a lantern similar to one which had until recently hung from Chauncy's corkscrew horn. Shadow and shimmer bounced over the uneven walls. To the lamp carrier's right, a figure pushed back its hood. I recognized the scarred face straightaway.

"Renford," Nimue said.

"Renford?" I whispered. "I thought it was Renegade."

Grace hissed at me to keep quiet.

Ren stepped forward. "Yes, Lyoness," he said, "I'm here."

Not Gran, not Great-Gran. I *did* feel sorry for him.

"Grace Irese," said Nimue, "I see you there, as well. How could I not? Come closer. Duncan, you too. He who does not believe himself brave."

So, the great-grandmother's replicant had witnessed our exchange at the campsite. I wondered how this was possible. For that matter, I still puzzled over a replicant's exact nature. Someone needed to explain. Knowing I would receive no answer right now if I asked, I moved up next to Grace. Once again, the three of us, Ren, Grace and I, stood aligned.

"And the girl? Where is she? Where is the thrice-gifted child?"

Grace's shoulders jerked. My own went cold, right in the exposed space between the blades, as if I felt a knife flying to me from behind. I almost looked back, to check, to be sure. Grace released her weapon with one hand, took my left one, squeezed my fingers hard, let them go.

"What do you want with her?" she said in a voice filled with challenge.

"I want nothing," answered Nimue softly. "It is you who requested sanctuary. I merely asked after her because she is young. The trail has, no doubt, been arduous."

Grace didn't believe her. Neither did I. Nimue had called Resa the thrice-gifted child, a designation first heard in Tiran's compound. Grace had told me about it, having heard the name from a warrior who had fought on her behalf inside. A woman likely dead now.

"You do not trust me," said the Wildron leader. "I can't blame you. But word of your reputation, Grace, and that of the girl, have traveled widely, even reaching us here. We mean you no harm. We offer only rest and safety for as long as you require it, as you have requested."

As genuine as she sounded, I still couldn't believe her. How often had I used inflection, earnest expression, false sincerity in a con? Every single time, that's how often.

I peered past Grace to where Ren stood, chin up, attention on the Lyoness. Feeling my gaze on him, he looked my way. His lips compressed. Something flickered in his eyes before he shifted focus back to Nimue.

"And you, Renford," said the Lyoness, "you and your three…friends will have to answer to me."

He blinked, nodded, squared his shoulders. A muscle in his jaw did a funny little twitch and the hand holding the unlighted cylinder shook.

Well, hell. Nothing good could come from any of this.

*Skelly*

Chapter Seven

How does it feel not to trust, sweet Grace? You and that dolt, Oaks. You should have been me. In life, I could trust no one. Not even you. I thought I could, but oh how wrong a stupid boy can be. You let me die.

I stop and think about that for a minute, about the fact you let me down in such a monstrous way. You said you would keep us safe. You made a promise. Not to me. Not to my face. But I heard you. All noble and heartfelt. Like you're something special.

A *warrior*. You think that tattoo on your face means anything? I've got one. All of us received one, right down to the newbies, the twelve-year-olds first learning how to mine. Well, not a tattoo, exactly. I'll admit that. A brand. They branded us all, in case of accident, you know? For identification.

I thrash around, screaming. Grace hears me. Don't you, Grace? You're fighting hard not to let me out.

But she doesn't. She won't.

I settle down, listening again. I hear the words from that scarred old woman. The words that make Grace tremble inside. She's afraid, afraid for them all, from that useless Oaks and his freak sister to the yellow-haired moron. Thinking she can protect them, save them, knowing in the dark places she never cares to seek out that she can't. But she'll try. Oh, she'll try. And fail. She knows this, too, and turns away from the knowing.

Grace, Grace, you're a fool. If you'd only let me out, I could help you. I would, you know. I did. I will.

*Let me out!*

You're not my friend.

Once upon a time I had one, a real friend. A kind friend. A gentle friend. Too gentle. We went to the mines together. And then he died.

Living sucks. I should be happy in here, away from all that.

But I'm not. You know that, Grace. I know you do.

*Grace*

Chapter Eight

I whisked my hand from my throat and the hidden bag beneath my borrowed tunic. Borrowed. As if I'd ever have the opportunity to return the garment to Senta. I'd wondered on and off where she'd gotten it, from which among her family members or neighbors she'd stolen the garments in order that my friends and I could leave our filthy, ruined prison garb behind. But return it to her? No. Likely, she was already dead, a girl younger than me, too young to have attained warrior status, yet determined to march out with her tribe next time they were called to battle.

Every time Skelly exclaimed, he got more difficult to put from my mind. He'd saved me once, whether he'd meant to or not. He wanted me to save him now. I had no idea how to do that. Not yet. I did recognize, however, how precarious, how dangerous to every living thing nearby he would be without a learned control. In action, he was nearly as frightening as Resa could be.

*Nearly?* he said.

I ignored him.

But I hoped to learn more, here where mage lore was reputed to be so prevalent. I'd never expected power to exist, too. After Hannah's revelation, I had no idea what we might encounter among the Wildron.

Both Duncan and Ren watched me, brows furrowed and waiting. For me to speak, I realized. I must have missed whatever the Lyoness had said. I looked to Duncan.

"So, we're going with them?" he whispered.

I sucked in a short breath and nodded. "We don't have a choice."

He squeezed past Chauncy to let the others know. Ren stood in silence nearby. Every so often his gaze slid in his great-grandmother's direction. When Duncan returned, he had Resa in tow, her hand in his. They ducked out from behind Chauncy, Resa's nose wrinkled at the creature's smell. In short order, Mika and Carina followed, then Ren's faction.

"All present and accounted for," said Duncan loudly, his usual flippant self when unnerved. He pressed up next to me, arm colliding with mine.

"Lyoness," I said to Nimue, "you lead and we'll follow."

Rather than join their fellows, the Wildron four stuck close to us. I suspected this had less to do with herding us along than steering clear of their own. Despite her gracious tones, I recognized Nimue's displeasure with her family member and his companions.

I found myself forced again to drop back to accommodate Chauncy's newfound proximity requirement, to prevent him trampling the others. The position didn't sit well with me. I'd grown accustomed to being in the fore and my inability to be where I could protect my friends added to my disconcert. Before long, the path began an upward climb and a dim daylight seeped into the tunnel, minimizing the artificial lighting the Wildron carried. Chauncy dropped his head down, hunching like a pouting child, his horn scraping the floor. Shoulders and hips bumped the rocky outcroppings. The tallest among us walked with heads bowed, although truthfully, we stood no chance of striking the stones above. Only Chauncy was hindered in that regard. I didn't know what I would do should he become lodged. Except for the area where he'd found us, no place existed wide enough for him to turn and go back. He wouldn't leave me, though, I knew that.

I noticed Hannah looking over her shoulder. After the third or fourth glance, she pivoted on her heel and strode back to me, her gaze warily assessing Chauncy. I could have told her she had nothing to fear, the *conjure* hadn't enough room for swift maneuver. But I held my tongue. Perhaps I felt it better for her to be afraid.

"Why are you here?" she asked, certainly not loud enough for anyone to hear, including her companions.

"What do you mean? In this cave?" A Duncan-like question, addressing the overly obvious first. It was a good tactic, throwing people off, although sometimes it made them angry.

Hannah was one of those, the latter. Her pale

eyes narrowed beneath a frowning brow. "In the Wilds," she hissed. "Once you'd rescued the girl, why didn't you go home? To your people."

"First," I said, voice low in response, "weren't you trying to find us? For a purpose? Second, how do you know we rescued Resa?"

Contrarily, she ignored the first, answering only the last. "Word travels far."

"Word travels fast, you mean. You speak of events no more than two days past. I can't see Tiran allowing such a story to be broadcast. It makes him look bad. His soldiers, too. Or is this something your Seer witnessed? I'd give a good deal to know the truth behind what you have told us."

Her facial muscles stiffened, expression going from irritated to rebellious. "You don't frighten me, desert warrior."

I studied her a moment, sighed. "I'm not trying to. I'm only trying to get some answers."

"So am I."

Chauncy twisted about in the confined area, rubbing his jaw against my head and making an odd, booming sound deep in his throat. Perhaps he attempted to soothe me, to calm me down. Hannah viewed his movements as hostile and danced away. Whatever his intent, he succeeded in distracting me, at least. He also made me smell worse than I did already, scenting my hair and shoulder with the saliva dripping in sticky rivulets from his mouth. I needed to bathe. Desperately. We all did. Last bath I'd enjoyed had been in the facilities on Emerald.

"Look," I said, "I can't go home. I would be bringing danger straight to my tribe, to my family."

"So, you thought you would bring it here to us instead."

"No!" At my raised tone, Duncan glanced back. I shook my head, turned again to Hannah, lowering my voice even more. "No," I repeated, confused by her change in tactics compared to what she'd revealed to us by the waterfall. I wondered if what the Lyoness had said, about them being answerable for whatever they'd done, something apparently not sanctioned, had made her cross. Or worse. Frightened.

"But crossing the desert would have led Tiran and his soldiers straight to my home, assuming we'd been able to outrun them," I explained. "He may still seek me there, but I am hoping the false trail the Ogdonians left in the opposite direction will keep him searching elsewhere for a while. He would never expect us to enter The Wilds. Who in their right mind would do so willingly?"

She snorted agreement. I hesitated before speaking again, my thoughts on the Ogdonians and the danger in which they'd placed themselves, for me, for us. Why? Originally, they'd wanted nothing to do with aiding us, honoring Neutrality. What had changed?

Hannah considered me through narrowed lids. "You keep secrets," she said.

"We all do, don't we?"

She made another noise, one that sounded almost like brief, contained laughter. "I suppose that is true." Running her hand through her red hair, she yanked at the short strands, increasing its spiky nature.

"Would someone do that for me?" I asked with a nod.

She pulled her fingers away from her head, turned her hand back and forth, squinting at the appendage. "Do what?"

"Cut my hair short."

"Truly?" Her eyes widened, as surprised as I at the change in topic.

I lifted the unkempt braid from my shoulder. "Yes. Truly. I can't keep this tended on the run. It's constantly tangled. I don't how Carina's hair looks so…not."

Hannah followed my gaze. "She does have lovely hair. Where is she from?"

"Tansi Islands."

"Ah," she said, as if my answer explained everything she needed to know.

We walked together in silence. I adopted my stride to her shorter one, keeping my gaze on the back of Duncan's head. He appeared taller than he had back on the prison planet, an illusion perhaps fostered by how thin he'd become. We'd all dropped weight. No surprise there. Due to lack of replenishment, our bodies depleted the caloric benefit from any sustenance consumed.

"The Lyoness," I said. "Is she angry with you four? It's hard to tell from her tone, but she did seem…displeased."

Hannah eyed me askance before returning her focus to the fore. I couldn't tell who she watched. Ren?

"We will be punished," she said.

"Why?"

"Disobedience. Unauthorized use of resources. Acting without orders. Shall I go on?"

"I don't understand," I said.

"You wouldn't."

"Why wouldn't I? Warriors live with tradition, rules, law."

"Not you," she said.

"Right. I suppose it doesn't seem I do, to you. But what I meant was that I don't understand what you have done. What rules have you broken?"

Chauncy moved his head. Hannah ducked away, flinching, and then straightened again. "I lied," she said.

"To me?"

"We all lied," Hannah added softly. Her nose wrinkled as if pushing back a sting brought about by threatening tears.

"About what?" I'd been wondering since our first meeting how much in what we'd been told might be untrue. Perhaps, she meant something not expressed to us, at all. Or, now that they'd been caught out, she worried about the consequences, wished they'd never had cause to search for us, bring us in.

Hannah shook her head, spiky hair jostling. "I don't want to talk about it. It's probably already too late."

"Too late for what?"

"I said I don't want to talk about it."

My left eyebrow shot up. I bit my lip and kept silent. Hounding her for an answer would serve no purpose. I'd give it a few minutes and try again.

Her eyes went front. "Do you like him?

Duncan."

"I love him," I said. I knew that wasn't what she meant, wasn't how she meant it. I let her think what she would, though. I didn't know what else to say,

A muscle moved in her jaw, a twitch tugging at her mouth. For another few minutes, we marched on without speaking until finally, with an awkward wave, she moved ahead.

"Wait," I said.

She halted until Chauncy and I caught up, then fell into step near me again.

"I had another reason for coming here, to The Wilds. One I haven't shared with my friends."

"Really?" she said, patently disappointed. I supposed she thought I might bring up Duncan. "What's that, then?"

"Mage lore. I've heard the Wildron possess mage lore. I hope to find answers from someone here."

Hannah considered, brows gathered close together, forehead wrinkling. We continued trudging along while she mulled over what I'd told her. "What answers?" she finally asked. She tipped her head in Resa's direction. "Answers to what *she* is?"

"No," I said quietly. "To what I am."

*   *   *

Hannah left me, returning to the others. I observed her for a time, anticipating she would hurry to impart what she'd learned. She said nothing to Joy-Li or Hugo, however, keeping a strange reticence. Ren stood too far apart for conversation. Duncan strode in front with him, Resa's hand in his, Mika and Carina nearby. Hannah looked back at me only once, her expression flat. I felt suddenly isolated, deserted, despite the *conjure's* gigantic nostrils snuffling at my neck.

*You're not alone, Grace. You'll never be alone. I'm here.*

I swore under my breath.

*Tsk, tsk, such language.*

The *conjure* nudged me harder, shoving away the hand clinging unconsciously to the hanging bag around my throat. I dropped my fingers.

I had to get answers, soon. The weight of the unknown perched like an entity upon my shoulders, weighing me down. I kept recalling how in the ship and later, after landing, the effect of the creatures from Emerald had continued to torment Duncan and me. Sometimes it seemed what Skelly had become managed to do the same, hampering my resilience, twisting perspective, raising doubts. But he couldn't have become the same as them. He couldn't have.

My concerns weren't only about Skelly, either. Resa needed…more. More than what we could give her. Carina couldn't continue to subsidize calm and peace when Resa lost her own. Eventually the connection would be too much, a break would occur, and whatever came next could be catastrophic.

Chauncy pushed his jaw against my shoulder, causing me to stumble. I looked up, realizing I'd fallen behind. The others had gone far enough their shadows now mingled with those cast by the Lyoness and her companions. Sunlight darted around them, glistening on the passage walls.

Alarmed by my lost concentration, my fading energy, I forced myself to walk faster. I spoke out loud in an attempt to lift my spirits. "When we're back outside, Chauncy, you can hunt. I'm sure you're hungry." *Conjures* had slow metabolisms, causing his kind to consume less than a smaller creature. However, I hadn't witnessed him eating anything since he first attached himself to me. I hadn't meant to be neglectful. I really hadn't. Intractable I'd often been called, but never negligent. And yet, I'd become this, the irresponsible, the unclear, the discouraged.

My steps lagged again. I pulled in a deep breath, let it out, found myself visualizing in minute detail the process Chauncy might engage in, where his appetite would lead, Surely, flesh rather than vegetation based upon his teeth, the placement of his eyes in predatory fashion, facing front. I visualized his long incisors ripping, tearing, almost tasted the iron of blood in my mouth. I made a face and spat on the ground by my feet. I assumed we could all rest easy, that *conjures* did not consume human flesh, but did I know anything, really? No. I acted on instinct, a flawed instinct, an instinct that had called Skelly Shane's spirit or whatever it could be down into the crystal, and by so doing had endangered us all.

I came to a complete halt and looked around, shoulders slumping. My *lathesa* slipped, scraping on stone. Chauncy had stopped at my back, head bowed, horn tapping the floor, a rhythm to the noise. The tunnel ahead echoed the drumbeat sound and nothing else. The faraway sunlight dappled the walls. No shadows moved within the light.

They'd left me.

I slid to the ground, my weapon clattering onto stone by my thigh, my head dropping, chin nearly on my chest. My shoulders shook as though I wept. Was I weeping? I might have been. In exhausted anguish, I opened my mouth, stretching it wide, listening for the sound of me, of my pain, my failure, to rush along the cavern walls. All remained silent. Even the comforting whuff of Chauncy's breathing had gone.

*I am here.*

"No," I said, the syllable overloud in my ears.

I whipped the silk cord over my head and lurched to my feet, hauling my arm back with one intent, one blind intent, to shatter the crystal into a thousand pieces on the wall, to relinquish my stewardship, to be done with it—

*And I will be free.*

Too late I recognized the mistake. Too late to latch onto the leather bag hurtling through semi-darkness. I lunged for it, slamming down hard and empty-handed across the stone beneath me. A rushing air swept by; a sound I did not recognize hurtled into my ears; a single footfall reverberated at my side, where my bruised ribs felt as though they might finally have cracked upon landing.

"Looking for this?"

Not Skelly. A human voice, echoing off the stone to either side.

I struggled upright. A hand appeared in my vision, long-fingered and filthy, the hand that belonged to a boy who once upon a time took so many showers, I thought he might strip his skin clean off. Attempting to wash away his guilt, I knew. In his grasp, Duncan held the leather sack, swinging it by the cord from his fingertips like a pendulum.

"You caught it?" I asked. Needlessly. Of course, he had. The proof was there, before my eyes, the bag intact, no fragments singing together inside; no dark intent looming overhead, freed to harm us all.

"Not me," he said. "Your buddy. I thought he'd skewer me when I came running in. I found it hanging from his horn."

I snatched the bag back from Duncan, slipped the cord over my neck. He offered me his hand, helping me to rise.

"Are you all right?" he asked.

I shook my head, crying again, or now, or still. He yanked me close. I bit back a yelp of pain, standing quiet instead in the comforting hug. I didn't often tolerate physical demonstrations, but from Duncan I did. From Duncan I always did.

*From the betrayer.*

*Shut it, Skelly.*

Ultimately, Duncan Oaks hadn't betrayed me. He'd betrayed himself. That distinction had to be so much harder to live with.

Chapter Nine

Duncan hadn't questioned the bag's contents, or why I'd thrown it. Sometimes he recognized when to keep quiet. Yet, they watched me closely, Duncan, Mika and Carina, knowing me well enough by now to understand I'd slipped, somehow; drifted away from the warrior they relied on. Resa watched me, as well. I had no idea what went on inside her head. For Duncan's sake, I wished I did. For his sake, I wished he did, too.

Once outside, Nimue and her troop had deliberately encircled the ten of us: our five, the four apparently disgraced Wildron, and Chauncy. A short time ago, Chauncy had wandered toward the boundary, the circle's members parting in a hurry to let him out into the forest beyond. Small animal screams followed his departure. When he reappeared, the Wildron gave him a wide berth. He walked beside me now, head held high, renewed and energetic and with blood flecking his jowls. Vegetation held no apparent part in his diet.

After Duncan's return for me, Mika had taken the time to rewrap my ribs and Duncan's fingers with strips torn from the clothes we would never return to their owners. Mika's erstwhile attention to his father's medical practice served him well. His inclination for major theft had not, although the knowledge gained in both activities turned out to be an invaluable asset to our group. Glancing at him sidelong, I wondered if he knew how much we appreciated him, and not only for his skills.

Obviously, he knew how much Carina did. Their closeness sometimes made me a bit prickly. I'd never had a relationship with a member of the opposite sex. Until Duncan, anyway. And even that wasn't a *relationship*. I supposed I'd been too busy. Training took up many hours in a warrior's life. Hours, and concentration, and dedication, and…

I thought suddenly of Mara.

Right.

As Duncan would say: moving on.

"What happened back there?"

I glanced aside at Ren, who'd ambled up to my right side by a circumvent route around Chauncy. He'd been walking there a while, not looking at me, definitely not looking at his great-grandmother. Clearly worried, he seemed diminished in some way, his brash arrogance stripped from him.

"Nothing," I said.

"Don't want to talk about it?" Hannah had been pacing slightly in front, ignoring us all until, at our conversation, she'd adjusted her stride, ending up beside Ren. "Were you going to run off, leave your friends? That's what Hugo said."

I closed my eyes, breathed in, breathed out. "I would never leave them," I said, lifting my lids to look at her. "Never."

Hannah and Ren remained silent.

"And she doesn't run away."

Heads jerked in Duncan's direction. I recognized an odd sadness in his expression. Duncan's arm dropped over my shoulders, giving the impression in its limpness that it belonged there. I didn't shirk it off, even when Chauncy turned an eye his way with the whites fiercely showing.

"Where's Resa?" I asked.

"With the lovebirds," he said. "Sometimes I think she rather have their company than mine."

Hannah spun to stare at Carina and Mika, walking backwards as she spoke, words drawn out, mocking. "Those two are together?"

"Yep," said Duncan. "Why? Feeling a little left out? A little lonely? A little jealous?" He tightened his grip on my shoulder. I flinched, recalling Hannah's interest in him. Snarling, Hannah pivoted front and stomped away. Duncan's arm dropped to his side.

"I guess I'm lucky she didn't fire-ball me," he said, and laughed.

I laughed, too, because he'd been funny with that last remark, not because he had hurt Hannah. I doubted he had any idea what she was feeling right then. Ren laughed as well, loudly. The sound, the sensation of my own in my lungs and through my body, shot like light into me, almost dispersing the dark, lingering disquiet. At that moment, if I closed my eyes yet again, I could have made myself believe we were all friends met through some unconceived circumstance and on our way to spend a morning together in a place where war and terror did not reign. In a place where cities hadn't been reduced to rubble and fire; where we weren't dogged by armed warriors; where I hadn't been falsely accused of treason; where Duncan had never given testimony to condemn me; where one of our number hadn't died in a manner too horrible for memory to bear.

But I did remember. Not his death. Only Duncan had been there to witness that. I'd seen what was left after. We all had.

I heard a scream. In my head. Skelly, shrieking inside the leather-bound crystal.

Laughter and lightness left me. Duncan's hand slipped around mine. "You'll have to tell me sometime. Tell all of us. Whatever it is."

"Desert girl," Ren said, "I wouldn't want to be you."

I wondered what showed on my face. Nothing pleasant.

*   *   *

Ren stayed close by, probably in an attempt to overhear any conversation we might have, and yet I couldn't be sure he wasn't there merely because he wanted the companionship. Or the protection. Or the illusion we could offer either.

As he'd been privy to the stories being told about our little group—and I could only imagine how swiftly-flown tales might become embellished—he likely imagined something far more impressive than the facts. Although if I were to be honest, we four managing to escape not only the juvenile facility but the horrifying creatures outside it, returning to Talia in one piece, could not be exaggerated. We had done all those things, and saved Resa. Extraordinary results, really.

Had my family heard the rumors? If not, they would still believe me dead. Duncan's grandmother had been told the same, that her grandson had met his demise. With no means to send a communication, this news could remain the truth for them unless—until—we returned to our homes.

Despite the dire circumstances with which we'd been existing, the thought of home caught in my throat, and not exactly in a joyful way. I longed for my family, my friends, to know they were safe, to be among them, to be safe again myself, yes, I truly did, but Duncan and his sister, Mika, Carina and I came from very different backgrounds, from places so far apart we'd likely never see each other again once restored to our prior lives. I would miss them. I didn't want to miss them. I wanted us to stand together, always.

*So, you'd be happy for war to continue? I could help with that.*

I shoved my right hand into my pocket, away from the insane, mystifying temptation to make contact with the bag, the crystal, with Skelly. I kept the *lathesa* in my left, angled across my shoulder. I'd expected the weapon to be taken from me when most of our supplies had been confiscated under guise of easing our burdens, but no one had made an attempt so far.

"Ren," I said, startling him from some reverie, "would your great-grandmother really see you punished for transgression?"

He frowned. "Who told you that?"

"Hannah."

"Oh. Well, then, yes, probably."

"Will it be bad?"

"Yes," he said, "probably. Unless I can convince her otherwise."

He threw the answer out as though he spoke about a commonplace occurrence and perhaps punishment was, indeed, commonplace. But he only pretended to be unconcerned. If nothing else, his enlarged pupils revealed a volume of unspoken sentiment, memories, apprehension.

The tribes, too, had punishments for recalcitrant conduct. These varied, but the intent was for them to always end up a lesson. The adults believed that, anyway. I'd frequently thought each and every earned punishment quite unfair. One would think that after having been subjected to enough of them I'd start to recognize their value. Yet, sometimes the knowledge consequences existed didn't always prevent the action they were intended to modify. I'd been guilty of such disregard, only to discover the penalties altered significantly for my benefit. Infuriating me, yes, annoying me, too, but I couldn't recall ever being afraid of a punishment.

I looked to where Nimue strode among what appeared to be an honor guard. The Wildron in her immediate vicinity wore cloaks with silver threading and an insignia on the breast. Everyone else wore simple, dark, and in some cases extremely worn garments. Ren and his three allies were no exception. Even Ren's boots had been repaired once too often.

Abruptly, I pulled my hand from my pocket, holding up the tangy contents I'd stored there. "Fruit?"

One by one, the dried slivers vanished, passed along to the others in both our groups. I stuck the last in my mouth, squinting one eye from the sharp flavor.

"You're like Gran," Duncan said.

Ren barked a laugh, his fruit slice flying from his lips. He managed to catch it mid-air.

"How so?" I asked, tone dry.

"Don't take offense. She always had some goodie in her pocket when I was little."

I smiled, chewing through the facial contortion, picturing Duncan with an older, maternal woman. I had no idea what she looked like. Him, a bit? It would be nice to meet Duncan's grandmother sometime. I never would, though. I understood that. I'd be lucky to ever get back to my own family, let alone to take a flight to the gambling moon, to Riley, where Duncan's Gran still lived.

As quickly as my mood had boosted, it plummeted down.

*Welcome to my existence,* Skelly whispered through my brain.

Something touched my arm. A small, pale hand, the rich blood in its veins standing out like paint beneath the almost colorless flesh covering them. Carina.

"Grace," she whispered.

I stared at her, my thoughts suddenly wordless,

filled only with images of the past days, of the manifestation in the compound, the crystal in its bag, my interactions since, the emotions, all drawn from my mind by Carina. Alarmed, I yanked my arm from beneath her fingers, my eyes meeting hers. Her irises transmuted to a vivid red.

Seeing them, too, Ren gasped. He stumbled a step or two away. "Transmogrification?"

"Ooo," said Duncan, "he knows big words. It's okay, Ren. I guess you just hadn't noticed before."

Ren shook his head, body poised for a hasty departure. Carina ignored them both, focused her unique gaze on me, asked in a low voice she hoped would exclude them, "Why did you not tell me?"

Brows lowering, Duncan's attention pivoted from Ren to me. "Tell her what? Is something going on here that Mika and I should know, too?"

I didn't answer.

"Grace," Duncan persisted, asking not for the first time and surely not for the last, "are you okay?"

I bit my lip.

"Please tell me you are."

My gaze shifted to Ren, who no longer looked like he might run off. He watched me closely. Alerted, no doubt, by a change in energy among us, Mika towed Resa closer. Hannah stopped, waiting for us to draw near, and Hugo and Joy-Li appeared from who knew where. I hadn't noticed their absence until now. Everyone had their own reasons for concern, for curiosity. I had no plans to oblige any of them.

"I'm fine," I said, and turned to Carina, repeating those words with emphasis.

"But you're not," she whispered.

I pulled her aside away from the others, gently because exhaustion seemed about to knock her to her knees. "And you are not responsible for taking care of me. Not now. Not right now. Hopefully not ever again. Because you have enough to handle with Resa. Okay?"

She closed her eyes, her white lashes shadowing her pale skin. She nodded. When she lifted her lids again, her eyes had colored like a sunlit puddle, more reflection than anything else. I had no idea what the hue meant or, for that matter, what color her eyes might be on a normal, untroubled day. They changed constantly with her emotions.

"Don't let them know," she said.

I glanced aside at Duncan, out of earshot. "I won't."

"Not them. Tell Mika and Duncan. Don't let any of them know." Her gaze swept the Wildron striding around us at the perimeter and within.

"But I need answers," I said. "And I think someone here might have them."

"I understand, but the portent—"

"You read portents, as well?" I interrupted. Some people did, predicting rain on the thickness of a *bulgar's* shed skin, or war on the flight of scavenging birds. The last, at least, might be valid. Birds who survived on decaying flesh would naturally seek out a battleground. "What have you seen?"

"Not that kind of portent," she said, her sweet voice marred by fatigue and, I suspected, impatience with me. "It is a Tansi word, *portent.* Like what you carry in here."

Before I could stop her, she'd reached up and tapped the place on my tunic beneath which the bag holding the crystal lay. Crying out, she jerked her fingers away.

*That little freak better not do that again,* Skelly's voice scolded.

"Oh, Grace," said Carina. I barely heard her. Her eyes rolled back in her head and she dropped to the ground.

I caught her as she fell, settled her onto the soil beneath my knees. Marching feet shuffled to a stop all around. Voices spoke. I did not heed their words as I smoothed Carina's tumbled, white hair from her brow.

"Carin—"

Mika blundered into me, knocking me aside. Blanched with shock, he crouched beside Carina, touching her face, her wrist, checking her pulse, laying a hand lightly on her chest to assess her breathing.

"What happened?" he asked me.

"I think she's exhausted and we were…we were talking about something that upset her."

"What? What were you talking about?"

I glanced around. "I can't tell you here, Mika. I'm sorry."

His face knotted with anger, breaking my heart. Grunting, he lifted her into his arms and stood. She was already coming around, blinking at him and murmuring what I recognized, with a start and a stab, were endearments. A hand grabbed my arm, hauled me to my feet. I clutched my aching ribs.

"Are you okay?"

Duncan, always Duncan. "It doesn't matter," I said.

He gave my arm a shake. "Are you okay?"

Resa stood behind him, peering around his hip, black braids swinging with her head's movement. She appeared relaxed, but at any moment her status could change. I tried smiling at her. My mouth wouldn't form the necessary curve. She looked away.

"I ask too much of Carina," I said. "Of all of you."

He swore, a particularly inventive conglomeration. Sweet, sweet Duncan. What would I do without him?

"Where do you think we'd be if not for you?" he demanded, nearly echoing my thought about him. "We *owe* you."

"No, please don't say that."

"We do," he said. "We voluntarily owe you, all right? Does that make it better?" He swore again in a frustration I recognized.

"I owe you all, too. None of this has been easy."

"I know."

His amber eyes held a heaviness I hadn't seen before, not in the worst moments we'd faced. The heartbreak begun at Mika's anger intensified tenfold.

Someone came along, a Wildron, and prodded us on. I hurried up to Mika, who still held Carina, her thin limbs wrapped around his neck, his waist, her head against him. Gently, I removed Carina's long veil from around her shoulders and prepared a sling, enveloping her in the sheer but strong fabric, tying the ends behind Mika's back. It would be easier for him to carry her this way. The entire time I worked, I avoided his gaze and didn't speak. Like a coward.

With a last tuck, I turned away. Fingers pinched my sleeve, pulled me back.

"Don't you break, Grace Irese. We need you," Mika said.

I looked at him, at Carina's head ducked

beneath his chin, at both of them staring back at me. My lip quivered. "I'll try not to."

We walked in silence after that, Chauncy lumbering along on my left, Duncan and Resa on my right, near to Carina, because despite her weakened state the proximity between Duncan's sister and our little island mystic remained necessary. Ren, Hannah, Joy-Li and Hugo separated from us, striding together in a knot, shoulders hunched, the threatened punishment no doubt clinging oppressively in their minds. I tried once to break the strain with a trivial question to Ren about a small creature flitting through the trees overhead. He looked up, arching his neck, seeking the animal, and then back down at me, mumbling a response I didn't catch and didn't ask him to repeat.

Odd shapes dotted the forest, covered in vegetation and hinting at the remnants from the shattered civilization. Sharp, manmade angles contorted branches and leaves, with many ruins cut straight through by trees grown old in the years since Olympian fell. Boots began to ring on stone. Beneath our feet an ancient road, nearly overgrown, ran on into the wood before us. I figured it must still be used with some regularity not to have disappeared altogether under the damp humus. In the desert, any roadway had to be constantly managed to keep the sand from obliterating it. No sand existed here, but it seemed likely the forest's growth would insist on thriving the way weeds did in my mother's perpetually-tended garden.

When the road started to climb, Mika stumbled. I rushed over, extended my arms.

"I'll take Carina for a bit," I said.

His eyebrows shot up. I think he'd decided I'd finally lost my wits.

"I have the strength," I reminded him.

"And a pair of possibly fractured ribs. You don't want them cracked completely."

He had a point. A very good point. But I wouldn't let it go.

"Just for a bit," I said. "Afterward, I'll give her back, I promise."

Carina shifted in his grasp. "You two do realize I'm right here?" Still sounding weak, tired, as if the brief respite from walking hadn't restored her. She'd have to be carried, and Mika needed a break. This wasn't like running from the compound with her on his back, where adrenaline had given him all the stamina he needed.

I shook my upraised arms at him. My insistence might be an affront to him as a male, reminding him also that up until recently he'd been sedentary and less than robust in the prison's confinement, but I couldn't waste time on wounded feelings. We needed to get moving again before the Wildron decided to do what Ren had only threatened: to leave Carina behind.

"Fine," he said. People said that a lot. Fine. It

was rarely what they meant.

Mika crouched down. Carina slipped her feet from the sling and stood, enabling him to maneuver the knotted end over his head. She wobbled on her legs. Mika seized her arm before she fell, propping her up against his body. My stomach dipped into my knees.

"This is bad," Duncan whispered behind me.

I knew it was. I would have to carry her. We had to go on. I wouldn't leave her behind. I wouldn't leave any of them behind.

Duncan stepped around me. "I'll do it," he said.

"You can't. Resa may need you."

Defeated by my reminder's logic, he backed away. I handed the *lathesa* to him reluctantly. He'd have to carry it now. Taking the silk sling from Mika, I shoved my arm through the opening, shifted the knot around to rest beneath my right shoulder blade. Mika lifted Carina, ready to assist her into position. A shadow fell across them both. Someone screamed.

I jerked back, startled, spun on my heel, extended one arm to push Mika and Carina to safety, the other to divert whatever was coming. I had no idea who'd screamed. I also had no weapon.

Ended up, I didn't need one. Chauncy pressed close, his smelly hide scrubbing across my face, my clothes. He planted himself in front of me with a distinct clop of his feet on the stone road, blocking my way. I exchanged a look with Duncan, who'd been knocked unceremoniously aside.

"Get that beast under control," a male voice shouted.

"Yeah," said Duncan. "As if." Not loud enough for the speaker to have heard. Only me.

"I don't know what Chauncy wants," I said.

"Ask him."

"What?"

"Ask him. It can't hurt, can it?"

I frowned, attempting to formulate a question that would make any sense at all, to the *conjure*, to me. The immediacy in our situation didn't leave me time for any obstinance from Chauncy. I opened my mouth, filling the cavity quite by accident with his scent, preparing to tell him to just get out of my way. I didn't expect he would comply. Why would he? Yet, before I could speak, he rumbled in his throat and bent his front legs, lowering his chest to the ground, settling in it appeared, and most unfortunately.

For a few seconds, I believed him to be looking off into space in some placid fashion, perhaps readying to sleep despite the awkward angle of his body. When I realized he was staring at Carina, I sucked in a startled breath.

"Mika," I whispered, signaling him with a discreet wave, "bring Carina here."

Again, he looked at me as if contemplating my present mental faculties.

"Slowly," I said, "but right now."

He started toward me with obvious hesitancy. Once he reached my side, I exchanged places, leaving him and Carina by Chauncy's ribcage while I walked around to the *conjure's* head. I stayed clear of the horn, but I was still so very, very close to the large, sharp teeth. I had a quick, unpleasant image and pushed it away, willing myself to remain composed.

"Carina," I said, "climb on top. Mika, help her please."

"What?" This from not only Mika, but Duncan, too. Carina, however, met my gaze, held it, nodded.

"Yes," she said. "Yes, of course."

I positioned myself between an animal that could, upon an instant, relieve me of my head, and the four people I cared about most in this strange, abandoned province. Mika assisted Carina onto Chauncy's back. The *conjure* accepted her presence with no more complaint than a small, soft grunt. Carina slid her fingers into Chauncy's thick fur, holding herself in place.

"Now Resa," I said, "if she'll go."

Duncan clutched Resa's shoulder protectively. "Are you sure?"

"Resa trusts Carina. It's best they stay together, yes?"

He nodded. After a moment, he lifted Resa up behind Carina. I looked at her, considered again her heritage. Mage blood would explain a lot, but it would also mean she and Duncan didn't share the same father. I hadn't yet felt comfortable enough to ask him this question. I couldn't quite understand why. We'd said things to each other that surprised me sometimes.

Resa wrapped her arms around Carina's middle

and leaned against her back, unperturbed, no doubt comforted by Carina's presence, if not her gift. Unbending first one leg, then the other, Chauncy rocked to his full height. I stepped away. An odd silence had fallen on the Wildron nearby. I glanced in their direction.

Duncan leaned forward, his mouth near my ear, tangled strands loosened from my braid flitting across my cheek when he spoke.

"They're afraid."

He wasn't wrong. They were.

Chapter Ten

We were treated differently thereafter, and not for the better. When people are afraid, they are frequently prone to attack rather than reason. I walked with my *lathesa* leaning against my shoulder, as if I did not sense the lurking danger, but kept my hand where I could swiftly utilize the weapon. Mika and Duncan strode one to a side next to Chauncy, Carina and Duncan's sister crowning the *conjure's* back like accomplished riders. I varied my position from front to rear in order to keep a constant eye, spotting our former companions but once in the following hour, still bunched together, still anxious and unhappy. Thus preoccupied, I found myself less troubled by the thing I carried concealed in the crystal shard, yet I didn't fool myself into complacency. I understood my active mind provided only a shield. I wasn't certain how long I could maintain the fight.

Duncan nodded at me as I passed him again to stride at Chauncy's head. Through the jumble of trees and ruin, I spotted something spread out along the mountainside above us. At first, the structures were hard to discern, looking more like stone outcroppings than dwellings, but then I spied roofs and windows, as well as a road, perhaps a continuation of this one, and movement upon it. I didn't believe this to be the City of All Dwellers. It appeared to be no more than a village, yet the first visible habitation I'd noted on our route; possibly a sign we were nearing the city.

As we drew close, the settlement's layout became clear. Stone buildings perched on the slope to either side of the road running through. No more than a dozen or so, varying in size and construction. Some had timbered upper levels; others were cylindrical in nature. Most, however, were foursquare, solidly built from gray and tan stones. Heavy-looking wooden doors barred any inside glimpse and the windows revealed little from our approaching angle.

The villagers already outside stopped, turned, gaped, pointed, mostly at Chauncy, moving on to the two occupying his broad back, then to Duncan, Mika and me. Others came out and joined them. In my long ago visit to Citadel during festival, I and my family had been among thousands witnessing a seasonal procession through the city streets. I felt like that, although more the center of the spectacle rather than the observer.

In time, stare after stare left us and alighted on the Wildron marching silently along before and behind. Gazes dropped to the street's cobbled surface and stayed there, as if afraid to meet their brethren's eyes. I assumed they considered themselves one and the same. The tribes were deemed one desert people but each possessed its own tribal identity and identifiers, so perhaps the Wildron segmented themselves likewise.

I noted they did dress in a fashion dissimilar to the Lyoness and her underlings, the people in this village. The long, hooded cloaks were absent, revealing clothing not unlike what the Ogdonians wore. Of course, I had no idea what our captors—yes, despite their assertions to the contrary, I knew what they were—had on under their cloaks.

"Grace."

My head snapped around. To my right, Hannah dogged my steps nearby, her red hair and pale eyes so similar to Skelly's in coloration. I don't know how I hadn't noticed before. My flesh shivered over muscle and bone beneath my somewhat sweaty tunic.

Hannah cut across to my side and reached out for my hand. "Take this," she whispered.

Initially, I repelled the force of her fingers into my fist, but then I relented, opening my hand as though to grasp hers. She wrapped her fingers around mine. "What is it?" I asked, feeling hard edges press against my palm.

"Don't look at it. Not now. Keep it safe." She didn't let go right away, I supposed to throw off any who might be observing her actions. She moved closer, leaning up on her toes and planting a strange, dry kiss on my cheek. "I'll be seeing you," she said.

I pulled her hand to my side, first, so no one would see when I released her and closed my hand around the object she'd given me, and second, to better look into her eyes. I didn't like the way she'd spoken those words *I'll be seeing you.* They sounded final, somehow, as if she expected she never would again.

She yanked her hand free. "I have to go." She darted away.

A minute or two later, enough time to avoid suspicion, Duncan ambled up to my side. "What was that about?"

I hadn't looked at the object in my hand, hadn't shoved it into my pocket, hadn't done anything but try to act as though nothing had been passed to me, swinging my arm to match my stride, my fingers in a loose fist, the way I often held them. I kept the object pressed to my palm with my thumb, avoiding probing the thing lest I drop it.

"I'm not sure. She gave me something, told me to keep it safe."

"What is it?"

"I haven't looked yet. I'm trying not to be obvious, Duncan."

"Got it," he said.

"I don't mean to be rude."

"No, I got it. I understand. Maybe when we get to the city. Do you think it's close?"

I glanced around at the villagers, their eyes stealing our way again in a scrutiny marked by awe, by fear, maybe anger. Was everyone afraid? Of us? Or was it something more?

"I hope so," I said. It seemed to me our arrival in the city might mark something definitive, perhaps answers, perhaps only an end to speculation. Anticipation frayed my nerves.

My gaze shifted to Chauncy, clomping along the cobbled road, eyes straight ahead, ignoring the stares from the people lining the street. Carina and Resa remained comfortably perched on his back, rocking from side to side in rhythm with his gait.

"How's Mika?" I asked Duncan.

"Holding up."

"Is he?"

"He's worried," Duncan said. "So am I."

Nodding, I acknowledged my own concern. I would not say the words aloud. Out loud, they flew free to stifle hope, and not only mine.

Pretending to adjust the *lathesa's* positioning. I slipped the item from Hannah into my left hand, then down into my pocket, giving it a quick onceover before I pulled my hand back out. It felt like a talisman, a small figure of some sort, but I couldn't be sure because the hard, sharp edges threw me off. Why would Hannah give such a thing to me? I searched for her, for her small group among the Wildron, but could find no sight of them. They were lost among the identically cloaked figures. Well, except for the Lioness and her presumed honor guard. They were easy to pick out, not only due to the distinctive markings on their cloaks, but the fact they were given a wide berth by everyone.

"What do you think we're going to find when we get to this City of All Dwellers?"

"I don't know," I answered Duncan. "I really don't."

"Frying pan or fire?"

My mouth twisted up at the corner.

"Cauldron?"

He grunted, a noise halfway between laughter and dismissal. "So bigger problem, less heat?"

"We'll see."

We continued on without speaking for a time, a comfortable silence not marred by unspoken words. We were each lost in our own thoughts regarding what might be coming, but I didn't feel overwhelmed by them with Duncan at my side. I don't think he did, either.

*Oh, please.*

Skelly.

*Yes, I'm back.*

*Have you truly been somewhere?* I asked him, curious at his remark and unable to help myself.

He didn't answer. After a moment I broke my thoughts away, pushing him down.

"Grace? Did you hear me?"

I shot a startled, sideways glance at Duncan. "Sorry, no. What did you say?"

"I was saying I'm surprised that Chauncy…you know." He dipped his head sideways toward the *conjure* and its passengers, twisting his lips in a manner that made me laugh. Just one, and short-lived.

"Yes," I agreed. "He didn't just allow them up, he instigated it."

"Why, do you think?"

"Me, maybe."

"You?"

"I'm injured and I was going to carry Carina anyway. Maybe this is something he sensed?"

"More protecting you, then, than them?"

"I don't know, Duncan," I said, fighting the exasperation in my voice. "There's so much I don't know."

He reached across the space between us and took my hand, giving it a hearty squeeze. "The only true wisdom is knowing you know nothing."

I snorted. "Gran?"

"Yeah, but I'm thinking she probably stole that adage."

I laughed again, this time hard and rather loudly. After, I wriggled my fingers from his and straightened my shoulders, shaking them a bit beneath my shirt to loosen the tension I'd allowed to build. I thought I glimpsed Hannah's spiked red hair ahead. A second later she'd vanished.

"Duncan?"

"Yeah?"

"Be kind to Hannah."

"What? Why?"

"She needs it."

"Don't we all?"

I turned my head, looked at him. His own shoulders drooped.

"Fine," he said. "You're more like Gran all the time. It's creepy."

"Yeah, well, get used to it, Duncan Oaks. She can't be all bad. She raised you to be who you are."

"A con-artist, you mean?"

I looked away. "No. You're so much more than that."

He remained silent a moment, thinking, I supposed, about what I'd said, about his Gran.

"To be honest," he went on, "she hadn't wanted me to join the Guild. Threatened me with everything she could think of, tried pushing me in other directions. I wished it had worked."

"Don't wish too hard," I said. "If not for that, it would have been someone else up there on Emerald with me, someone I couldn't count on, couldn't trust. Someone I'm sure I wouldn't have liked half as much."

I punched him lightly on the arm, as though I were joking, and to show him that really, after all was said and done, I wasn't.

*     *     *

We'd left the village and gone straight on, the village being only an outlier to the city. Like an animal sensing home, the Wildron's pace picked up. I worried Mika, and therefore the rest of us, wouldn't be able to keep up with them. Not that they would have permitted us to fall behind. We were theirs now. Sanctuary seemed a label designed to accommodate what we were expected to believe. But we weren't stupid, not a single one. I sensed the knowledge, the wariness, in all of us. Even Resa had become restless. Duncan stayed close.

Ahead, the road ended at a craggy ledge. Beyond it, the treetops peeking up from below disappeared into a misted blue haze. To the right, a jagged fall of rock lay in a jumble at the bottom of a steep incline. I stared upward, looking for a path that wouldn't put my companions and me at risk. Chauncy, too. After he'd braved the blackness underground to find me, I wouldn't turn him away again. I saw no path, not even the evidence one had ever existed.

The Lyoness and her guard had pressed to the fore, stopping beneath a deep outcropping. The late afternoon sun glinted on the silver adorning their cloaks when they turned to face the remainder coming up behind. Sunlight highlighted Nimue's scars as well, shadowing them in such a way they reminded me of my people's illustrative and deeply colored tattoos. Nimue spoke, her voice echoing off stone.

"Grace, you and your companions come near."

I obeyed, my friends and the *conjure* following. I switched once again the hand clutching my weapon. Eyeing Nimue's guard, I halted our party at a defendable distance.

"Despite what you may be thinking," she said, "you are welcome among us. I know you had a rough start with Ren. I promise that shall be amended. There is nothing to fear here."

I had so many questions, yet asked none. Except for one. "Where is here?" I looked around. "We're standing on the edge of a cliff."

"Step forward," she said.

"I'll decline." Beside me, Duncan sniffed in a

short breath, suppressing something. A laugh. Shock? Perhaps both.

"There's nothing to fear, as I've told you." The Lyoness continued, "We will back away. I wish you to see where we are going."

Together my companions and I walked forward, not to the ledge and the forest below, but toward the tumbled boulders, to the place Nimue directed us with a hand's sweeping motion. I saw at once the rocks had been blasted away, broken, jagged, adorned by trees which had sprouted long ago in the rubble. The road took a sharp turn here, invisible from where we'd been standing, and ran between two towering stones; carved stone, the images worn, cracked here and there, pieces missing from what might once have been faces. I barely spared a glance for them, my eye drawn instead to what lay beyond cupped in a geological bowl surrounded by a barren circle and forested hills.

Duncan whistled. The piercing sound echoed off the twin stones and was answered, it seemed, by a raptor crying in the air above the wooded valley behind us.

"Welcome," said the Lyoness, who had come quietly to stand next to me, "to the City of All Dwellers."

*　*　*

The city contradicted all I had been told about this place of ruin. The rumors regarding a devastation from which the territory had never recovered were frankly untrue. The bare bones of

130

the former civilization had been scrubbed clean and stood stark and lovely in the green, green forest, the remnants rising well above the treetops, and between, around and inclusive of them stood the new city. A city fashioned from glass and history.

I stood a moment without speaking, disturbed by its strange beauty. Desert born and bred, I quite preferred the open spaces I'd known, the low-lying abodes, the combinations of unexpected color where residents like my mother managed their gardens. Even Citadel, the only city I'd ever visited, had possessed before it's destruction elements more easily recognized by association. Sand-colored stone, stucco, cool blues and other pastel elements, the structured, courtly gardens. Here, I found none of that. The City of All Dwellers was lush, wild, encapsulated beauty.

It totally unnerved me.

Duncan, on the other hand, appeared enamored. "Cool," he whispered, another word he'd brought with him from the gaming moon. He uttered it on those occasions when he couldn't quite summon up the vocabulary to express his feelings. I wished for a similar but opposite word, one that Duncan would understand and the Lyoness would not.

"We should keep moving," Nimue said. "I'm sure you are tired and hungry. We must remedy that."

The Lyoness and her immediate entourage led the way and we followed, the remainder trailing after. Unperturbed, Chauncy lumbered down the incline with his passengers, once again between Mika and Duncan, me at his head. Sunlight struck his horn, reflecting a semi-clear calcification I hadn't noted before, a fine, jewel-like dusting. His hooves clattered on stone. Birds fluttered above the road, their song loud, but neither they nor our noisy progress managed to disguise the low hum vibrating through the air. Power. Mechanical power.

"Lyoness," I said, approaching her. Her guard stepped in, close, but she waved them away. "It is my understanding you receive communications here. At home, all systems were down. Tell me, what news of the outside world? How do the desert tribes fare? My friends would like to know of their homes as well, I'm sure."

She squinted at me from the burned side of her face. "Who told you this?"

I took a small breath, marshalling calm. "Lioness, you did, unless I misunderstood you. At the campsite, you said you had heard of me. I assumed there is only one way to have done so." Not exactly lying, but fishing for the truth. I hoped she wasn't as adept at reading my face as she seemed.

"Ah, yes, quite right," she said. "When we meet for the evening meal, we will see if we can update you on events, yes?"

I thanked her and dropped back to stride alongside my friends.

"What did you ask her?" Duncan whispered.

"For news of home," I said. I had made the request because I'd hoped to determine how she'd heard about me, about us, but the possibility I might receive some news regarding those I'd left behind, for good or bad, made my empty stomach churn. I swallowed, hard, fighting down bile. "For all of us."

"What did she say?"

I shrugged. "That we'll see, at the evening meal."

Mentioning food was all it took. Duncan's stomach rumbled. "I don't suppose you have any more fruit lurking in your pocket?" he asked, a bit like a plea.

"No. I'm sorry. And dramatic sighs aren't going to change that," I added, when one escaped him. The only thing my pocket held now was what Hannah had given me. I reached into the catchall in my trousers and palmed the object, pulled it out, glanced down. My breath caught, fingers jerking. I quickly stashed the hooded figure on its small plinth away.

"So?" said Duncan, witnessing my action. "What is it?"

"It's the Crone," I said.

He shook his head, jerked a shoulder. "Yeah? And?"

"Old magic. Among the desert peoples, the Crone is the beginning and the end of everything."

His breath stuttered from his mouth and he tried to catch it back. "I don't understand. Why would she give you that?"

"I don't know," I said, "but you can be assured I will find out."

Duncan's gaze met mine, held a moment. His face split into a grin. "From Hannah, you mean? I'm looking forward to that."

"Duncan," I said, "please. She's…"

"She's what?"

"Never mind."

I walked away from him, back to Chauncy's head. We continued our descent toward the city along a road swept clean and bordered by trees. Lanterns hung from the branches, glowing brightly as the sun dropped below the mountainside. Illumination started to fill in behind the glass walls, too, like stars in the shadows. Until then, I'd been unable to pick out living spaces. With a start, I realized there weren't any. Not in the way I knew. The pathways beneath the trees were filled with movement, but above, within the bowers, platforms and boxes nested in the branches or wrapped around the prior structure's skeletal remains. The city spread out to either side, points of brilliant light shimmering inside. I wondered if where we headed had a similar function to the Quadrate, a government office, and quarters for living and other purpose continued off into the distance.

I gave up on speculation when we arrived before an enormous gate parting open. We went through into something resembling a courtyard, the hum in the air inside less intrusive. Heads turned, eyeing Chauncy with fear, horror, disgust. I stayed close to him. To Carina and Resa, too, as the latter began to study our surroundings, staring, brown eyes wide.

I had no idea what her routine had entailed among the Sisterhood Duncan spoke of, but I knew her time with Stone Tiran had likely been a horror to one who had previously been protected, understood, cared for by the Order. The city she observed now had to be unlike any other she'd known. I wondered what she would make of it in her unique mind and how long it would be before she slipped control again. Duncan had said frustration and fear were often triggers. I couldn't imagine what I would feel with her abilities, frequently unable to communicate clearly with those I loved and yet seeing places and hearing conversations inside my head far beyond my immediate surroundings and the life I daily led.

I noted Duncan watched her, too. Always watching her, his guilt and worry evident. He'd talked quite a bit about his family life with me. Mika had, also, touching on his past in our conversations together. Carina had said nothing about hers. Perhaps she had nothing to say. Or perhaps it was too painful.

I turned away, taking the measure of our surroundings. Beyond the gates, the courtyard spread out around tree roots and the ravaged, now polished remnants of once tall buildings. Stone-framed glass rooms had been fitted in between at ground level. I did not think myself wrong in believing this area to be lodging whatever governing body existed. I saw people inside these box-like rooms, uncloaked, busily attending to matters. Their heads lifted as we passed, staring in the same manner everyone else had done. I had a sudden vision of the glass box into which I'd been placed during my trial. Much smaller, unframed, making me visible to all who'd come to observe me, to hear testimony, to see me condemned.

Duncan turned his head my way. His expression hit low, like a blow to the belly. I could tell he, too, was recalling the box, the trial. As he would. As he must. My forgiveness hadn't erased his remorse. Only he could do that.

"This way," said the Lyoness, and led us off to the left. With the exception of her guard, the others drifted away. I tried to catch sight of Ren and Hannah, Joy-Li and Hugo, but couldn't. It seemed odd to me that Nimue had brought so many Wildron with her when she came to collect us under sanctuary's guise. Had she expected we would fight rather than follow? We'd already come a long way with Ren. Perhaps, as with many leaders, a powerful display was deemed necessary. Such spectacle did not impress me. I thought it unlikely to impress anyone.

My mother often scolded me for lacking respect. Her lectures hadn't been entirely unwarranted. I did lack respect. For the undeserving. I suppose my mistake rested in the belief I could discern the difference. Still, I hadn't been wrong so far. Ren lacked respect, too. I remembered thinking so, when first we met. In his case, his lack blanketed all he encountered without regard for cause or instinct. I thought about them again, the four to be punished. Some disconnect existed between their plans and Nimue's. I couldn't discern why or what it might be. We were here in the city now, after all. If such had been the mutual intent, Ren and his companions reaching us first shouldn't matter. Because I did understand we'd been sought out and brought here for a purpose. Duncan's request for sanctuary had only made it easier to achieve. I'd wanted to seek out the Wildron, but I would have preferred to accomplish it on my own terms.

We passed into a tunnel-like construct; a natural one formed by the closely grown tree trunks here and the branches twining overhead. Chauncy's spiral horn caught once or twice, showering us with leaves.

"Soon you will have to part company with the *conjure,*" Nimue said, brushing a golden leaf from her shoulder.

I'd expected that. Of course, I had. Expectation didn't make the command easier to take.

"Is there a place nearby where he can be housed? He is not hostile to being in a paddock. His former driver kept him in one. I would like to know he is nearby when we are ready again to depart."

She hesitated, taking and expelling a long

breath.

"I will look after him," I said. "There would be no trouble to anyone else."

Back at the campsite, she'd appeared generous, or at the very least, reasonable. I'd lost my assurance somewhere in the hours we'd been traveling with Ren and his companions. I couldn't be certain why, but right then her long pause served to give me further concern.

"Very well," she answered at last. "We can make arrangements."

"I'll have to bring him," I said. "He won't go without me."

She dipped her head in curt agreement. "As you say. The beast does appear uncommonly attached to you."

I thanked her, though it suddenly galled me to do so, my accompanying smile no more than a meaningless gesture. The frayed thread of hope that my initial trust might be restored had unraveled. I couldn't fathom what lay ahead for us at all.

*Duncan*

Chapter Eleven

She'd been gone a long time, Grace had. Mika and I were stuck in this glass-walled room, like exhibitions in a museum. Like Grace had been on that day that seemed so long ago now. Unlike then, with a hundred spectators in tiered seats glaring down at her, Mika and I were partially concealed from pedestrians on the pathway outside by some huge shrub with red berries. My mouth watered, looking at the bright fruit. A probably poisonous fruit. Good thing the glass kept the branches from my reach.

Gods, I was hungry. But I was more worried.

At least we had eye contact with the room where Carina and Resa had been placed. We'd been told the housing arrangements were based on gender. Okay, I got that. But we'd all been living together on the run, so I found the restriction rather ludicrous now. Still, if it had to be this way, I was thankful Resa and Carina had been kept together. If the Wildron decided to part them, they'd better be prepared with a broom or two, because I had a feeling Resa would bring those walls down.

Resa's power was frightening, more than frightening, yet part of me experienced a small thrill at knowing she possessed it. Like Carina with her mysticism, Grace with her warrior's training, even Mika and his appropriated medical knowledge, this made her...*other.* These gifts made the four of them, somehow, more. Not that they wouldn't be special enough on their own, without the added benefits, and Resa might be better off without hers altogether, but still. Life had given them all something it hadn't given me. I admired them for it. I felt marked a little by their glory. And I felt a jealous pricking in my bones when I least expected it.

I hated myself just a little—sometimes a lot—for recognizing it there.

"I don't like this," Mika said, not for the first time by any means.

"I don't either."

"Where do you think Grace has gone?"

"Mika," I said, "do I look like I own some comprehensive knowledge of every culture, just lurking in my head for questions like that?"

Mika shrugged, smiled crookedly. "I guess not."

No, I thought, I don't even have that. But Resa probably did.

I jumped up off the floor, resumed my pacing alongside Mika, who hadn't yet stopped. Spare and uncomfortable-looking beds stood against the glass to either side, but we hadn't bothered to sit on them yet. Our supplies hadn't been returned to us. Besides being hungry, I really longed for some water, preferably ice-cold, although I'd have taken anything right about then. Even body temperature spit would have worked, but I realized I couldn't work up much of that in my mouth, either.

"Ah, crud," I said.

"What?"

"Frying pan or fire. I really should learn to keep my trap shut."

"Am I supposed to know what you're talking about?"

"No," I said, and walked on, leaving Mika to catch up in our circling around the room, or not.

A short time later two guards appeared at each room, standing outside the transparent doors. The nearest lifted a bundle and shook it at me. "Clean clothes," he said. Apparently, the walls were not soundproof. I heard him fine. Reminder to me: Watch what you say.

"And we're supposed to change in here with the whole world watching?"

The guard frowned. "You are supposed to accompany us," he said, "to the bathing facilities. The way you smell you'd not be welcome to dine at any occupied table, let alone with the Lyoness."

"I see Ren comes by his pleasant manners naturally," I mumbled. The guard gave me an indifferent stare. The other reached out and opened the door. They both stepped back.

We hadn't even been locked in. Neither Mika or I had tried the door. We'd just assumed we were prisoners. Force of habit, I supposed.

We met the girls at their door, Mika reaching out to give Carina's long white locks a flick. They looked at each other reassuringly. I looked away, taking my sister's hand.

The bathing facilities were nothing like on Emerald, nor at home, nor, really, anywhere I'd ever been. They possessed this nature-tech vibe, with flowing streams and a large pond and rocks and trees all around, but nestled among the trunks were narrow, empty chambers for changing, enclosed showers and toilets areas. I figured they had proper drainage, but I eyed the pond anyway and decided not to go in it, no matter how enticing it appeared.

Carina curled her fingers, indicating to Resa to follow her. Resa looked longingly over her shoulder at the rippling pondwater. Several Wildron who had been floating in a relaxed manner glared at us as they climbed out. They'd had no qualms about pipe drainage, and honestly, the water held no scent but that of green, living things. But we weren't here for enjoyment. We were here to bathe and put on clean clothes and join, according to the guard, the Lyoness for dinner. My grumbling stomach insisted delay would not be an option, even if I'd been foolish enough to believe thwarting Nimue's time schedule was.

I lingered anyway—just for a minute, I told myself—watching the sun spark on water, on ripples like shining ribbon. And then I was in it, quite like that, no notice, no thought, propelled through the air by something slamming into me from behind. I went under, sucking in liquid, floundered to my feet, thrashing and swinging in an attempt to ward off another blow. It came anyway, along with Mika's voice, Mika's laugh, and his hand, helping me up to stand once more.

I shook the hair from my eyes. Glared at him. Shoved him hard and watched him fly with a splat onto the water's surface.

After that, we were undone. We couldn't help ourselves. Didn't want to. Our interaction degraded into a clumsy, soggy wrestling match marked by grunts and hooting laughter. I heard a separate splash and then another, blinking through streaming water to spy Carina and my sister side by side. From a distance they kicked and splashed water at us, Carina egging us on. I dunked Mika again, dragged him up and he returned the favor, taking my legs out from under me. I'm not sure how long we could have gone on, how long we would have been allowed to, had I not suddenly felt myself lifted from my feet. Not by a hand. By the air itself.

Mika and I spun on a waterspout, borne above the churning pond below. With each rotation I spotted Resa, hair whipping, hands uplifted, her face contorted in concentration—no, not concentration, happiness. I recognized the joy in her face, wondered when I'd last seen such joy in her, wondered too how much higher we would rise. On the next spin, I saw Carina reach out to her and braced myself, shouting in warning to Mika.

It was a long fall, longer than I'd realized, accomplished in an instant. Impact with the water hurt, but also saved us. I rose up, dashed my sodden hair away, reached back a hand to help Mika, all the while with my eyes on my sister. Carina had her hands on Resa's shoulders, but Resa hadn't been taken down to sleep. She stood watching me, calmly, and when I neared, she broke free from Carina's grasp, splashing forward into mine. I nearly wept, idiot that I am. Maybe I did. Who could tell with the water streaming from my hair?

Who, I realized, would care? Not these friends. They understood.

"That nearly looked like fun."

Grace. I whipped my head around to face her. The guards stood a dozen feet behind, still holding the clean clothing, their stares far from indifferent now. Their eyes went from us, from what they had witnessed, to Grace, who looked like…I don't know what.

Not like Grace. Not like the Grace I'd come to know. Not like the Grace of prison uniforms and battered, borrowed desert garb. Not the Grace who for so many days now had been smeared with dirt and grime and worse. Her hair, the curly, dark, ever-tangled braid, was gone. She'd cut it short. Or someone had. The change made a difference. I couldn't quite figure out what it was, but I liked it. Her bronze skin shone with scrubbing. Most startling of all, she wore a dress. A *dress*. She didn't seem quite comfortable in it. I doubted it had been her garment of choice.

Spotting her boots peeking out from beneath the hem, my mouth twitched.

"Don't," she said to me. "Don't say a word."

I arched a brow and remained silent.

"Get dressed. We have to hurry."

I supposed we were cleaner now than we had been. All of us hustled away to strip down, dry off and put on the clothes being provided. When we emerged a few minutes later, Grace still stood where we'd left her, staring out across the pond.

"Chauncy?" I asked.

"He's okay. He's in a fenced enclosure just outside the boundary wall. Not happy, though."

No shock there. The brute had grown as attached to Grace as the rest of us. "And you?"

She turned her eyes to me. Nothing else. I understood.

*     *     *

We entered the glass-enclosed dining hall where a clear ceiling rose far above us. I arched my neck, squinting at the place where it ended in a sharp peak. I could see the trees through it. Probably by day the hills and mountains beyond, too. There were shadowed spaces where the room didn't reflect and I glimpsed stars there, shining in the night sky.

Rectangular tables lined a stone floor, butted up one right after the other in three separate rows. The chairs and long benches weren't filled. Most folk gathered near the far end, where I detected Ren's great-grandmother. She raised her scarred face in our direction as we approached with our still nervous escort. Holding their hands against their sides, not quite hidden in their cloaks, they made signs against enchantment. Annoyed, I urged Resa around to my right. The moisture from my damp bandages left marks on her borrowed shirt.

"Why is everything glass?" I mumbled to Grace, who walked on my other side. "I mean, it's

145

nice and all, but it can't be the easiest thing to build with."

Her lip quirked up at the corner. "They mine it."

"Mine it? How?"

"There's a place called Crystal Arena, where the desert runs into the forest. All the sand was made glass in the war that destroyed Olympian. Some weapon, some enormous amount of heat, converted it."

I frowned. "Where'd you learn all this?"

"The Lyoness. She wanted me to understand certain aspects of the new city's history."

"Really? Why?"

"Because she was asking a lot of questions, too, and trying to disguise her intent. She's hunting for information."

"Ah," I said. "So, be careful what I let out of my mouth."

Grace lowered her voice even more. "Especially about Resa."

"Might be too late for that. Between what Ren and his cronies witnessed and now the guards, she has to know Resa is no ordinary kid."

"I think she already knew," Grace stated. "The thrice-gifted child. Where did that name come from? From someone who knew the extent of her powers."

"Not the Sisterhood, surely?"

"Remember that woman who was with her? The one you thought might be a Sister? She could have been forced to reveal everything."

I released a long breath, thinking about the

woman from the images. I had no idea what had happened to her, only that in the end she'd no longer been at Resa's side. "This still doesn't explain how anyone here knows."

"The power of rumor," Grace said. "It travels faster than wind."

"We're not any safer here than on the run in the desert, are we?"

"I don't know. We need to be prepared."

"To run again? Not in that ridiculous get-up, I hope?" I forced a grin.

"Did you look in the mirror after you changed your clothes, Duncan?"

I had, and she was right. "Shut up."

She laughed. A genuine laugh. Heads turned in surprise. She ignored them, as did I. Together, the three of us, Mika and Carina behind, strode up to the empty seats we'd been told were ours. Grace stopped, inclined her head, seeking, I supposed, permission to be seated. Perhaps she'd been instructed. Perhaps this was merely a courtesy she knew.

"You may all take a seat," said a man to Nimue's right. We sat. My stomach growled.

All up and down the occupied chairs, heads turned, studying us, a bunch of fugitive teenagers being seated at their leader's table. I remembered what Grace had said, about no one leaving The Wilds once inside its boundaries. I fancied our tablemates were mulling over ways to kill us. I mean, they could have been pondering something as innocuous as how to assimilate us into their society, sure. No one appeared particularly homicidal. Still, my bet was on the first. It would always be on the first. Again, habit. The thing a person got used to.

Food was served to the Lyoness and then down the line, which meant plates were set before us right after hers. A few words were said in ritual, a very few words, enabling me to dig in almost immediately. Our last full meal had been two days ago, when Mika had cooked around the fire. I couldn't remember another since leaving the prison facility. I couldn't remember another tasting this good, not really, not since Gran's cooking. No offense to Mika, who'd done his best. He'd outshone me, anyway. I'd been cooking for myself in Citadel before the uprising and war. I'd often wondered how I managed to stay fit, or even alive, eating that swill.

We didn't speak much, all energy focused on much-needed consumption. I didn't imagine Ren's great-gran would let us go on too long without following up on the question-and-answer session she'd had with Grace. I slid my gaze sideways, watching Grace cut her food, transport it to her mouth, chew. She gave a good impression of being focused on the task, but I knew better. She listened, assessed, probably cataloging a thousand scenarios in her mind. Planning. Preparing. Even without her weapon, which she'd had to leave outside the dining hall, I knew she'd probably taken the chair's measure for use as a substitute, or the cutlery, or the hefty, metal, soup-filled bowl nearby. I really wished the lessons she'd started with us hadn't been cut short. Yet it seemed to me we were learning, every day, through an uncanny osmosis-like process.

None of us were who we'd once been.

Finally, I lowered my utensils. I noted the Lyoness had finished her meal some time ago. She watched me, a small, strange smile visible on half her face, the other half tight and immobile. She nodded at me.

"Better?"

"Much," I said. "Thank you."

"You're a polite boy," she said in her raspy tones.

"My Gran raised me right."

Her eyebrow lifted, the one she still possessed. "On Riley, yes?"

I suffered a swift, cold twinge at my nape. "On Riley," I said. "Yes."

"Lyoness," Grace interrupted, "how do you know this?"

"You are all famous among the resistance. Did you not realize?"

"The resistance?" Carina and I echoed together.

"What is the resistance?" Grace asked, formulating the actual, fully-worded question we were all thinking.

"Any and all who fight against the false Revered, of course," Nimue explained.

"And how do they know?" Grace persisted. "About us."

"Words spreads. Not only from those who fight against him, but from Tiran's camp itself. I believe if was from there the particulars came."

A muscle in Grace's jaw danced. "I have further questions," she said.

"Proceed. If I can answer them, I will."

The hall had gone still, all conversation among the Wildron ceasing. Mika leaned forward, peering toward the table's head, his elbow planted by his plate. Resa remained focused on her food, taking tiny bites from everything.

Grace pushed her plate away, folded her hands in the vacated space. "How do you receive your communications?"

"Ah," said Nimue, "so we come again to this."

"Yes," Grace said. "We would all wish to know how our loved ones fare. Perhaps even contact them to let them know we are alive, if it's possible."

"In due time, Grace. Our communication system operates sporadically, as you might expect in these times. As of this moment, it is inoperable. I have my best people working on getting it running again. Perhaps we then might be able to accommodate your requests."

I didn't believe her. Grace didn't believe her. Mika, rumbling under his breath, didn't believe her. Carina stared at her. I would have given the meal I'd just eaten to know what she could or couldn't glean from the Lyoness's thoughts.

"Do you have more questions?"

"Yes." Grace shoved back from the table and stood. Nimue's personal guard rushed her. Grace spun toward them, her stance, perhaps her expression, causing them to halt, circling warily. Grace dogged their movements. I clambered upright from my chair.

Nimue snarled at them to retreat. I sat down again.

"Grace," Nimue said, "don't threaten me."

Still standing, Grace inclined her head. "Such was not my intent, Lyoness. I expected I could speak better upright."

Nimue chortled like a throaty bird. Her guards backed once more to the wall. "A full belly?" she asked.

"It's quite uncomfortable. I haven't eaten much for some time. Thank you for the meal."

Nimue waved away the gratitude. "Then stand and speak. More can hear, anyway."

Grace loosened the belt on her dress and began to pace in double strides away from the table and back again. She ran her fingers through her shorn hair, making me think of Hannah. I glanced around the table and saw none of her group seated there.

"Will you tell us how this conflict began? Because I don't really understand it," Grace said. "Stone Tiran made a forced and violent bid for government control, usurped the true Revered's place, his power. That's all I know. There has to be more than that. Why did he do it? Power, I assume, but where did he gain all his backing? His soldiers? His weapons? His confidence he could possibly win?"

Nimue began to cackle, loudly. Grace stopped her pacing and stared from beneath frowning brows.

"I'm not laughing at you, Grace," Nimue said. "You said you had questions, and you most certainly do. I wish I had an empty seat among my counselors. Despite your tender age I would put you there. They don't speak half as well and with as much intelligence behind their words as you do in the heat of the moment."

Grace drew a deep breath, let it out. She relaxed her shoulders, visibly forced them down. "When Stone Tiran came to my parents, to our tribal leaders, seeking their influence, a bonding with me, his plans weren't even a whisper in the wind. Had they been, my parents would not have agreed to even entertain him in our household, I am sure."

Nimue tipped her head to one side, waiting.

"I knew there was unrest in Citadel. Bombings and skirmishes between the Citadel forces and the dissident attackers. Citadel had been burning for many days before my parents and others went as emissaries to the Quadrate, to address the disquiet, the violence. But Tiran had not been named in those issues. Duncan," she said, moving her head to indicate me, "told me he had heard rumors for a while before the first attack, about Tiran's ambitions, his associates. But I knew nothing. Not until he arrived in my home with my parents in shackles. How, Lyoness? How did this happen? Do you know?"

I gaped at Grace. Obviously, she'd been wanting to get this off her chest for a good, long while. The possibility she could receive answers had driven her into a near-manic, vocal frenzy. She took another deep breath, lifted her hands to her hips for a moment, and then flopped back down into her chair.

She nodded again at Nimue. "Lyoness," she said.

Nimue clapped her hands together, the sound

ringing through the hall. I watched them, age-spotted and wrinkled, and thought of Gran's hands. Gran had never handled anything more dangerous than a broom handle, occasionally swung without contact when I'd severely crossed her in some way. This woman's hands had wielded weapons, doled out death to her enemies. She was a warrior, like Grace. But unlike Grace, I feared her.

My hand stole under the table toward Resa, ready to snatch her from her seat, ready to flee, to fight our way out. The heavy meal I'd just eaten threatened to find its way back into the world.

Grace remained calm, however. She leaned forward in her chair, her half-blood green eyes studying the Lyoness expectantly.

The sound from the woman's clapping died in the air. "You are eloquent, Grace Irese, and you are brave. But you are also naïve, perhaps even a fool."

"How so?" Grace asked, her voice remarkably steady. I would have been stuttering like a buffoon.

"Stone Tiran never possessed the influence or ability to carry out this plan on his own. There are those more powerful who backed him. Back him still, without revealing themselves, so that he alone shall be held responsible should he ultimately fail."

Grace's hand lifted toward her throat, hovered there, drifted back down to the tabletop. "Who helped him?" she asked. "Name them."

"Can you not guess?"

Something slumped against my arm. I turned and found Resa, barely conscious, clinging to my sleeve. Beside her, Carina shook her head.

"I didn't do this," she said. "Her food."

I snatched Resa from her chair, onto my lap, up against my chest.

"I cannot guess," Grace said. She lied. I knew she lied, even as I rose with Resa in my arms, Mika and Carina behind me. Grace stood also, her eating utensils in her hands. She whipped the chair out of her way with her foot. "Why don't you tell me?"

The Lyoness rose also. "Well, for one, there's me," she said, showing her teeth in a crooked, humorless smile, nearly lost on her marred face. "But I think you knew that."

Chapter Twelve

Two days had gone by. Two days without Resa, without Carina, without Grace. My sister had been wrestled from my arms, dead asleep, drugged, and then Mika and I had been subdued. That's what Nimue called it. Subdued. In reality, we'd taken quite a beating. To be honest, it might have gone easier for both of us if we'd complied. We hadn't. My fingers were re-broken. Mika's whole left side had discolored into a purplish-blue blossom, where he'd been kicked. He had a black eye, too. Some of my hair had gone missing. Just a fistful. I had a seething hankering to get my hands on the coward who thought that was the thing to do.

I sat in the darkness listening to Mika snore. He'd finally dropped off from sheer exhaustion, after battering himself against the only door again for way too long. Not glass. Glass would have been nice. Glass would have given us a view into the outside world. Nope. Wood. Solid wood. Solid, splintered wood. We'd both been picking slivers from our skin ever since we'd been thrown in here.

I could hear voices drifting from out there

somewhere. The dense cave walls didn't let noise through, but space existed above and below the door to let me hear. Someone was crying, male or female I couldn't tell. At times, it would have been me, because I'd done a bit of it, weeping. Mika, too. Worried, scared, frustrated. Tears were a release when battering that door became too painful. When rage felt like it would burst a heart.

Shifting around on the stone floor, I tried to find a more comfortable position. Not so I could sleep. Mika slept, I watched, and vice versa. Habit, too, but a darned good one, a necessary one, even here, where we'd hear the door open if someone came in. Necessary, because we both worried we might not.

I swore, softly, so as not to disturb Mika. The words fluttered over stone, some of them familiar, not as mine, but desert words Grace sometimes used. I had no idea where Resa, Grace and Carina had been taken, what was being done to them. Grace had fought, too. Nearly every piece of crockery in that place had been shattered, most on the heads of those who'd stupidly placed themselves in her path. Chairs. Forks. She'd been outnumbered, though. We all were.

Sanctuary. Why hadn't I kept my big mouth shut?

Grace had said something to me before we'd been separated. A word group, like a mantra. Like mine. Like what I always said to her.

It'll be all right.

Except it wouldn't be. I couldn't see any way clear to a place called all right. A place like that didn't exist, hadn't for a long time.

Lurching to my feet, I started to pace. I stumbled once over Mika's leg. He didn't wake. I made myself remember where I'd tripped, even in the dark. I couldn't afford to hit my head against the sharp rock I kept feeling beneath my hand in various places on the walls. Mika needed me alive, and I needed him.

We'd been given water, a thin tray filled with it shoved beneath the door. The first time we'd lifted it, trying to tip the liquid off the edge into our mouths. Ended up having to suck the water from our clothing. Now when it came, we lapped at the tray like dogs.

No food though. Well, I supposed we'd had enough on that the night we were betrayed. I would have said we'd been fattened for the slaughter except I didn't think killing us was the plan. I could feel something else creeping up, something we'd find out soon enough. Hopefully before we both lost our minds in here.

Then again…

Letting out a long, whistling breath, I eased back down onto the floor. I pulled my knees up to my chin, wrapping my arms around them, avoiding clutching my broken hand with the whole one. Mika had done his best to reset and wrap my fingers again, but it had been difficult to see in the dark, especially with one eye nearly swollen shut. A hint of light came from somewhere, though, making the floor beneath the door glimmer like silver mist. Odd light. It didn't really illuminate the cell at all. Usually, in pitch blackness, the smallest shine gleamed like a beacon. Not this. I couldn't imagine what was making it.

It helped, though, the silvery dark glow. Occasionally I set my hand down in it, the good one, and studied fingers, knuckles, torn and filthy nails, to make sure I was still whole, still alive, still solid. Gave me something to do, too. Time passed in here without the beat of life to it. I only knew two days had come and gone because the last time the water got pushed inside, I'd asked. Asked how long we'd been here.

The answer could have been a flat-out lie.

While Mika slept—sleep he required more than I did—I sat in the dark worrying about the girls, about my sister mostly. And about what Nimue had said to Grace. *But you knew that.* I couldn't believe this to be true. Grace would never lead us willingly into such danger. She wouldn't.

But Grace had suspected something. She'd said so, again and again.

And yet she came. For answers. What answers? What did Grace need?

I jumped to my feet, lurched toward the door, ready to batter it uselessly one more time. Beating myself nearly senseless against the barrier provided me with purpose, an illusion I could make a difference. I couldn't, though. I knew I couldn't. Slumping to the floor, I pressed shoulder and head against unyielding wood. A raised splinter jabbed into my scalp, revealing a bruise I'd not known I had.

I found myself holding my breath. Listening. Listening hard. The crying had stopped, and the muttered voices. Instead, I heard a tapping at a distance. A long distance. I thought water might be dripping somewhere and I swallowed, my mouth dry and foul-tasting. But no, the noise didn't possess the metallic ping water made when plopping down onto stone. It had a repetitive design to it, though, the same sort Chauncy had made with his horn, a sound I'd since come to believe had been an alert, a calling, a pattern that meant something. I reached across the floor, shook Mika's boot.

"Mika, wake up! Listen."

He mumbled, shifted on the ground. I heard his clothing rustle. I shook him again.

"Leave me alone," he said.

"Listen," I repeated. "What do you hear?"

"Nothing." He hadn't even bothered to lift his head.

"Mika, Mika, buddy, don't give up." I stood, fixing my ear against the door. Closer now, the tapping, louder. I pictured the great, lumbering beast making its way in the dark for us, and Grace with my sister and Carina. The five of us together again. It didn't matter where or how far we'd have to run this time. Whatever it takes, Grace, I whispered silently. I will give whatever it takes.

I turned my brow against the door, my fists to either side of my face, my eyes squeezed shut. I realized I was praying. Praying to whatever deity would listen.

Come on, Grace. Come on. We're here.

Right. She needed to know where. I started pounding the door with my unbroken hand, kicking it, kneeing it, shouting. The sounds in the corridor grew louder, steadier, closer. Resolving themselves into something else, something more recognizable, something I understood, that made my flesh burn cold.

A hand closed around my arm.

"Stop," Mika said.

Outside, booted feet marched to a halt. Doors started flying open, banging against the stone walls. One after the other, like a storm headed our way. I stepped back, Mika with me. Back as far as we could, up against the rear wall. The door opened, blinding light pouring in. I threw my arm up to block it, unable to see a thing. Someone stepped inside.

"Time to go, boys."

Amused. Cruel. I much preferred the cybernetic units that had hounded us on Emerald. We'd learned a way around them. We weren't going to be so lucky here.

*     *     *

Hands bound, we stumbled along through shifting light, surrounded by others in the same condition. Disoriented, tied, prodded, made to nearly run. Occasionally someone fell. You'd hear first a grunt, a cry, then a scream. I made certain I stayed close to Mika, just in case. If he went down, I'd have him up before anyone could get near him.

In time, we exited the underground into the forest. I managed a glance behind and saw the city's gleaming surfaces very far away, starlight inside glass and starlight above. Before us, a track ran downhill between trees, their shadows thick and moving with a sullen, damp wind. I thought I caught the glimmer of dark water below. A river, maybe. Looked slow moving, so probably fairly deep. It seemed the path led straight to it.

"Where are we going?" I asked a hooded Wildron striding to my left. He raised a weapon, nothing like the mechanical bow Ren and the others had carried, waving it threateningly at me. I thought about Tiran and his soldiers, wondering if we were being taken to them. But why all these prisoners? I would think he'd want us, with good reason in his eyes, but not them.

Of course, prisoners could be handy for any number of uses in war.

While we hustled down the hill, I kept searching for a place where we might slip away. I didn't think it likely, though. We were accompanied by nearly as many Wildron as prisoners, all with eyes on those they'd rounded up. Besides, I couldn't be sure how far Mika could run at this point, and I wasn't going anywhere without him.

Soon, I spotted boats on the water. Heard them, too, over grunts and pounding feet. Moored to the banks, they bumped together in the river's flow with a sound like drum beat. Metal fittings gleamed. I glanced up toward the stars, caught a breath. So far from Citadel, the Emerald's fixed point sat in a slightly different position in the night sky, but I could see it clearly glowing with its greenish tint, blinking in and out behind a few flying clouds.

Mika muttered something. I looked at him. "What?"

"Do you think they could be sending us back

there?"

"Oh, gods, I hope not," I said.

The thought hadn't even occurred to me, but now it stuck like a biton-leech in my mind, sucking hope from my brain matter like blood. Mika had been incarcerated there a lot longer than I had, at least two years longer, having been remanded when he'd been little more than fourteen years old. "That's not going to happen, Mika," I whispered. "I'm not going to let that happen."

But what could I do, if this was their plan?

Nothing.

I blew out a long breath, sucked another one in, continuing our harried pace downhill.

When we reached the riverside, the guard split us into groups. I stayed close to Mika, ending up in a wide-bottomed, open boat with him. I quickly scanned the occupants in the other craft, searching for the girls. I didn't believe they'd been imprisoned with us, because the battle in the dining hall had obviously been designed to separate Resa, Carina and Grace from Mika and me. I didn't understand why the Lyoness had waited so long. There'd been ample opportunity to do so, and probably with much more ease, many other times. Hell, once we'd been divided into our rooms, someone could have just locked the doors.

Unless she'd hoped for cooperation. Some content in her conversation with Grace either before or during our meal must have tipped her off that Grace wasn't the cooperating kind, and neither were we.

Forced to sit down, I dropped my hands

between my knees and started working on the material binding my wrists. Not rope, but some slick textile I couldn't break or untie. I continued to struggle, carefully, quietly, and with frustration. Beside me, Mika did the same. The mooring ropes were cast off, thumping down onto the dirt above. Boats rocked into the water's flow. Yet they weren't at the river's mercy. Something silent powered them, steered them. I watched the bank slip away.

A while later, not sure how long, Mika bumped his elbow into mine. "Wake up."

"I wasn't asleep."

"You were. You were nodding like a bouncer in a seedy bar. Remember those? I used to sneak in on occasion. Not for any particular reason. Well, there was a reason. Sometimes they had those flight simulators in there. Fun for the customers, but surprisingly accurate."

I'd forgotten Mika had been born and raised on Riley, like me. Our paths had never crossed. A lot of people lived up there, on the gambling moon. Even more came and went, only there for the games.

"Is that where you started learning?" I asked. "Setting yourself up for stealing the real thing?"

"Don't knock it," he said.

"I'm not. We'd never have made it back to Talia without you."

"Thanks," he said. "Thanks for saying so."

"It's true."

He grunted, looked away.

I would have clapped him on the back, but my

hands were still tied. I hadn't been able to manage to work them free before I'd drifted off. I blamed the rocking boat, for both.

"There are lights over there," Mika said. "Do you see?"

I looked up, followed his lifted hands. The trees had thinned out at some point, exposing barren land right up to the river at each side. I did see the lights, still some distance away. We sped closer to them, bouncing in the heaving water shooting out from beneath the boat in front. "How long have we been on the water, do you think?"

"I don't know. An hour? Two?"

I swore, thinking about how far away we were now from the City of All Dwellers, from Resa, Grace, Carina. I dug my fingers, the ones I could still move, into my palms. A mechanized hum carried through the air, followed by a ship rising in the distance above the lights. Black against the night sky, it moved almost invisibly toward us. I ducked my head when it neared. Yeah, like I could be picked out and recognized among the fifty others filling our boats. I couldn't help it, though. Mika started straight up at it, his face twisting.

"We're not going back to Emerald," I insisted, determined. "We're not."

He lowered his head, stared at me. "You're right, we aren't. Didn't you see the insignia on the bottom of the aircraft? I think we're all being taken to work those mines Grace mentioned to you. We're on our way to the glass fields."

Very soon, the boats eased toward the left bank. A structure prodded the water, rocking in the current. A structure we were meant to climb onto, stand upright on, traverse to the scarred, barren bank. I'm ashamed to admit I contemplated throwing myself into the river, allowing the swift undercurrent to drag me under, never to return to daylight, to brutal reality. For an instant I witnessed the same consideration in Mika's eyes. But then we both turned, remembering my sister, Grace, Carina, and followed the others onto dry land.

Once there, I stood in utter silence. I didn't even breath. Not until I had to, until my flaccid lungs forced me to suck in the rancid air. Mika went down on one knee, his head momentarily on his hands. I heard his rapid respiration and bent down next to him.

"You okay?"

He nodded. "Yep."

I helped him up. We waited side by side, surrounded by strangers. Wondering what was coming next.

It didn't take long to find out. The biggest guy there, hooded and hulking and who would have made more than two of me, shoved stragglers into line before positioning himself up front. To be seen. That was his tactic, stand and stare at everyone until the shifting, the muttering, the intermittent sniffling ceased.

"What are we doing here?" someone asked.

"Stupid question," another hissed at him. "Shut up."

The big guy, the hooded giant, turned his head quite slowly. His eyes glittered in the shadow beneath his hood. They lighted on me.

"Was that you, boy? Asking that question?"

Until he spoke, I'd wondered if he might be a metal-head after all, given his size. But no, human, or something akin.

"No," I said.

He waved a hand at his reasonably-sized cronies. "Find him."

The hunt was swift, the punishment for transgression even more so. I turned my face away, thinking about Grace, how Grace would step in, her training to protect never forsaken, the risk to herself never foremost in her mind. My shoulders slumped, a shudder taking my whole body. All eyes somehow found the ground. Stayed there, even when we were forced to walk past the kid lying crumpled on the harsh, cold soil. Because he was a kid, just a kid. I'd known so by his voice, but I'd tried not to think about it, tried not to think someone half my age had been dragged off to this place.

Lesson learned, for everyone. Keep your mouth shut.

Chapter Thirteen

They fed us, if you could call it that. Wouldn't do any good to starve the workforce. The gray stuff in the bowls would fill a belly, but only if it managed to stay there. The consistency and smell brought to mind a concoction my mother had once tried to get me to eat. Funny, my remembering that. You'd think I'd recall something more touching about my mom when facing a slim chance of survival. But no, I recalled only how angry she'd gotten when I set the spoon down and refused a single mouthful. Gran had done her best to enlighten me as to why my mom had been so mad. Short explanation, she said Mom had been trying to be the mother to me I needed, even if she didn't know how to cook worth a darn. Gran didn't expect me to accept what she told me, but she was always one for clarifying things. My mother left again a few days later, maybe a few months—hard to measure the time back then—not coming back until she found herself ready to give birth to Resa.

I had no idea where she'd gotten herself to after that. Neither did Gran.

"Eat," whispered Mika, next in line on the bench, crammed up next to me. "It's not as bad as it looks."

I made a face, shoved a spoonful into my mouth, realized I didn't have to chew and forced myself to swallow. The mash went down. Stayed put, too. The fact it was warm helped.

We were in some type of metal hut, one of many in a fenced enclosure, and curving like an arch from side to side. Whispers slipped along the metal roof in the long, dimly-lit building. No one dared speak louder. Mika and I consumed our meal without further conversation. Every time I lifted the spoon to my mouth, the welts on my wrists and hands glared in reminder. We all had them, crisscrossing flesh like angry red tattoos. At least our hands were free now, to eat this crap, to scratch an itch, to reach out on occasion for assurance.

To work.

The lot jammed together inside the metal shelter hadn't started yet. After eating, we had training. The way the Wildron said the word, I had a feeling training entailed nothing more than throwing us into the task and hoping some survived. I figured I might be wrong, though. It wouldn't be wise management practice to lose all one's laborers in one go.

A bell rang, an annoying single tone. We'd all heard the alert before, signaling us to sit, to eat, so we all rose in response without questioning it. In single file we traipsed outside. Half were siphoned off, directed somewhere else. An oddly chill wind blew unimpeded across the cracked, gleaming plain.

The glass field spread as far as the eye could see. Places existed where the light didn't. Hollows, perhaps, deep and black. I couldn't imagine how deep. Didn't want to, because I very much feared one of those black places would be our next stop.

Our next stop, however, happened to be a huge metal bin set right up against the fence. Two doors at the front stood wide. Shivering in the clothes I'd been given by the Wildron, I stood beside Mika, frowning at the bin's contents. My initial reaction to the sight was revulsion. The bin appeared to be filled with bodies. A moment later, even before the Giant spoke, I realized my error. Not bodies. Suits. Heavy suits, the material thick enough to maintain shape and bulk. Thrown into haphazard piles, they hadn't been cast aside by prior users. Such disorder by the workers wouldn't be permitted.

In his bored baritone, the Giant confirmed my suspicions. "Choose wisely and be quick about it. Those suits are designed to keep your limbs in one piece, if you're careful. Their previous operators won't be needing them anymore."

Necessity overrode horror. Everyone charged forward, yanked out the protective uniforms, tossing back the damaged ones, the ones with missing sleeves, pant legs, obvious and gruesome stains. It was difficult to judge what might fit in the rush, in the dark, but no one delayed overmuch, yanking on whatever appeared would serve.

"Gloves, masks, light sticks over there."

We hurried to the smaller bin, not caring if the gloves matched in size, as long as they covered hands. Only then did I realize how hindered I would be by my broken fingers. I stood with two gloves held tightly in my left hand, trying to figure out what to do. Turning me so the guards couldn't see, Mika worked to get the right glove shoved over my curved, bandaged fist, then pushed the left on, too. After affixing his mask, he swept his uniform's head covering into place before tugging up mine. We queued up with the others at the gate.

"Thanks," I said.

"No problem."

"Did you take your meds?"

He rolled his eyes, huge and misshapen behind the mask's shield. "Of course, I did. Carina would have my hide if I didn't. Grace, too."

We both went silent. I turned away, gazing out over the glass fields. Something sorrowful and hopeless moved through me, seeping into every cell.

"We stick together," Mika said. "No matter what happens. Got that?"

I nodded. "Got it."

*     *     *

I thought it more likely the miners rather than the Wildron had named the trails across the glass fields. It didn't seem to me the Wildron would care. The miners would. Oh, yes, they surely would. We trudged along the raised 'safe-way' with absolute care. What had looked smooth and level at a distance, turned out to be pitted and jagged and deadly to anyone who slipped off the path. Or was shoved. Or just decided to pack it in.

No one in our group did. We made it safely

across the field to a staging area positioned at a hollow's edge. We formed a row in sight of the long, black drop to await our next instruction. I figured part of the training had been managing to get a garment to protect yourself, followed by traversing the safe-way without dying. Two very essential skills. I'd been counting steps and turns, as well. Despite the impossibility, I had no plans to give up on escape if the chance happened to materialize.

Giant—he hadn't introduced himself and my title for him stuck—faced us. In truth, faced me, singling me out yet again. I made certain not to move a muscle, not a facial twitch, or a flexing finger.

"Who's the strongest here?" he asked, still looking at me. No one spoke. Keeping my gaze respectfully on his chest rather than anywhere near his eyes in what he might construe as challenge, I thought, you're mistaking me for Grace. You're mistaking me for someone with two whole hands. You're mistaking me for someone who doesn't realize strength is probably going to come up badly, in the end.

He pointed at me anyway, and three others.

I swore. Not out loud. Despite my thoughts to the contrary, I still valued my life.

"Pair up. You'll man the winches. The rest of you, form a line and get ready to be lowered down."

Breathing in and out, mouth closed, nostrils flaring behind the mask, I marched over to the winch. The air rushed from my lungs in relief when I spotted the mechanism. Brute strength wouldn't be required for the operation. It had a motor. Our function appeared only to be in assisting the others into the swinging baskets and to push buttons. Okay, I could do that. I'd make sure everyone stayed safe. I'd perform the best darned winching job I could, because I'd be expendable if my injury were discovered. I wasn't about to let that happen. Mika was counting on me. So was everyone else on the platform with us.

The baskets held three occupants each. The guards shoved them forward, making entry into each conveyance a haphazard affair. Paired as two holders to a basket, we wrestled them steady against the shifting weight, allowing them to fill, closed the door, pressed the appropriate button to lower the basket down, and down, to an impossible depth, and brought them back up again, empty.

Finally, with only a few prisoner-miners remaining, I knew Mika's turn had come. He stepped up next to me.

"I'll see you down there," I said.

He smiled behind his mask, crooked and unsure, leaped in, moved to the back. Two more followed. I watched the basket drop until it disappeared from sight.

"You four next."

When the baskets returned, I got in. My balancing partner pushed in beside me. The final two climbed into the other basket. We began our descent, the wide night sky, the brilliant stars slowly contracting the deeper we went. The metal bars held the last dull gleam from above, but the occupants were soon invisible. Suddenly, both winches screeched to a halt. The baskets swung, clanging together. I managed to stay upright, but the guy with me tumbled to the floor. Far, far below lights showed, pinpricks like glowing dust particles. From above came laughter, muted by distance.

I swore again, this time out loud. The guy on the floor scrambled upright, flailing back and forth in the swinging contraption. He reached out, grabbed my uniform. I felt him rather than saw him, clinging to me with both hands.

"Back off," I said. "We need to distribute the weight."

He did and the pendulum effect slowed. With a jerk, the conveyance began moving downward again.

"I thought they were going to let us fall," said my basket-mate. "That they were just going to let the line go."

I sucked in a breath, reached into my uniform and yanked out the light stick, resorted to pulling my glove off with my teeth, leaving it gripped between my lips. I flicked the small switch bare-handed, caught the glove on the flopping fingers on my other hand as it slipped from my mouth.

Ren.

He laughed. Shock, I figured. If I hadn't convinced myself of that, I probably would have punched him.

"Is it just you?" he asked, bending to pick up his mask.

"Mika, too," I said. "The girls are in the city still. At least I hope so. I'll need to know where to find them once we get out of here."

He shook his head. His yellow hair fell into his eyes. "We're not getting out of here. You work until you're dead and then they bring the suits back up."

I stared at him. "I don't believe you."

"Believe me."

"But your great-grandmother wouldn't let you—"

"It's her orders. Families, huh?" He sneered, lip curling. "She's got about thirty of us great-grandkids. She doesn't need the rebels."

My mouth opened. Only air came out. I slid down onto the cage bottom. Pity and anger made me wince. Gran would never do such a thing to me. She'd give her life for mine, I knew she would.

"What do you mean rebels?" I asked, flipping the light back and forth in my fingers, dancing Ren's shadow over the two in the other descending basket.

"Remember I said we wanted to intercept you? Can you think that far back?"

Oh, it would have been so nice to open the door and tip him out. But I wouldn't do that. Not to him. Not to anyone. He needed to control his attitude, though.

"Yes, and you were pretty evasive."

"We were trying to reach you before the Lyoness did."

"Well, you could have said."

"It was too late, as soon as her replicant

showed up at your camp. Way too late. I tried to pretend afterward that I...that I was bringing you to her, in case she found out. To prevent something like, well, this." He waved a gloved hand. "She did, as you know. Find out, I mean. Didn't believe me innocent either."

"Obviously," I muttered, standing back up as the lights below neared. "Where are your pals?"

"Hugo and Joy-Li are here, already below. I don't know what happened to Hannah. We tried to convince the Lyoness to just banish us. She wouldn't go for it."

"And this story about the Far-Seer, is that true? Does that have anything to do with why the Lyoness wanted us?"

"She didn't want you," Ren said. "Didn't want Mika. Only the girls."

"What for?"

He gave me a disdainful, impatient look. "You know what for."

Yeah. I did.

*　　*　　*

I mean, I knew why she'd want my sister and Carina. The same reason Tiran had wanted Resa, to use her powers, the long-view sight and hearing, the ability to manipulate objects with her mind. And now Carina could keep her in balance until called upon for some weaponized use. As for Grace...

Grace was a warrior. Grace would be trouble. Grace wouldn't tolerate any of it. The one reason Nimue might want her would be to—

Turn her back over to Stone Tiran.

I almost threw up, right there in the miner's cage, the only thing stopping me the sudden jolt as it hit bottom. I shoved open the door and staggered out. Mika was there, waiting. He reached out an arm and grabbed me, kept me upright. Beside me, Ren grunted. Someone had run into him, pummeling his chest with small fists.

"This is your fault! Your fault!"

Joy-Li.

I spun about. "Shut up, both of you. I need to think."

I looked around, blinking in the glitter from the many small lights along walls made from heaved and sparkling glass. It seemed impossible, glass and rock interspersed so far below the surface. But what did I know? Nothing. Exactly nothing.

"Why do they mine the glass down here, instead of above? Seems to me that would be easier," I said, not because I wanted to know, but because I stalled, afraid no plan would come to me.

"Sometimes they need the denser stuff, for their machines."

I couldn't tell who'd spoken. It was no one I knew.

"Yeah," said Ren, "for the replicators. The

crystals have to be just the right density."

I turned in a slow circle, glanced up and down the ranks of suited prisoners. "Are there no guards here?"

"Why? They wouldn't," someone said.

"No need," said another. "If you don't do what you're supposed to, then you die down here."

"You die anyway," Ren murmured. I heard him. Mika, too, and Joy-Li, who released a whimper.

"The ones who were left behind when the last lot went back up top will teach us," said yet another voice in the crowded area.

"No one goes back up top," Ren hissed. I told him to stop talking.

"And where are they?" I asked. "The ones left behind. Hello? Could you come forward, please?"

For a minute no one moved. I heard shuffling, then a slow tread as a suited prisoner made its way through the crowd. He or she appeared tall, taller than me by a few fingers, but so thin their wasted condition was obvious even beneath the suit's padding.

"I'm all that's left." A male voice, or so it seemed to be.

I moved closer. "Do you want to tell them the truth?"

He shook his head. "No. A promise was made. If I stay and show the next batch, I'll be brought up top.”

I watched him through the shield’s ripple effect.

“I’m hungry,” he said.

A rage burned suddenly, fiercely, right through me, so volatile it could have ignited the suit I wore. I swore, and swore again, my voice echoing off the mine’s walls. I heard a crack behind me. A brilliant glass sliver fell to the ground.

I stared at it.

“How do you mine this stuff?” I asked. “Are there tools?”

“This way,” he said.

The company parted to let us pass, Mika and Ren at my heels. Joy-Li, too, clinging in fear to Ren’s uniform sleeve. I wondered where Hugo was, but not for long. I had enough whizzing through my brain.

The starving leftover took me to a stockpile of strange-looking implements. I pushed at one with my foot. “What’s your name?” I asked.

“Levon.”

“Levon,” I said. “The guards do come down here sometimes, am I right?”

“Yes.”

“To retrieve the suits.”

“Yes,” Levon said, quietly now.

The rage still lit me up, from the inside out, but I felt like a flame in glass. Nothing to disturb the combustion. “How often?”

“Every few days.”

“That’s all it takes, a few days to die?”

“Yes. Some last longer. I did.”

I said nothing.

"They promised me."

I sucked a breath in, blew a breath out, listening to the sound of moving air inside my mask. "And the glass you collect. How is that returned to the surface?"

"Over here," Levon said. We walked on.

A good distance along the mined area, another tunnel entered from the right. Metal carts lined the narrow interior, wind rushing down its length. I yanked off my mask, scenting the chill, musty air. Something else caught me, another smell. A putrid, undefined odor came not from the tunnel, but from somewhere further along. I started in that direction.

Levon plucked my sleeve. "Don't go there."

"Why not?"

He dropped his shaking hand. On his ill-fitting suit, the catches and buckles jangled like unfinished bells.

"What's back there, Levon?"

His chin lowered toward his chest, his gaze gluing to the ground near my feet. "The pit," he said. "It's where they all end up."

The flame in me roared, battering its imagined containment, threatening to suck all the oxygen from my lungs. I continued on with my light stick held high. Eventually the light reached a darkness it couldn't penetrate. I picked up a stone and tossed it over the dark's edge, counting seconds until the stone hit bottom.

I drew in a breath, spat it back out. With a grunt, I pressed my mask into place before breathing again. Levon wandered up next to my shoulder. Others followed, hesitant, silent and scared, every single one of them.

"Did you help put them there, Levon?" I asked.

He nodded. "They promised."

The flame sustaining me went out. I stood before the pit of the dead without any life of my own left inside.

*Skelly*

Chapter Fourteen

I hear them. So many voices. Grace, do you think I can't? Everywhere you go, I go, so sure, I hear them all.

You have to understand, though. Oaks' freak sister and that spooky island mystic aren't your problem anymore. Stop listening. Shut your mind to that noise. We can't control everything. If I could, you know what I'd do first thing? I'd make you let me out.

Yeah, I feel you fighting me. I feel you fighting even those simple words. Words are not action. Wouldn't life be just hunky-dory if they were. Could you imagine? Wave a hand, speak a word, and done.

No words are going to bring me back. My time in the world is ended. I am what I am.

Soon, I won't be the only one.

And you know what that means, Grace?

# THE THRICE-GIFTED CHILD

Everything that's happening is your fault.
You ought to own it. It's the least you can do.

Chapter Fifteen

I ground my teeth together, my elbows on my knees, my palms pressed flat against my ears. It didn't help. If nothing else, I recognized the cowardice in my actions.

Four days had passed and my body still ached from the battle's ferocity in the dining hall. I had no idea where Duncan and Mika had been taken. To a cell somewhere, I'd been told. Questions yielded no further answers. I knew where Carina and Resa were housed, however. I'd been allowed to see them.

I shut my eyes. Tears leaked out, despite my efforts.

*It's your fault, Grace.*

"I know it is."

*Let me help you.*

I didn't answer Skelly, not out loud. I didn't have to. He knew my response, railed against it. I ignored him, jerked up from the mattress where I'd been resting up until a short time ago, not asleep, staring through the roof overhead at the stars. At home, I would often lie out in the garden observing the inexorable, twinkling movement across the sky, picking out constellations between the *celia* bush branches, the delicate embrace of the *banya* beside it. The vastness and beauty in the night sky frightened me when I was very young. I'd felt as though I'd been forced, somehow, to awareness of the infinite.

Releasing a long, slow breath, I stood, crossed the floor, came back, sat once more on the mattress edge. I reached into my pocket, pulled out the talisman Hannah had given me, rolled it in my fingers. I knew it as the Crone, but that didn't mean the figure meant the same here. I wouldn't ask, though. Hannah had given it to me for a reason and I wouldn't endanger her with questions to the wrong people.

In this long row of single rooms, the ceilings, the walls front and back were glass, crystal clear, the walls between each made from some opaque material. Not soundproof. Every night I heard weeping, scream-filled dreams, voices crying out for help, for comfort, for reason. Prisoners, like me, yet not like me. I'd been told the very first day that all possessed mage blood in this block of what amounted to little more than cells. Separated. Persecuted. No wonder Ren had been so angry with Hannah's display. She'd endangered them all, I supposed.

Rising again, I strode to the rear wall and pressed up close to the glass, folding my hands behind my back. In the unlit tree-corridor outside, I could see the guards, count them. I'd been watching them every night, their movements, the shift change, in which direction they headed when they left, from which direction the new ones came. One turned my way. Our eyes met. I resisted the urge toward rude gestures and kept my hands under control behind me. He looked away, but not before he'd taken my measure and I, his.

It would be hard, escaping. Not for me, not alone. I'd noted numerous opportunities each time I found myself removed from my cell. But four existed within my guardianship as warrior, four who were my friends. All, or none. Escape wouldn't happen any other way.

I stood until my legs grew weary, until the sky above the trees began to lighten. I turned, then, and began my daily exercises, my routine for so very long and what seemed so very long ago. I needed my strength, my flexibility, my endurance intact, because soon, quite soon, a move toward freedom must be made. I would not die here. I wouldn't let my friends die here.

*　　*　　*

A guard came for me a short time later. I asked him where we were going.

"To see the Lyoness," he said.

"Is there a reason?"

"You do not need a reason."

True. I didn't. Not now. The requirement for reasons had been negated as soon as I'd been placed in detainment.

I walked behind him, passing once again the other containment units and the detainees lying defeated on their bunks, or pacing as I had been. They were nearly all my age or younger, confined for the evidence of their powers. I had wondered on it during my sleepless nights, and concluded these rare mage gifts did not vanish upon reaching a certain age. Rather, the older ones had only learned better how to keep them hidden. What still baffled me was why they should. Among the tribes, mage kind were esteemed. Although they lived apart, ofttimes odd in their ways, as a people we respected them, and not only for their gifts. They possessed knowledge, wisdom, learned through meditation and studies in their reclusive lives.

We passed the tree-formed tunnel at the other end of which Chauncy had been released into a paddock just outside the city limits. I'd not been permitted to see him since. For the briefest instant I considered knocking the guard to his knees and running along that long, shadowed lane, breaking through the paddock fence with Chauncy, running and running and running as far away as I could, mounted on his back like Carina and Resa.

As I said, my thoughts were fleeting. A momentary weakness. Picturing Carina and Resa on Chauncy's back cut short my irresponsible fantasy. I had my duty, and even if not, I had my friends. I would not forsake them.

I followed the guard through the maze that was the city, stopping at one of the strange staircases that wound around the massive tree trunks to the bridges above. People used these bridges for access to the various raised chambers. I'd only seen them from a distance, because thus far I'd been conducted nowhere but to the governmental area at ground level, to be interviewed by Nimue. The interviews, though unpleasant, had not yet resulted in bodily injury. Each time I gleaned a little more regarding her intent. Each time, I fashioned my answers to keep as much from her as I dared.

The guard moved to stand behind me, prodding me toward the staircase wound around the tree's trunk. I frowned, studying the steps with their elongated, triangular shape. The space between one step and the next seemed a little higher than it should be, the point nearest the tree too narrow to hold a foot. The steps down to the cellar at home were nothing like this. Cautiously, I placed my boot on the lowest tread. The guard shoved me again. I fell against a metal edge, lurched upright, spun to face him.

"Don't," I said.

"Don't what?"

"Push me."

He did anyway, jabbing a finger hard against my collar bone. I snatched his wrist, whipped him around and thrust the heel of my palm between his shoulder blades, releasing him to sprawl across the ground. He scrabbled upright, two more guards hurrying over. I managed to back up the misaligned staircase to a defensive stance.

Nimue's voice echoed down from above. "Leave her be!"

The three guards jerked back and away from me, snapping into immobility, eyes filled with anger. Nimue's voice continued to filter down.

"Come up, Grace. Take your time. I'm sure

you've never seen a staircase quite like this before." Friendly. Welcoming. So, this would be today's tactic.

About halfway up the spiraling stair I found a rhythm to my climb, no longer clunking along like a toddler in new sandals. Nimue waited for me at the top, holding her arm out to usher me forward. Old friends, well met. Right.

We crossed a narrow bridge to a series of wooden-framed, glass-walled rooms. The door to the first stood open. Nimue entered first, waving me inside. I shut the door and followed her across a brightly-patterned carpet that made me think, with a twinge to my heart, of home.

"Grace, sit down."

I walked around the room, an inordinately elegant and inorganic room, one that didn't seem in keeping with what I had seen elsewhere, and chose a seat far from hers. I couldn't stand to be near her. I didn't trust myself near her. She sat directly below my *lathesa,* now hanging on her wall. Again, I was reminded of home, where once my original *lathesa* hung in a place of prominence above the hearth where fires burned on colder nights. I glanced at it and away, looking outside the glass to other chambers elevated in the trees. All contained people going about their daily lives. Well-fed, well-dressed Wildron, unlike those who toiled below in their tattered garments, some looking nearly as thin as I and my companions had become.

No privacy up here, though. I noted some had halted their activities to stare across into the Lyoness' chambers. To stare at me. I crossed my arms and stared back.

"Don't do that, Grace," Nimue chided. "They think you an oddity already. No reason to reinforce it. I'd rather they came to think of you as one of us."

"I'm not one of you," I said, continuing to glare through the glass, fighting, as I had earlier, the urge for rude gestures.

Nimue sighed. "You are still such a child."

My jaw tightened.

"And I have an offer."

I spun about on the chair. My hands dropped to the intricately carved arms. "Why?"

She blinked, taken aback. Good.

"Why?" I repeated. "Why would you offer me anything? What have I to give in return?"

"The Revered—"

"The false Revered, you mean? Tiran."

"Of course, that's who I mean," she snapped, and took a deep breath, regaining control over her emotions. "Grace, he does not yet know I have you here. I shall keep it that way, as long as you help me. Do you understand? He would very much like you back, this time for public execution. It was I who convinced him not to have you killed following your trial. I don't think he cares what I think on the matter anymore. I believe you've wounded his pride for the last time, my dear."

I suppressed my surprise; curbed also the growl forming in my throat at her tone. "I don't understand," I said. "Why would you interfere in that?"

"Because I admired your courage, Grace Irese. Your feistiness even when enclosed in that glass box."

My mouth dropped, astonishment ripping free in verbal accusation. "You were there? In the courtroom?"

She sat back, pleased she'd caught me off guard. "I was watching," she said. "My replicants can go far, when we have the proper materials."

Unable to sit still any longer, I jumped up from the chair, began to pace. Nimue leaned forward.

"I can show you how the replicants work, if you'd like."

"They are holograms. I don't need to see. I assume you use them to inflate your number in battle. An illusion." My gaze shot to the *lathesa* and away. I went on pacing, maintaining a distance far from Nimue, from my weapon. "I still don't understand your interest in keeping me alive."

She rose, came stiffly to stand in the floor's center, to block my way. I veered around her into a new course. She turned from me to look out through the glass. The curious hurried to return to their undertakings.

"Back then at your trial? A whim. But now," she said, "there are rumors among the Tainted."

I stopped pacing. The Tainted. A reference to those with mixed ancestry in their veins, ancient mage blood from the desert tribes. How often had I been called half-blood, for more recent lineage than those among her people. What must she think of me? Not that I cared. Not that I cared what anyone thought about my heritage.

"Persistent, troubling rumors," she went on, watching my reflection in the glass. "Rumors about you and your friends. Can you not imagine what they might be?"

I shook my head, wanting her to think I held no concern at all, with any of it.

She smiled, seeing right through me, the smile that lifted only half her face. "It is said among you are powers far beyond what the Tainted can attain."

"You've locked them all up. Why? Are you afraid of the powers they possess, lesser as you may believe them?" As I spoke, I heard my mother's voice in remembered reprimand, cautioning me on my outspokenness.

"Afraid?" Nimue scoffed. "No. What they display is the failing blood pool of a long dead kind. They are of no use to me. And yet they think—" She stopped herself dead, her scarred face wrinkling further in annoyance at what, I thought, she'd been about to reveal.

"After lengthy consultation with my counselors, however," she hurried on, "these rumors appear to offer great benefit to the present cause."

One breath, two. I steadied myself, took a single step closer. "What is it you think I can do to help you?" I asked. So far, the crystal in its bag remained with me, undiscovered. If these rumors, or prophecies as Hannah had called them, had contained any reference to what I carried, I doubt I'd still be in possession.

Nimue reached out, tapped a finger to the glass. A small insect on the other side darted away, tapered wings flashing. She appeared to be giving my question some contemplation, when I suspected she already knew exactly what she planned to say.

"To begin with, you can assist with the work I have planned for the little witch and the thrice-gifted child." At my look, she added, "They trust you, don't they?"

"They have names," I said.

"You'll introduce us properly, then. It'll be so much better than what you'll allow them to go through if you don't."

*This old coot's cracked.*

*I don't need this now, Skelly. Please.*

*If you say so.*

I considered. Not for long. I didn't want them to suffer more as a result of my indecision. The one thing, the most important thing, was to be together again. A chance to speak might present itself, to discuss a way free from this mess. "Very well," I agreed. "However, I'll require Duncan and Mika with me, too. If Carina senses I'm worried about them, so will Resa. Things will go a lot more smoothly without that."

*Oh, you liar.*

I shut him down, trying to maintain a demeanor that didn't scream falsehoods, reminding myself Carina really would sense my worry. No distortion of truths there.

Nimue returned to her seat, lowered herself onto the opulent cushion with a grunt. She stretched her legs, her battered face twisting in pain. "Too much walking," she mumbled.

I could imagine Duncan's response to her complaint. Not my problem, he would say. She'd be furious. I schooled my expression, fighting back a smile.

"Lyoness?" I prompted. "Duncan and Mika."

She waved a hand. A man appeared from nowhere, brought her a glass. I had no idea where he'd been hiding. She drank, handed the glass back, sat a minute longer. Her eyes glazed. "Those boys have been sent to perform a job for me, for us."

My stomach sank, at that point just a little. "Bring them back, then," I said.

The man holding the glass bent and spoke a few words in Nimue's ear. Her gaze shifted to me, held. She nodded at him. He departed.

Standing once more, Nimue made her way toward me. Her expressions were so difficult to read, hidden as they could be among the deforming folds from her injuries. But I saw something there. Something that made me take a step back, hands lifting, not in defense, but to ward off what was in her eyes.

"Grace," she said, slowly, almost gently, "I'm afraid that's not possible. I've just been informed they died, yesterday, in an unfortunate occurrence at the mines."

Skelly started screaming inside my head, the boy haunted by his prior life.

Except it wasn't him. It was me.

Or maybe it was us both.

Chapter Sixteen

I, not she who had sent them to their demise, had to stand before Carina and Resa and give them the terrible news. In truth, I wouldn't have wanted anyone else to speak those words and yet I couldn't imagine myself saying them either. They didn't seem true. They couldn't be true. But I had no cause to doubt them. I'd seen too much to foolishly believe we, our group of odd and wonderful companions, could be immune to death.

*Tell me about it,* Skelly said, jabbing his anger into my grief. *And I wasn't even your friend. I wasn't anyone's friend.*

*You were Mika's,* I thought back at him. *And you could have been mine.*

He went silent. I was glad.

Carina and Resa had been kept separate from the others in containment, separate from me. I followed once again the guard I had thrown to the ground. He seemed a bit more wary. Given my present state of mind, he needed to be. More likely, though, he'd been warned off by Nimue. She wanted my cooperation.

My mother used to read and sometimes recite to me at night when I was quite young. While I strode with lagging steps toward the place Resa and Carina were kept, a phrase kept repeating itself over and over in memory. An ancient phrase carried forward by my mother's distant forebears from a world so far away I couldn't really fathom it. But the words I understood, especially now. *Rage, rage against the dying of the light...*

I didn't realize I spoke them aloud until the guard turned his head and growled at me to keep silent.

*Don't let him tell you what to do,* Skelly said, almost a whisper in my ear. For the first time, I felt comforted by his sentiments.

Still, *I must,* I said. *For now.*

We rounded an area marked by particularly dense foliage, striding on over the stone pathway. Ahead, the huge, oval room came into sight. Unlike the others, which contained mostly glass in their structure, the walls along the back side were made from some white material and only the curved front had been fashioned from glass. Even so, the vast surface provided ample viewing. Wildron stood about, rude in curiosity, staring in at the occupants. They hurried away upon our approach. I stopped at a short distance. Carina and Resa lay on the smooth floor beneath the strange and ever-constant light, curled around each other, the veil Carina had managed to keep from her prior attire stretched across them both. They appeared to be asleep.

The witch. The thrice-gifted child.

I bowed my head, fighting back tears.

"In you go," the guard said, like I was an animal being coaxed into a crate. I went anyway.

The door shut behind me. Neither Carina nor Resa awakened. I could hear them breathing along with the rushing air through the vents, like dull, voiceless whispers.

What could I say to make this all right?

Nothing.

I removed my boots. I don't know why. Perhaps to make my approach kinder, less intrusive. Dropping to my knees, I crawled across the floor until I was only a foot or two away. Sitting back on my heels, I watched them for several long minutes. Peaceful, they looked, both of them. Soon, when I told them one's love, one's brother had been swept from this world forever, that peace would be shattered. So, I waited. And waited.

The guard hammered on glass, making me jump.

Pivoting at the waist, I swept my hand out in a powerful fury, my whole body wanting him gone. He staggered back, shocked, I knew, by my expression, my rage. I didn't care. Even if it brought punishment on me, I didn't care. We stared at each other for longer than he could stand. His gaze shifted away and he turned, his back now to the door.

Inhaling, exhaling, I released my anger. Without it, grief full-blown returned. I crept closer, reached out, my fingers settling on Carina's shoulder. She rolled over, blinked a few times, looked at me.

"I had a dream—" she mumbled, and stopped.

Her pale skin turned to ash, her iris darkening until no pupil remained. "No, Grace. No."

I gathered her into my arms and we wept together while Resa slept on.

*     *     *

"Is there any chance Nimue has lied to me?" I asked, voice low and hoarse, smeared tears lying cold on my face.

Carina shook her head, pushing her damp hair from her cheek. "I don't know. Why would she? About this, I mean. But there's something about this room. My connection to…to what's beyond is gone. It feels gone."

"When you looked at me you knew—"

"Because you're here, inside the room with me. Besides, your face doesn't hide things well. I knew, Grace. How could I not."

We rocked together a while longer. I fought the howling pain until my stomach ached as if I'd been kicked.

"But my dream," Carina whispered after more time had passed, time in which I wished the room itself would collapse in on me. Not them, though. Not Resa and Carina. I had to give up the grief-wish for my own demise, because I would never see them hurt. A small hope, a tiny gratitude, swirled through my consciousness at the realization I could still care, that caring for another wasn't about to rip me open from head to toe.

"What about it?"

She shook her head. "I was dreaming we were together. All of us."

We cried again in a pattern that continued until Resa woke. When she did, before she sat up and saw us, we quickly scrubbed away all evidence of sorrow, fixing on our faces not a smile, but serene anticipation, having agreed without words not to let Resa know. Not yet.

Resa signed something to Carina I didn't quite catch. Carina lifted her head. "We need the facilities, please, and food and water."

I closed my eyes at the knowledge they were being so demeaned Carina had to request these things. Even on the prison planet, food had been available at all times and each cell contained a toilet, a sink. Privacy.

Because they were back, the gawkers, the curious, the rude and insensitive. I shot to my feet and marched over to the glass.

"Be calm," Carina called after me. I stopped short before verbally condemning them all, turned my back. Yet, I couldn't help looking over my shoulder and positioning myself to block their view. Again and again, until they straggled away.

"Oh, Grace," Carina said. Her lips twisted.

"They're tangling with the wrong warrior."

"You sound like…" Her voice trailed off.

"Duncan," I said. "I know."

Again, silence. We both averted our heads, away from Resa's curious gaze. A fist knocked lightly on glass. I turned to find three women, young ones, perhaps two years my senior. They signaled to Carina. She and Resa went out. I was not permitted to accompany them.

Alone inside the oval chamber, I paced off its

dimensions, first circumference, then diameter, for no reason other than my need to keep moving. The floor felt cool beneath my feet, like desert sand after a long, chill night. The sounds I made in movement seemed loud but muffled, which appeared odd to me, as I would have expected the glass, the floor, the rear walls to bounce noise around in continuous echo. The deadened atmosphere made me feel lonely. I needed to get Carina and Resa out of here.

When they returned, damp strands clung to their cheeks, a clear indication faces had been washed. Carina's hair looked as smooth as ever, but she'd also taken time to detangle and re-braid Resa's dark locks. I rubbed some grit from my eye, ran my fingers through my thankfully short hair, and considered how lax I'd become. If Duncan could see me now, he'd—

I sighed. Carina caught my eye, caught my thought, touched my sleeve in passing.

"Did you eat already?" I asked.

"Yes."

"That didn't take long."

"It wouldn't," she said.

We sat together against the rear wall, in a circle, facing each other. Resa asked several times in her way where the boys were.

"They'll be back," I said, signing those words as best I could. Lying, as best I could. Resa produced something from her pocket, held it out to Carina. Carina broke off a handful of hairs from her own head, tied them to the object and began weaving them, while Resa intently watched. After several minutes she handed the item back to Resa, for her to continue the work. I'd made a hair bracelet for Carina back on the Emerald, to celebrate her birth anniversary. I couldn't recall if I'd ever given it to her.

Carina sat back, arms extended behind, leaning on her palms, still graceful despite circumstances. "What does the Lyoness want from us?"

"Everything." Carina's eyebrows arched. I explained in a voice little more than a whisper my conversation with Nimue, her distaste, indeed her fear, regarding those who had been dubbed the Tainted, the plan she'd revealed as I wept over Duncan and Mika, her plan to use Resa's gifts with Carina to control her, to reveal all Resa learned and saw and heard. Yet, I suspected so much more than that. Given Resa's ability to toss physical objects around with her mind's furor, Nimue had to possess plans for this ability, as well.

"And what has this to do with you?"

"I am to lull you into a sense of security, so you'll cooperate. Convince you this is the best course of action for all."

"Well, then," she said, "you're doing a fine job."

I smiled, shocking myself. Up until that second, I hadn't really expected to find I could.

Carina glanced over to make certain Resa remained occupied. She sat up, leaned forward over her crossed legs, folded her hands together with a typically Carina movement, like feathers drifting. "So, what is it we're really going to do? What's your plan?"

I held her gaze, willing her to understand what

I was about to say, to realize my fear, to know my reasoning.

"We cooperate," I said. "It's all we've got."

Carina's white brows lowered over eyes as amber as Duncan's had been. Pain jolted through me. Could it be a memory manifestation? I looked away, though, unable to bear it.

"Cooperate," she said.

I nodded.

"Okay."

I clambered up onto my knees and hugged her. She returned the embrace with her small, narrow arms around my neck. Another pair slipped over us both. I looked up into Resa's face beside Carina's, her black braids twined in Carina's white hair. She smiled at me. Smiled, right at me. As if she were happy. I only wished Duncan could have seen it.

Chapter Seventeen

Within the hour, I'd cajoled the Lyoness into moving Carina and Resa into a less-exposed location. I insisted the atmosphere where they'd been housed resulted in Carina having to keep Resa in an altered state. Another lie. I was getting good at telling them. In truth, though, Resa experienced some form of serenity in Carina's company, a composure I thought might have more to do with their interaction than Carina's mystic abilities. Carina kept her busy in gentle ways. They touched often, communing. And, in the end, Resa had to recognize the safety net Carina represented when she lost control. Duncan would have liked to have given his sister all these things himself. I truly believed so. Sometimes, families didn't communicate, relate quite the way one might expect, the way they hoped.

The new room possessed several things the old had not. Beds, for one. Three beds. I would be staying with them. Another thing I had insisted on. I didn't believe Nimue to be stupid, but I did know she wanted results and had likely decided not to risk delay in achieving them.

A liquid computer monitor, the kind they'd had in the library in the prison, sat on a desk. No controls, though. Visible in a chamber opposite on a heavy console another had been positioned, along with the apparatus conducive to its use. None of it looked new. Duncan would know best about that, though. Of course, he would and I could never ask him now.

A small unit on four legs had been stationed in a corner. I'd peeked inside and found fruit, a jug filled with water, some other foodstuffs I didn't really recognize. A closeted area contained a toilet and a sink. On further inspection, I located a small image carved into the bathroom wall, a crude face, and two words beneath: *don't trust*. I didn't. I wouldn't. Seeing evidence from former use, I wondered if Nimue had attempted this scenario before with mage-blood Wildron. Unsuccessful attempts, or she wouldn't require us. I wondered, too, what had happened to those who had failed. Hopefully, they'd been added to the incarcerated in the long row of cells where I'd previously been housed. I wouldn't contemplate other alternatives in this hostile place.

I exited the closet and took a turn around the square room, studying ceilings and corners. On Emerald, I'd been unable to spot the interface which had eerily, sometimes annoyingly, provided me with instruction. If any existed here in this space, I couldn't see it, either. We'd have to be careful in our conversations.

Carina watched me. I forced a small smile to

my face, hoping to reassure her. I had no reassurances. The smile slipped away. Footsteps sounded outside, cracking against stone. Carina touched Resa's shoulder. I turned around to face the door.

Nimue paused there with three others. Two moved on to the next room, went inside before Nimue came into ours. She didn't knock. I hadn't expected she would.

"I see you're all settled in," she said.

I kept my hands at my sides, my face immobile. Standing before her, I felt on the edge of something I might step over with no chance for return.

Nimue strode past me. I followed her with my eyes, then turned my shoulders, my waist, finally shifting my feet. She stood a moment staring down at Resa and Carina sitting side by side on one bed. "You'll be happy you complied. Is the child ready?"

"Resa," I said, much as Duncan would have done. "Her name is Resa."

"Resa," Nimue echoed. "And she can't hear me?"

"She cannot, Lyoness," Carina said softly, her eyes on Nimue's.

"Good. Then listen. Listen well. As long as you can make sure she does what's needed, you will all retain your status here in this room. If not..." She let the sentence hang theatrically. My muscles tensed. I circled around Nimue to sit beside my friends. I, too, met Nimue's gaze, doing my best to control my expression. She took a step away nevertheless. I looked past her to the man now standing at her back.

He looked different than anyone I'd met here so far. Not only his clothing, which resembled more the garments worn by someone residing in Citadel before the flames had taken it, but his markedly sharp yet delicate features, his silver eyes. Like Skelly's—no, more like Hannah's, and yet not quite. Not a pale gray hue, but an actual silvery gray, lighter even than his hair. I thought he might have something on them, something to disguise their true color, but I couldn't see any indication this was so. In his hand he clasped a device, a loosely woven metal cap with multiple wires hanging from it.

"This is the physician," Nimue said, with a dismissive flick from her fingers. Was there no one she didn't view in disdain? "He will ready the child—Resa," she corrected herself, "for testing."

She walked out without another word, not to the room beside ours, but in the opposite direction. I turned to the physician. "What is your name? What are you called?"

"I am called doctor," he said. "My name is Symick. You may call me that."

"I would feel wrong calling you that," I said, motivated by a brief picture of my parents' reaction should I address a physician by his given name. Habits learned, not easily cast aside. "Where I come from doctors are esteemed. You must have a title."

"I had once, long ago. I've forgotten it. If you would feel better, call me Doctor Symick, yes?" He placed the cap on the table, spread the wires, separating them into some order not apparent to me.

"Doctor Symick," I said, "are you going to hurt

her?"

He blinked, shot me a glance from eyes that in profile resembled water. "That is not my intent."

I released a quick breath through my nose.

"Nor," he added, "do I anticipate you would allow it."

It was my turn to be surprised. "I…I wouldn't," I stammered before collecting myself. "Be assured, I wouldn't."

"Then we have an understanding." He straightened from his task. Resa watched him, watched him extend a hand to her. Rising from the bed, she took his fingers. He pulled out the chair from beneath the desk with his other and she climbed onto it. I exchanged a look with Carina, a chill moving across my shoulders to converge at my nape.

"Doctor Symick," I said, "where are you from? Not here, I think."

"Not here," he agreed. He held the metal cap up for Resa to examine before placing it on her head. After, he pulled a box from his pocket and connected the leads to their proper receptacles. Stepping back, he swiped his fingers across his face, closing them into a fist against his chin and lips. Reaching awkwardly beneath his right arm with his left, he rapped on the window between the two chambers.

"We'll begin," he said to Carina and me. My shoulders relaxed a little. I thought, *we can trust him*, until I remembered the words carved into the bathroom wall.

* * *

I'm not sure what I expected. Something invasive and upsetting to Resa, for certain. It didn't begin badly. Doctor Symick explained that Resa would be reviewing images, directions which I then related to Resa, aided by Carina's direct interpretation by touch. These images started to appear right away on the monitor for Resa's observation, innocuous depictions, such as trees, water, the night sky, people. Strangers, in locations I didn't recognize. The speed with which the images changed increased until they were coming quite fast. I noted the injection of harsher images among the others, picking out a burning Citadel between two other pictures of the city whole and beautiful. They only got worse from there. Resa seemed to freeze, transfixed. Carina moved closer, pushing away Symick's hand when he reached out to stop her. She knelt beside Resa's chair.

Suddenly, Resa's small hands flew up toward the monitor in frantic motion from side to side that changed, became symbolic, filled with meaning, words and phrases too fast for me to read. I tried, recalling what Duncan had said about her frustration and wanting to help her. Carina reached out, too, to settle her down, but Symick shoved me aside, lurched across behind Resa, thrust Carina away. I grabbed his stiff, white coat sleeve, yanked him back. The desk, the monitor, the box with the wires attached, all began to vibrate, preparing for gyroscopic flight.

One word left my lips. One single syllable, directed at the doctor. In an instant, he found himself sliding down the wall. Not at my hand, although I'd felt the surging power in my mind. At Resa's. Both Carina and Resa stood now within a dying eddy, nothing broken, nothing thrown, except the physician. I walked slowly across the room and extended my hand to help him up.

"It could have been worse," I said, glancing back to the open-mouthed pair in the opposite room.

"How much worse?" he asked, leaping to his feet, his oddly damp hand still in mine. I released it, wiped my fingers on my dress.

"You're still breathing. Contemplate not."

He nodded, clearly shaken. His silver-gray hair fell across his forehead and he shoved it back with quaking fingers. "Perhaps that's enough for now. I'll come back later and we'll try something different."

"Whatever you think best," I said with false sweetness and deep satisfaction. "Will the Lyoness agree?"

"She must, if she wants results."

I walked him to the door, the way I'd been instructed to do at home whenever seeing a guest out. I hadn't always done it, particularly with Mara, who used to come and go at will before the uprising. Remembering Mara, regret surged, reminding me how little I'd thought about her these past months. I said a quick silent prayer for her well-being and at the same time wondered if, when we met again, she would recognize me as her friend. I'd changed. I would likely be a stranger to her.

When we were again alone, the two in the

chamber next door having also departed, Carina skipped over to me, the way she used to back on Emerald. Incarceration hadn't dampened her spirit. Everything after had.

"Idiot," she said. "Maybe he'll know better now."

"I hope so."

Resa appeared beside me, signing as she came. I watched her hands carefully, my head tipped to one side. I found I only had to ask her to repeat a portion, more because I wanted to make sure my interpretation wasn't based on expectations than because I believed I'd misunderstood. Beside me, Carina gasped, way ahead of me, of course, having delved into Resa's thoughts.

"Duncan?" she said.

I nodded. "I saw him, too, in those images. Cruel way to get a reaction. Even more brutal for us than Resa, I suppose, because she expects him—"

"To come back," Carina finished.

"Yes."

"How long are we going to let this go on?" Carina whispered.

I turned to Resa, offered her a weak smile. "Until I can figure out something else."

Later that evening, Doctor Symick returned. He came alone, carrying a portfolio under his arm. In it were maps and what looked like pages torn from illustrated books. He spread everything out across the floor, then sat down among them, cross-legged. He asked us to join him.

We made a rough circle among the items he'd brought. I couldn't help looking at them myself, searching for something familiar, perhaps comforting. With a cry, Carina pointed out a sky image showing a brilliant white star beyond Riley.

"That's Carina Excelsior," she said. "I was named for that star." She'd told me so when first we'd met. I provided the information for Resa now. At least, I hoped I did. I struggled with my signing.

Resa picked the paper up, tucked several braids behind her ear and nodded. Before returning the image to the floor, she pressed a finger to the gambling moon, to Riley. My breath stopped.

"Ask her what she sees," Doctor Symick directed.

I didn't want to, because I feared I knew. Her Gran, her home, her brother, Mika, all of them from Riley.

"Please," Symick said.

I did, or tried to. I held no assurances what I intended to impart would translate through my fingers. Yet, the request was a simple one. *What do you see?*

*Home,* she said back. Home. I wondered how she formulated that word-image in her head, how she understood it, attached it to what she'd been shown. Resa baffled and amazed me. I told the doctor only her reply.

"Anything in particular?" he asked.

"She has memories of the place," I said. "So naturally, she would see many things in her mind."

He held my gaze for many seconds. "Understood."

"Where are you from?" I asked again.

"Why does it matter?"

"I don't know. But it does."

"Not here," he said, repeating what he'd told me when asked before. The response sounded different this time, somehow.

"Well, then," I said, "why are you here?"

He released a long, slow breath. "I have a job to do."

Dismissed, I stopped asking. He pulled out another page from the many littering the area. We continued this way for several hours, working slowly through the images and maps strewn about. Occasionally, Resa frantically attempted to explain her reaction to a face, a place represented, a word, a name on a drawn map. I couldn't keep up with her. Carina did her best to fill in the gaps, but Resa's scattered comprehension, her rapid, convoluted impressions made it impossible. Carina said it was as though Resa viewed these distant places through some strange and mysterious kaleidoscope. More than once, Carina pressed her forehead to Resa's, instilling calm, close to shutting her down. Doctor Symick made no attempt to stop her doing so. I supposed he'd learned his lesson the first time. Smart man, even if he couldn't be trusted.

He mixed the papers up again, shuffling them around across the floor between us. I supposed he hoped Resa would somehow gain a different perspective. Suddenly, Resa shot forward on her hands and knees, snatched a picture from near his knee. She held it up to her face, close, as if she couldn't see it properly, then slowly lowered it, looking at me. Doctor Symick reached out for the image, but I got there first. Resa released it into my hand.

*Home,* she signed.

I looked down. Mine.

And there I was, a tiny thing, beside my mother. Holding her trouser leg with one hand, a stick in the other.

"Where did you get this?"

Doctor Symick said nothing.

"Where did you get this?" I repeated.

"The library."

"There's a library here?" Carina asked, coming to peer over my shoulder.

"Yes," Doctor Symick said. "Some of the older forms are archived, the physical books, what's left of them. These images and maps were stacked and waiting for me. From the Lyoness."

I noted an intriguing hint of distaste in his tone. Not as interesting as discovering my picture as a child had found its way into the archives in the City of All Dwellers library.

"Why was this among them?"

"I don't know," he said.

"How?"

"I don't know."

I stared at the image, ran my fingers over it, holding them overlong on my mother with her deep auburn hair, her green eyes—my eyes—and the smile that always seemed to hold something else beyond joy, humor, affection. Her secret smile, my father called it. Not as if she kept secrets, but as if her smile encompassed more than we could ever know.

"How is she, my mother? My father? My

brothers?"

"I don't know," Doctor Symick said once more.

"I wasn't talking to you. I wouldn't expect you to know," I said, fully cognizant my words reflected discourtesy and disrespect. If I suffered punishment for them, so be it. "I was talking to Resa."

"Who can't hear you," he reminded me with an odd gentleness. I glanced at the silver-eyed, silver-haired physician. Tears pricked my lids.

"Grace," Carina whispered.

I turned away, from her, from him, and met Resa's gaze. I lowered the picture to my lap, signed family, me, hoping she understood. She did, reaching out for the stiff paper. I settled it into her hands. Her face contorted, eyes squeezing shut. She seemed to be trying to will something into being. I'd never seen her do so before. From what I understood, the places, things, people came to her. She didn't call them. Yet she was trying. For me.

Finally, she looked up. Her eyes filled with tears. I bolted to my feet.

"No!"

Carina's tiny fingers slipped into mine, squeezing. "Grace, it's okay. She's crying because she doesn't know, because she can't find the answer for you."

My heart split into tiny pieces, for so many reasons. Shattered, feeling like it, like I, might float away, all the fragments disappearing and not even sure I would care. I crouched down next to Resa, smoothed back the tangled, wisping strands from her forehead. I placed my lips there, to the warmth, and allowed myself to grieve again, not only for

Duncan and Mika, but for everything that had come to pass.

"I'll leave this one here, shall I?"

I glanced through watery eyes toward the desk, where Doctor Symick placed the processed image near the edge. He'd already gathered up the rest and with a nod, withdrew, striding the short distance to the door and out.

I stood, crossed to the cabinet containing food and water, opened the door. "We'll have some fruit and a drink before bed."

"That was a ritual at home," Carina said. "Gilda fruit sliced in a bowl. We'd sit outside and watch the sun go down while we ate it."

This was the first Carina had really spoken about her life. I paused with the door still open, studying her. "Who is 'we'? Your parents? Do you have brothers and sisters?"

She shook her head, silky hair flowing fluidly around her shoulders. "I do, but I haven't seen them in a very long time. I mean the other girls," she said. "The dancers-in-training. I learned many things there, like how to pick pockets, and locks." She glanced toward the door. "I wish I still had the kit I appropriated outside Citadel, but Duncan's been…was holding it for me."

My lips curled up and then down. Remembering Duncan. "Why not Mika?" I asked.

"He was hoping I'd reform." She laughed with a little snorting sound and burst into tears.

I couldn't remember the last time I'd wept so frequently, so long, so much without a hope there'd ever be a reason not to anymore. We held onto each other for minute upon minute, not wanting to let go. On the floor, Resa continued her study, frowning down at the picture of me, my mother, our sand-colored desert abode in the unrelenting sunshine. Sluggishly, I turned my head, nagged by the idea I'd missed something. Turned, and turned again, toward the desk, pulling away from Carina.

"What's this?" Not my home. Resa still had that one in her possession. I picked the sheet off the desk, pivoted the image in confusion, a frown creasing my brow. I couldn't begin to understand what I saw, until—

"The glass mines," I said.

I dropped the picture, betrayed by a man I'd started to believe might be kind. Why would he leave this here? Resa's hand shot out, snatched the picture as it slipped from the desk and fluttered toward the floor. Too late for me to retrieve it, to save her the pain she'd surely find with her unimaginable, inner eye. Too late, I realized, to save us at all.

Chapter Eighteen

I couldn't be sure how much longer these light sticks would hold out. How much longer we would all hold out. No food since the gray mush, no water. No idea how far the tunnel stretched into darkness before us.

Some had wanted to start mining, still believing they would be released back to the above-world after labor. I'd done my best to convince them otherwise. It killed me having to give up on those who still refused to listen in the end.

They were gone now, anyway. Shortly after we started climbing up the side tunnel where the carts were lined up waiting to be filled, it sounded like one of those cages had come crashing down. Glass and stone roared into the main corridor where the holdouts stood dutifully clutching their tools. I tried not to think about those we'd left behind back there. No one could have survived. That was my hope, anyway. The alternative couldn't be borne, by any of us. If we talked about them at all, we talked about them in the past tense.

But we didn't talk. Not much anyway. The

occasional grunt while we forced ourselves past the carts, up and up at a steady incline, or a whispered encouragement if someone lagged. We carried thick glass slivers, like crystal blades, in case we needed them. A few, me and Mika included, had also pinched cutters, the tool with its concentrated laser used to remove the glass from stone. Those would come in handy. If nothing else, I anticipated a barricade or gate at the opposite end of this treacherous shaft.

Mika, Ren, Hugo and Joy-Li stuck close behind me. Levon, too. I hadn't thrown him into the pit. Odd, because I'd visualized doing it so clearly.

I had my doubts he'd make it to the top, though. He'd been almost without strength even before we started up. Yet the further we went, I realized he might succeed, he just might, from stubbornness. Maybe given a chance, he'd do something to redeem himself. I had to remind myself his actions weren't entirely his own doing. In his mental and physical state, he'd been convinced he had a chance as long as he cooperated. They were already dead after all, those poor kids. Still, considering doing what he'd done wrenched my nearly empty stomach into contortions that sucked it right up against my spine. I liked telling myself I'd have died rather than strip those bodies of their suits and dump them over the edge, but really, what did I know. I hadn't been there, in his place. I didn't plan ever to be there.

This tunnel had to lead to somewhere on the outside for cart collection—carts that would remain empty since the main tunnel's collapse. The tragedy might work in our favor. With nothing expected to come up, no one would be there to oversee unloading. I began to feel a teensy bit, perhaps even legitimately, hopeful. I had no idea where this tunnel exited, but anywhere had to be better than down where we had been. Another lie to tell myself? Could be. But I planned to stick with it.

We all felt the change in the air as we climbed, and most removed their masks. It made breathing easier, even though whatever intermingled with the wind barreling down the tunnel stung the nose and throat. Carried a scent with it, too, reminding me there were living things out there. I hoped someone among us would recognize where we were, might navigate by the stars, the sun, be familiar with the surroundings, and could point Mika and me in the right direction. Because we planned to head back to the city. The rest could do what they wanted.

My conscience, a really tiny part, experienced some guilt over abandoning this group to make it on their own, but unless they opted to come with me and Mika in our mission to save the girls, that's how it would have to be.

And what would Grace say to that? my conscience argued. I ignored it and scrambled on up the incline. Now that we'd left the carts behind, we were able to use the crossties on the tracks for traction. Which helped. A lot. Most of us were bone-tired, breathless, needing hydration and sustenance. Most? All.

Although we'd find air outside, we'd not likely find rest, food or water. Somehow, it always came down to frying pan or fire. It was like those words were meant to haunt me. Like I really, really, really needed to stop saying them.

Mika gave me a sudden poke in the arm. I looked at his finger lifting, pointing, away from us to somewhere up ahead. I squinted, dazzled by the lights we all held in our fists. "What?" I asked. "Do you hear something? See something?"

"Both," he said.

I lifted the hand holding the light stick, high enough for everyone to see, and shut off the beam. Without the need for instruction, everyone followed suit and shuffled to a halt.

"What is it?" someone whispered. Ren the Impatient. I shushed him like I would a two-year-old and listened.

I'd learned a word long ago: susurration. A word that sounded like what it meant. A whisper, a murmur, a soft rustling. I used to say the word a lot when I first discovered it written in something I'd been reading. That's what I heard now as the constant, rushing wind died away. Though soft, the sound was pervasive, a distant soughing. Another good word. More importantly, the sound accompanied a welcome sight. The night sky.

Framed by the rocky opening, stars glittered in absolute brilliance, meaning no artificial light shone in the area. I had the word passed along that we'd come nearly to the outside world and instructing everyone to tread carefully. We didn't know what to expect out there.

Ren made to push past me and I thrust my arm out, blocking him.

"You're not the leader," he growled, trying to

shove my arm away. Mika stepped in to impede him as well.

I had all I could do not to laugh at Ren and his stupid complaint. "I don't care," I said. "That's never been my intent. But I'm also not going to let you get us killed. Got that?"

Taking a deep breath, I tried to channel Grace. Give him a job, is what she'd do. Make him feel important and not slighted.

"I could use some help, though. Can you keep everybody back there quiet, calm? Mika and I will go a little ahead and you bring them up behind. I want to get a good look outside before the rest of them go running into the open."

"Fine," he mumbled, but complied. Mika and I moved forward.

"Good one," he whispered. "She's rubbed off on you, after all."

I said nothing, struggling against a grin, moving carefully toward the opening with a glass knife in one hand, the darkened light stick in the other. Both would work as weapons, the former best if some vicious animal awaited us. I didn't think about using it against a Wildron guard. I hadn't yet had to fight in that way. I didn't plan to if I could help it.

From the opening, the tracks ran off to the right in a curve to a platform raised off the ground below. A hulking ship body sat atop it, dark, looking at the moment to be unmanned. I jerked my head in the ship's direction. "Could you—"

"No," Mika said, before I could finish. "I wouldn't dare." He nodded at something beyond my sight. I leaned forward and peered out. Distant lights made a dull glow beneath the sky. It looked like the base where we'd been brought for our descent into the mine. We'd come far. Even so, we'd be spotted the moment we made an unauthorized takeoff.

I looked to the left, where the forest grew dark and shadowed along a curved ridge on the barren field's edge. I figured the ebb and flow of sound came from the leaves. It certainly seemed louder now we were standing on the precipice formed by the opening. "We could hide in the forest for a short time," I said, "rest, maybe find some water. Just have to figure a way to climb down to the ground. Right up against the rocks seems to be flat, safe for walking once we get there."

Ren appeared, extended his arm straight out between us, fist closed, one finger pointing. "What's that?"

I frowned, studying where he pointed. "A reflection from the sky. Glass? But more broken up than what's nearer."

"No," said Ren, anxious now. "It's moving."

He was right, gods, he was right. I stared at the strange formation. Row after row, what appeared to be lit, almost bubbling strands rolled forward in a haphazard formation on the horizon, disappearing as they got closer to where the glass field took a sudden dip. The sky was darkest just beyond where the anomalies appeared, the stars gone, an almost perfect delineation between stars and blackness. As I watched, though, an occasional thinner glowing line appeared in that blackness. Farther away, perhaps. Was it land? Was I mistaking where the sky ended?

Mika swore. Mika, who never swore. I snapped my head toward him.

"What?"

He shook his head, sounding on the verge of laughter. "It's the ocean," he said.

"The ocean?" Ren repeated, stepping forward. I had to grab his arm to keep him from going off the ledge. "I've never seen it."

"Not even images?" Mika asked him.

"No. Well, not like this. I would never have guessed… I didn't think we were anywhere near…" His voice trailed off as he stared, dumbfounded. Suddenly, he licked his lips. "There's water there. Plenty of it."

"Salt water," I said, because I believed Mika. I'd learned about oceans, too, although I hadn't seen one in real life. No images had depicted what I saw now, either, but Mika was smart like that. He knew things.

"So?" said Ren. "What's a little salt going to do?"

"The salinity would kill you. Trust me," he said to Ren, who was about to object, "I know. My father's a doctor."

Ren blew out a long breath. The others ambled up behind him, peering around us, looking out, looking at me, waiting for me to tell them what to do. Waiting for *me* to tell them what to do.

I crouched down in the stiff, mining suit to get a better look at the stone face, searching for handholds, footholds, steps, for crying out loud. If we could make our way along the tracks, they did descend on their way to the platform to a drop that wouldn't be half as far, but we'd be crashing down onto heaved and razor-edged glass. We had to find a way to the cleared pathway right here.

I stood. "I don't suppose anyone's got a rope?"

Mumbled negatives, some shuffling as suits were actually checked. "I've got a belt," someone said.

"Me, too," said another.

I slapped my waist, remembering what I wore beneath. "Me, too."

All told, we ended up with about fourteen feet of belts. We needed roughly twice that much. I thought some more.

Levon wandered up. "I can climb," he said.

I looked him up and down, trying to contain my instinctive, troubling reaction to him. "What are you saying?"

"I'll find a way down. Toss your suits. I'll pile them up." He drew a deep rattling breath. I almost expected it to be his last. "Use the belts for as far as you can. I'll direct from down there. Everyone can slide or drop when they can't do anything else."

He wheezed a few more times, clearly having expended his energy getting those words out. Despite the sane content of his plan—when he hadn't sounded at all stable back there in the mine—he didn't possess the strength to see it through.

I did, though. I looked at Mika.

"Okay," he said.

"You and Ren make sure these belts are secure.

Everybody else, get out of your suits and be prepared to throw them down. The tools, too. Bundle them up in something. Levon—" I glanced around for him. "Levon?"

I hurried to the ledge. Levon's pale face looked up at me from about ten feet below as he felt around in the rocks for places for his boots, his hands. His breath rasped in the night air. "Levon," I said.

He kept going, not answering. He probably couldn't. I removed my suit, handed it to Mika, and headed over myself.

It wasn't easy. I couldn't believe Levon did it. Every step constituted a major fight against gravity. My muscles, still sore from the dining hall battle and everything before that, screamed at me in protest. I dropped when still about four feet from bottom, stumbled backward, knocked Levon to his knees. I helped him up, feeling bones and little else beneath the padded suit. I hated myself for hating him.

"Sit down," I said. "Rest. I've got it now. I'll...I'll let you know if I need help."

He managed to lower himself onto a flat rock and hunched over his knees, his hands folded, tightly clasped. I caught the suits, including the ones in which the tools and glass daggers had been secured. Those I set aside, but the rest I piled up, glancing every now and then at Levon where he sat.

"That's the ocean," he whispered at one point. "I heard you say. I went there once. Not here. Elsewhere. With my mom and dad. I swam in the waves."

I tuned out his wistful voice, concentrated

instead on making sure no one dropped to their detriment from above. One by one, they all made it with only a few, minor mishaps, Mika and Ren coming last, the same way Levon and I had done, freehand. I caught Mika as he dropped feet first, helped him to stand, then waited for Ren.

"Check on Levon, would you?" I asked Mika, reaching out to keep Ren steady. The others started gathering up pieces of their suits, I supposed against the night's chill. Weapons and tools were redistributed. I walked over to where Mika and Levon sat side by side. Mika had adopted generally the same position on the rock's flat surface, leaning forward, hands folded between his knees, his gaze on Levon, just watching him. Levon's eyes remained on the distant water.

Mika reached over and closed them.

Chapter Nineteen

We buried him, under stones. Like a cairn. We couldn't do anything else. The parents he'd mentioned would never know. I felt awful about that, but for us he didn't even have a surname. I couldn't imagine how we'd get the news to them anyway, about him, about any of the others who'd perished. By the time we'd finished, the sky had started to lighten. The long night had ended. Time to go, to get ourselves hidden, to make the next plan.

After concealing the suits no longer needed, we hurried into the forest and made rough camp. No fire, no food, only a place to take turns sleeping, while others set about foraging for something edible, for water. At least, that was the intent. Implementation? Another matter.

I finally plopped down on the ground, put my head in my hand. Swore. Quietly. In exhaustion, most had fallen asleep where they'd landed. The ground vibrated. Someone sat beside me. I thought it might be Mika or Ren. I felt too tired myself to even look.

"Thank you."

I opened my eyes, turned my head. "Joy-Li," I said, surprised to find her there, my eyes drawn to the tracks along her filthy cheeks, from tears, maybe, or sweat. "What for?"

"For saving us."

"I didn't—" I started, but then thought about it. Only briefly. I had no desire to dwell overlong on the last hours. "Okay," I said. "You're welcome. It wasn't just me, though."

"I know. I thanked Mika, too."

I nodded. Mika, the doctor's son. Mika, pronouncing a guy no older than the two of us dead. Not quite the same as setting and splinting a couple fingers, wrapping some ribs. Not the same at all. I searched for him, found him sitting against a tree trunk, head back, eyes closed. Not asleep, though. Every so often his mouth moved, answering Ren, who sat nearby jabbering away. I couldn't hear what either said.

"You'll want to go back for the other three, I expect."

My eyes slid again in Joy-Li's direction. "Yeah," I said.

"We'll go, too. Ren, Hugo and me."

"Why?"

"Why not?"

I sat up a little. "Someone's got to lead this lot to a safe place. Ren—"

"No."

I released a breath through my nose. "Not to be rude, Joy-Li, but I don't exactly trust you three."

She scooted closer across the ground. For a shocked second, I thought she was going to try to cuddle me, but she merely shucked her sleeves into a more comfortable position on her arms. She'd yanked the top from her miner's suit earlier and wore it like a jacket.

"I get that," she said, "I do. But there are things you don't know."

"Obviously," I answered with sarcasm. She frowned.

"The prophecy—"

"I don't care about any prophecy. Don't really even believe in them, okay? So, nothing you're going to say about that is going to sway me."

"Really? I'm telling you anyway. It refers to the warrior, the witch and the thrice-gifted child."

She had my attention now. Begrudgingly, I listened.

"Those three should never have been allowed to get together," Joy-Li continued. "Or maybe I should say they shouldn't have been brought together. The prophecy is unclear as to the purpose, but it is quite clear that they must—"

"Joy-Li."

I glanced up at Ren. Joy-Li didn't even turn her head. "They must go into the mountains," she said.

"Why?" Always why, but I needed to know.

"So, they won't be used," Ren said. "That's what I believe anyway."

Though deliberately cryptic, I recognized an urgency in them both. I heaved a sigh, shifted my position. Ren, at least, didn't seem into the prophecy hype. I asked him what he thought it was all about.

"There are legends," he said. "Stories. I'm sure they have them wherever you're from."

"Yeah," I said, but really, we didn't. Not so

much. The occasional spooky story, or embellished talk about something we'd all witnessed, but there weren't any ritualistic tales. None that were repeated, passed on through generations, believed to be truth.

"Well, they always vary anyway, to suit the teller," he went on. "But the Far-Seer—one with Hannah's bloodline, not mine—has been spouting, recounting really, the old tale about the witch, the warrior and the thrice-gifted child. It's come up a lot, and not just here in our land. The tale is growing. The Far-Seer said that the three had come together and that they were not alone. That got people talking. Because legend is..." He paused, frowning.

"Go on," I said.

"Legend is," Joy-Li finished for him, "that together they can stop the darkness."

"The darkness?" I echoed. "What exactly is that?"

"Dunno," said Ren, "but I believe we might be pretty much living it."

He had a point. But there was no way Resa, Carina and Grace could put an end to the cruelties implemented by the Lyoness, let alone the war. "Wait," I said. "Is it your great-gran's intention to stop them from doing that?" My heart started to pound, thinking we might already be too late to save them.

"No," said Ren, "she wants to use their supposed power. Once the rumors began, she started testing all those with mage blood. I think she was counting on an army of freaks."

"Don't call them that!" Joy-Li cried.

"I'm not. She does."

"So, you four came to find us to do what exactly?" I asked. I began to realize just how much they'd hidden in the explanation they'd previously provided. "'Before someone else did' isn't good enough."

"To keep you out of her hands," Ren said.

"To take you to the Halcyon Range," said Joy-Li. "To Ogof O Cysgu Chwedl."

"And that's what when your tongue works properly?" I asked.

She shot me a dour look. I hadn't meant to insult her. I really didn't understand. "The Cavern of Sleeping Myth," she said. "In an elder tongue, I am told. I practiced hard to pronounce it, and I hope it's right. Don't make fun."

I straightened my spine. "And why would we need to go there?"

"For answers. Someone among the three is seeking answers."

A chill tripped down the alignment of my bones. Grace. Grace sought answers. She'd said so. I started sucking in short breaths though my mouth, letting out longer ones. My jaw clenched. Crap, crap, crap.

This couldn't be true.

"We'll be coming with you," Ren said. "We started this. We'll see it through."

I shook my head, waving my hand toward the others, lying about or sitting, looking confused and frightened and pushed to their limits. "What about them? I don't think they've camped out often."

"Done what?"

"I don't think they'll survive out here on their own," I clarified for Ren. Speaking slowly. "They need someone."

"Who cares?"

I bent my legs, pushed up with my hand and stood, facing Ren across a patch of grass in the sun. "Ren," I said, "your attitude stinks."

His fists clenched. "Should I be afraid?"

Joy-Li lurched upright. "Enough."

We both turned and looked at her, almost like she wasn't there, like she was just a shadow voice in the early morning air. My muscles tensed. We wanted to fight. No getting past that. Needed to, maybe, to settle something between us, something unknown, something burning like a sore in a place you couldn't reach.

Mika appeared from nowhere, wedged himself into the space where we stood inches apart. "Do you hear that? Are you even bothering to listen? There's activity out in the fields. We need to get moving."

We roused everybody with minimal noise, hustled them deeper into the forest. Before long, however, we encountered a ridge, tall and impossibly vertical, as though the land had heaved up like a rug in a push from a gigantic broom. We couldn't climb. Not again. No one had the strength. To our left, it towered back in the direction from which we'd fled. To the right, well, to the right, I couldn't see an end to it either, but at least it took us away from the fields, the mines, the manufactory. We headed that way, silent and sullen.

"Anybody know what wild berries are edible in

these parts?" I asked. It was the same as the rope question, muttered responses, but without the volunteering. Of course not. No one had been secreting berries in their pockets.

"Fine," I said. "Keep your eyes open for water."

From that point on, many walked with their heads down, scanning from side to side, stumbling because they weren't paying attention to anything else. I wondered how long they'd been imprisoned to have become so desensitized to their natural surroundings. The two—had it been only two—days Mika and I had been in the dark had nearly brought about our undoing. I could only imagine what it had been like for all of them. Worse. That's what it had been like. Far worse.

The fury I'd experienced when first we'd entered the mines, the rage at the situation, at Levon, bubbled up again. I pushed it down as best I could. Anger could make a person careless, reactionary. Foolish. I wouldn't be able to help anyone if I gave in to it.

So, I thought about Grace, going over in my head what she would do, not realizing I had started speaking out loud until Mika commented. I mumbled an apology.

"No problem," he said. "I'd give anything for us all to be together again, but at least Grace is with Carina and Resa. One less thing we have to worry about. They'll be all right."

I nodded, silent now, not as confident as Mika sounded. He probably wasn't either.

The ridge continued for a very long time,

giving us no opportunity to get on top, to move beyond it. Stragglers began to drop, pleading for rest. I finally called for a halt, hearing no one in pursuit through the forest. Finding cover beneath the trees where we wouldn't be seen by any ships above, I left them all and took Mika to search for water. At the very least, we needed hydration in order to go on.

"How are you doing?" I asked him as we walked. His face twisted in annoyance. He didn't want me asking anymore. I got that.

Still, he answered with a curt, "I'm okay."

I gave him a smile, a light clap on the shoulder, puffed up my cheeks and blew out a long, slow breath. Along with the risen sun, I'd been hearing a chorus of birdsong as we all trooped along. Suddenly, with only Mika and I on the move, I heard none. I heard something else, though. Running water.

Mika became aware at the same time and started forward. I held up a hand, put a finger to my lips in a rather dramatic manner. We crept forward quietly, closer to the gurgling, liquid sound. I heard something else, then. A snort, a growl. We stopped dead, peering through the undergrowth.

*Conjure.* Not one, a half dozen, drinking from the running stream. Heads bowed, their long horns dipped into the flow, occasionally rapping out a rhythm on the many stones in the streambed. I watched them slurp up water using their very large tongues and swallowed, my own much smaller tongue rasping in my dry mouth.

"Maybe we should just go get the others and

bring them all here. The beasts will be gone by then," Mika said in a barely audible voice.

A twig snapped. A *conjure* lifted its fearsome head and I spun around. Ren stood behind me.

"Why aren't you with the others?" I demanded, more loudly than intended. Beyond the undergrowth great bodies heaved.

Ren lifted his arms, multiple empty gloves hanging in his grasp. "I came to lend a hand." A joke. He was making jokes. I'd never understand him.

"Keep still," Mika hissed.

"Have you found water?" Ren whispered. "These gloves will hold it for a while."

I jerked my thumb in the stream's direction. "Can't get to it just yet. Crouch down and shut up."

I thought he'd argue. I had told him to shut up, after all. Instead, he dropped without a word to his knees, clutched the gloves against his chest. They were a good idea, the gloves. I only wished I'd thought of them myself. Returning to my post beside Mika, I saw the animals had begun to retreat from the waterside, their huge hooves gouging holes in the soil. Shuffling and shoving, the herd meandered downstream. Not much longer and it would be our turn. My throat contracted in anticipation. Turning my gaze away from the *conjures'* vanishing backsides, I checked the other direction. My heart performed a funny bump, like it had decided it should be anywhere but here, in my chest, pumping blood into my body.

Across the water, silver eyes stared out from the green, green leaves. Stared right into mine.

I muttered two words, stepped back. Ren yelped behind me. Part of me thought I'd trodden on him. The other part knew better.

"Oaks," he said, a squeak cut short. Mika turned in his direction, swung an arm, caught my wrist, bone to bone. I didn't look. I didn't need to. Across the stream a body had emerged to accompany the eyes, tall and thin and silver-haired. I only blinked and there were four more. Dressed in a hide-fabric combo, all with the bright silver hair, the silver eyes, and making their way across to where we stood, apparently not as hidden as I'd thought behind the rampant growth. I heard more behind me, sounding as though they wrestled with Ren.

"What do we do now?" Mika whispered.

Frying pan. Fire. I was beginning to hate the implications of that adage. Of my life.

I lifted my hands up to about shoulder height, palms out, turning on my heel to check Ren's condition. He'd opted not to fight, but hadn't released the gloves either, even though two sets of hands tried to take them from him.

"Have we trespassed?" I asked, attempting to sound reasonable, like we had the upper hand and they were just...I don't know. Unexpected.

Ren mouthed a word at me, three times until I got it. Kanon.

Several spoke at once, to each other, not me. A strangely gabbling, rapid-fire tongue I couldn't understand.

"Hello," I tried again. "We didn't mean to be here. Believe me."

One from across the stream ambled up next to me and Mika. Unlike the others, who held long, metal-handled, finely-honed blades, he clutched a pliant length of polished wood, much like Grace's *lathesa*, except each end had been lodged into a rounded stone. For balance, maybe, or to increase speed or deadliness. Or maybe decoration, some indication regarding rank. They certainly all watched him as though they expected him to instruct them in their next move.

"Where are you from?" he asked.

A breath rushed from me in relief. My bladder's contents almost did the same. I couldn't imagine enough fluid existed in the organ to do so, or why. I wouldn't have wanted such an awkward thing to happen in sight of Ren and Mika, these Kanon. Because I wasn't scared. Not really. They hadn't killed us outright, the hunters Joy-Li had threatened us with. That meant something.

"We escaped the mines," I said.

A muscle flickered in the man's cheek. "You three?"

"No," I answered. "All who would come. One died, though, once we were on the outside. And some stayed back in the mine. There was a collapse afterward." Why was I telling him all these things? It seemed an excessive information dump directed to someone who might very well kill us all in a minute or two.

"Where are the others?"

I jerked my chin. "Back there. They needed rest. We were seeking water."

He said something to his companions in his

native tongue, sending several into the woods the way we'd come. Ren struggled to look over his shoulder, then back at me.

"You gave them up," he said. "I can't believe you just gave them up." He glared at the man beside me. "You're not going to get much meat from that lot," he snarled and called him a name. I didn't know what it meant, but the insult behind stood out loud and clear.

The Kanon leader responded with a noise in his throat. Not language, not even their language. A stuttering, repeated rumble. He paused, said something to his company. They reacted to his words in the same fashion he had to Ren's. Startled, I realized they were laughing.

"Boy," he said to Ren, "we are not cannibals. Who has told you such a thing?"

Stubbornly, Ren refused to answer. His face went red.

"The Lyoness, no doubt," the man said. "She and her counsel have been spreading rumors. Even before her time your people were made to be afraid of ours."

Captive between the two Kanon still holding him, Ren glared at the man and spat on the ground.

"And just to prove the rumors false, we will feed you and your runaways, and not to each other. You look as though a meal would do you good."

He spoke well in the language not his own. I wondered if he'd been educated somewhere else, somewhere he'd learned other languages. I wondered, too, why he'd come back to live as an outcast in The Wilds.

"My name is Duncan," I said, "and this is Mika. That's Ren," I added, swinging my thumb in Ren's direction. I felt oddly at ease around this guy. I couldn't tell his age, except that an unlined face didn't seem much in keeping with the silver-white hair. I only knew we hadn't been subdued on sight, or thrown into a cell, or been treated badly in any way. I had to hope meeting the Kanon would turn out to be a good thing.

Ren, on the other hand, struggled against the two holding him. I understood why they hadn't let go. Everyone was calm except him. He looked like he wanted to take a swing or run, neither of which would do him or anyone else any good.

"Ren," I said, "I think it's okay. I really do. Calm down."

With a grunt, Ren jerked away and the two stepped back, eyeballing him. Ren crossed his arms, the gloves somehow still flapping in his grip. He glared at the man next to me. "What's your name?" he demanded. "You have ours."

I remembered something Grace had once said, how giving someone your name also gave them power. I didn't quite get the reasoning behind her belief, but it occurred to me the Kanon might share the same. The guy spoke up without hesitation, though, ending my speculation.

"In your tongue, my name is Kerrick," he said. "In mine—" and here, I couldn't even follow what he said. He introduced the others still with him in baffling sounds that meant nothing to me and which I'd never be able to imitate.

Ren glanced around at each man introduced as

though counting them before returning a hostile frown on Kerrick. "And who's side are you on?"

"We take no sides," said Kerrick.

"Like the Ogdonians?" I asked. We'd been informed they were neutral, too. Yet when we were fleeing Tiran's soldiers, they helped us. We'd believed or hoped to find neutrality or at least not condemnation among the Wildron. That had been a mistake.

"Yes," Kerrick answered, "for longer than the Ogdonians have existed as a people."

Ren exhaled in disbelief and looked away. The other Kanon returned with our remaining group, who strode slowly between them, wary and afraid. The brief rest had done some good, I saw, but many remained weak and stumbling.

"They should drink sparingly," Kerrick said. "Too much will make them ill after so long without."

Under his watchful eye, we all drank from the stream. I wondered why he took our care upon himself. We were nothing to them. Runaway slaves, really. Maybe, despite his declaration to neutrality, he saw some profit or reward for our return whole and sound. A moment later, however, he quieted my doubt, seeming to read the suspicion on my face.

"I have brothers and sisters out in the world," he said. "I would like to hope they are cared for, as well."

I inclined my head. "I can understand that. We, Mika and I, have friends, family we're worried about right now, too. They're in the City of All Dwellers."

He shot me a look I couldn't read and said nothing.

A tramping downstream caused us all to turn. More silver-haired Kanon made their way in our direction, carting several huge somethings slung on poles between them. Joy-Li, having quietly crept to my side, whispered:

"I know what those are."

"What, then?"

"Creatures. From the ocean."

"Fish, you mean?"

"Yes, fish," she said, with a scorn not unlike Ren's. "What else would I mean?"

"I don't know," I said. "That's why I asked."

She apologized in a small voice, watching with hungry eyes the group joining us. "They'll filet them and cook them, I expect."

"I expect so, too." My stomach grumbled. I had a flash image in my mind, a swift and rather detailed fantasy about eating the meat raw, because I was that hungry. Some did, I'd heard. I'd never had fish, though, uncooked or otherwise. Still, I wouldn't turn it down. Gran hadn't raised a fool.

The new arrivals gave us the onceover, eyes narrowing before addressing Kerrick. Several lifted the implements they held in their hands, waving them in our direction. Kerrick answered them before turning to me.

"They are concerned there will not be enough food. I have assured them there is plenty. A party will be going back out again tomorrow. I will send the strongest among you to join them. They will teach you how. You may as well earn your keep."

"Yes, sir," I said. We totaled about two dozen more mouths to be fed, so I understood. I certainly did. However, Mika and I wouldn't be around long enough to learn fishing. Neither would Ren, Hugo and Joy-Li, once they noticed our departure. Whatever their motivation, I believed they wanted to see the girls safely away from the city, too. We had that in common. I might have to work with it, trust it, until we figured out what was really going on.

At Kerrick's command, we all moved out, heading away from the ocean and deeper into the forest. We followed paths I would never have noticed. Each seemed to be overgrown, not a track at all, until you stepped on it and saw how it curved unnoticed behind brush or around a huge rock or under a fallen tree. These were not the obvious Wildron trails we'd followed to the city, but secret ones and, in an odd sense, incredibly ancient. Not in terms of the footpath's actual age, but in the way they were followed. As if the Kanon had spent many lifetimes perfecting the art of being hidden.

When we reached the settlement, I stared around at it, amazed. The Kanon village resembled in essence the City of All Dwellers, but I realized the city was only an awkward, modernized imitation. Larger by far than this one, yes, but the idea for it had been born here. Where the Wildron in the city pretended to live among the trees in their glass cubes, here the Kanon literally did, without glass or steel and almost invisibly.

Kerrick observed my face and made the rumbling, stuttering sound in his throat, amused, I supposed, by my open mouth and staring eyes.

"Are there more like these?" Mika asked. "Other communities."

"Throughout the Perimeter," Kerrick said, "and beyond. Some nearly on the doorstep of All Dwellers, unseen."

"Really?" I said, impressed.

"Yes," said Kerrick, "really."

I had a suspicion I'd offended him, but I didn't know how to go about apologizing for something I didn't quite understand. Instead, I asked more questions. "Where are your people from? Originally, I mean?"

Oh, yeah. Offense taken for sure. Again. "I'm sorry," I said, but he shook his head.

"You shall be forgiven your ignorance. Yet be careful what you say. Understand?"

I nodded.

"As for your question, we are from here. Always. We are…" He paused, seeming to search for the word. "Indigenous," he said. "Like the desert tribes, we are the original peoples of these lands, since time before memory."

"So…The Wilds. They're yours."

"They should be. Before Olympian, they were."

His face closed down then. I recognized our discussion had ended. We started walking again. "My friend Grace, she's a desert warrior," I said.

At my statement, he slowed, turned his head, looked at me. "This Grace, is she one of the three about which you are worried? Living at All Dwellers?"

I nodded. "Not living there. Not by choice.

We…we were taken there." Abbreviated account, but accurate enough. "She's being held there along with my sister and another friend."

Mika, blatantly listening to our conversation, grunted at my mention of Carina. Kerrick glanced at him and away, to the women exiting the various dwellings and making their way toward us. In contrast to every male present, they had hair as dark as pitch. No females traveled with Kerrick's group. No hunters among the females, then. No warriors. Grace would be displeased.

"We will speak more on this later," Kerrick said and hurried forward to greet a Kanon female, who threw her arms around him in greeting and mashed her lips hard onto his. My gaze shot to the ground, observing where I placed my feet instead.

In short order, the tools and the glass knives were taken away from us, put into an area where those weapons and implements belonging to the Kanon were kept. We were promised their return. I didn't know whether to believe it.

Those of us who could, helped with the meal's preparation. We ate cross-legged on the floor in a common area with squat tables. They spoke a lot, the Kanon, and through the occasional translation I understood they were talking about the day's hunting and us, the impending storm possibly headed in off the ocean, numerous other details of the day and more about us. I don't think we paid attention much. Food claimed all focus, even though we'd been warned against overeating. Did I listen? Nope. I ate so much I wanted to vomit. Almost did. No lie. Even hours after what appeared to be the main meal for the Kanon, I still felt an uncomfortable distension in my stomach.

We bedded down under a roofed, open-walled pavilion beneath the trees, still sated to the point of being sore, and even more exhausted. The Kanon provided us with blankets and other items for use outside. No room existed indoors for us. At least, that's what we were told. I had a feeling the truth leaned more toward not being entirely welcome in their midst. I couldn't blame them for that. We were strangers and considering the story I'd related to them about where we'd come from, our presence was surely problematic.

When we all readied to sleep, I expected we'd split off into factions. To me, it seemed likely some had known each other before being imprisoned. Yet, the pack mentality prevailed here as it had with Grace, Carina, Mika and I, since we'd departed the Emerald. Everyone bunched together for comfort. For warmth. Reassurance. The fact we were alive. Same old reasons.

Conversations drifted drowsily around beneath the sloped roof. I couldn't pick out words, but I recognized certain voices. Joy-Li. Hugo. Ren. Plotting, or maybe only talking about home. I turned my head on the folded arms beneath it and looked at Mika. He lay flat, arms at his sides and his head tipped slightly to the side against the ground, eyes wide open and focused on the night sky beyond our shelter.

"Hey," I said, "are you al—"

"Stop asking."

"Okay."

We all grew silent after that, drifting off one by one. Even Mika eventually closed his eyes, his light snores keeping time with some night bird's sawing call in a nearby tree. Maybe it thought they were communicating. Smiling at the idea and still uncomfortably full, I slipped away into my subconscious.

And into nightmare.

I knew I was dreaming. Sometimes you don't, sometimes you think you're really there in your imagination's bizarre construct. Either way, whether through the awareness you're dreaming or the shock caused by violent extremes, you awaken. I tried, but I couldn't.

In my dream, I found myself once again on the Emerald, populated by its horrifying creatures, facing the worst of them, those humanoid beasts who reached into your brain and twisted it, who possessed the strength and the power to rip a body to pieces. Dark, they were, like shadows. Only Grace and I stood in the murky twilight with them. We'd lost the others, lost them forever in ways I didn't have to visualize to understand. As I turned to Grace, seeking a plan, she, too, vanished, and in her stead a creature stood. A creature with her eyes in its fingers and her *lathesa* in its other hand and it said in a voice so much like hers, *we are all the same.* I recognized with revulsion the truth in what it said. *We are all the same. We are, all of us, monsters.*

Waking, gasping, I threw off the blanket and stumbled upright, lurched away into the trees. Doubled over, I spewed the meal's final remains onto the ground. My mind, my heart filled with fear and hopelessness. Because people were cruel, people were heartless. I knew that. Even if I hadn't known, I'd learned. Wiping my face against my sleeve, I fought the terrible feelings overwhelming me, refusing to believe we were all the same. We were not all monsters. I knew people kind and good and honorable. Gran, for one. My sister. Grace, Mika, Carina. Countless others I'd met in my life. I had to focus on that, not the duplicity of so many.

Yet a lot of bad existed in the world, too. I couldn't deny it. I'd be foolish to deny it. This was what we were facing, bad things.

Shaking, I went deeper into the woods, exactly where I shouldn't while afraid. Every shadowed movement made me jump, forced me to think of the creatures lurking in my dreams. Like the worst of what we all were, the bad without the good, the evil without the hope for deliverance. At a noise, I turned. My heaving stomach clenched. A black, familiar shape stood before me. Filled with stark terror, I staggered back, stumbled, anticipated the confusion, the mind manipulation used to disable prey. Instead, the thing blinked, turned, dropped onto all fours and scurried away, half the size it had appeared to my nightmare-addled mind.

I bent forward, hands on my knees, huffing out air, chugging it back down.

"Bakkak," said a voice behind me. Or at least, the sound seemed to make that word. "Nothing to frighten you there."

I straightened, turned, met Kerrick's silver eyes. Lifting my arm, I wiped prickling sweat from my forehead.

"I wasn't afraid," I said. "Not of that animal. Of something else. My memory of something else." I pointed toward the night sky. "From when we were up there, on the Emerald."

I heard the gruffness in my voice, a sound like impatience. I wasn't. Fear still held me in its grip, tightened my vocal cords. I cleared my throat, turned to make my way back to my abandoned blanket.

Kerrick reached out a hand, stopped me. "You were imprisoned?"

"We all were. Me, Mika, our two friends. Not my sister, though. She was still down here."

His hand dropped to his side. "What was your crime?"

I considered. "I gave false testimony at a trial. That wasn't why I was sentenced. I was sentenced so I couldn't recant it. That, and so I would be faced with what I'd done, every day. So that I'd never, ever forget."

"And have you? Forgotten? Now that you're down here."

"I'll never forget," I said. "But I've been forgiven."

I turned my face away. I didn't want him to witness the anguish and shame I carried with me, even now. What had happened to detachment, a Grif-Drif's detachment?

I knew the answer to that, of course. I'd never had it. I'd worked hard at pretending. Had to. Got good at it. Being a Grif-Drif called for a specific frame of mind. Tiran had seen through me.

Managed to manipulate not just me, but many he met with that ability. Grace had seen through it, too, uncovering me in the process.

I wondered if she'd ever know how grateful I was.

"Where were you going?" Kerrick asked.

"What?"

"Just now."

"Nowhere," I said. "I'd had...a bad dream. I was walking it off."

He nodded, his head moving a bit from side to side, too, as if to say he understood. Like maybe he had a few hauntings in his subconscious, as well. "You shouldn't wander. Even though beasts such as the *bakkak* are harmless, other aren't."

"Good to know. Thanks for the warning. I'll get back now." I still sounded impatient. Maybe I was.

Kerrick looked at me in the darkness. His was a face that hadn't expressed much until that moment. It reacted now to my tone. I saw a dozen changes cross his features in less than a second, reflecting who knew how many thoughts rushing through his mind. His features finally settled into a stern, reproachful glare. "I'd like you not to leave yet. I have more questions."

I heaved a sigh, one he plainly heard. Grunting, he stepped to the side, swept his hand out, clearing the way for my passage, if I chose. I studied his face, not moving.

"What questions?" I asked, defeated in my intent. "I'm guessing they can't wait?"

He said nothing, his silence reminding me that

he and the others had been generous, sharing food, bringing us out of danger. My shoulders slumped.

"Okay," I said. "Ask away."

"Follow me."

I did, curious, perhaps a little relieved for the company. I dreaded sleep again so soon after nightmare. I knew I'd fall right back into the same. Honestly, it surprised me I didn't have such haunting dreams every night. Every time I closed my eyes, in fact. I wondered if Grace did. Outwardly, she displayed a practical viewpoint. Deal with things and move on. I'd recognized that a long time ago. Yet what we'd been through had to catch up to her at some point, might have already.

"This way," Kerrick said, stepping beneath overhanging branches. I ducked, too, staying close behind. We walked on ways only he could see. I'd never be able to find my way out without him. In time, the invisible path opened up, revealing a clearing bounded by stones standing upright. Their positioning, the way they leaned inward, made me think of people frozen in action. Or those creatures. My heartbeat stuttered and I looked again, just to be certain.

Beyond them, pale trees towered. They possessed a pitted, peeling bark marked here and there by nearly black striations. Each tree seemed filled with small creatures leaping from branch to branch, chittering down at us. No, not at us, at something in the circle's center. I did a double-take, halting so quickly my feet slid on the packed dirt.

Surrounded by stone and shadow, the Lyoness watched me from beneath her dark hood.

Chapter Twenty

I cast about for anything I could use in defense. My hand flapped down onto the nearest branch and I broke it free. At the loud crack, Kerrick turned.

"You've betrayed us," I said. I hefted the makeshift club over my shoulder, ready to swing if necessary. I had to get to the others, warn them, get them up and running. I might already be too late.

"I don't understand," he said. His brow furrowed. He appeared genuinely confused. I figured he was just that good at pretending. The way I once was.

"Liar." I turned on my heel, realized I had no idea how to return to the place Mika and the others slept, unaware.

"What is it you think I've done?"

I frowned, spun back, pointed. "You brought her here."

The Lyoness hadn't moved. At all. Kerrick did, but slowly, following my finger.

"The Giver has been in that place for hundreds of years," he said. "I did not place her there. What is your objection?"

I frowned, took a step closer. My breath rushed out, recognizing an inanimate object. I mumbled an apology for my mistake. I could see now the figure wasn't the Lyoness. It wasn't even alive. Not in that way. It appeared, however, to be grown from living wood.

I tossed the branch to the ground. "I'm sorry," I said again. "I didn't...I thought... Might I look closer?"

In response to his cautious nod, I strode forward and around the figure, my hands at my side. From what I could tell, the whole thing remained green and thriving beneath white bark. Certain parts had been forced somehow to grow into the various shapes. Very small leaves dotted branches that had been trained, contained and trimmed, possibly for many years. Longer branches twisted to produce a hood, a cloak, a belted gown beneath, all covered in the same tiny leaves. I believed him when he said the figure had been there for hundreds of years. Something in the meticulously managed growth showed its age.

I could also be forgiven the impression the thing had been watching me, because as I strode around the figure it still appeared to be doing so. Not only watching, but turning to follow my movements as I passed. An illusion. Of course, only an illusion, yet still, I stopped short more than once, attempting to catch it in the act. Feeling like an idiot, I eventually backed away, went to stand beside Kerrick, shoved my hands into my pockets. Inside the right one, I felt the hard edge to the box Carina had asked me to hold. The tools had been useless in the city and the cells below ground. I didn't know why I still held onto the darned thing. A talisman, maybe, like the Crone Hannah had given Grace. A link to something else. In this case, Resa, Carina and Grace.

"What is she?" I asked with quiet respect. I didn't want to be insulting. Not after I'd just threatened him.

"What do you believe it to be?"

Odd wording. I considered. My thoughts went again to the small figure Hannah had entrusted to Grace. They did look similar. "The Crone?" I suggested. We didn't have such icons on Riley. There were others, though. Good luck charms for the gambler. Sold them in every gift shop. Visitors to Riley didn't tend to be particularly spiritual, or if they were, they kept the fact to themselves.

Kerrick shifted his stance, shoulders moving beneath his shirt. "What do you know of The Crone?"

"Not much. Only what Grace mentioned."

"Ah, yes," he said, "the desert warrior."

I didn't like his reference, as if her heritage possessed some disturbing element. "Yeah, the desert warrior," I said. "A darned good one."

"I would expect no less."

I shot him a look from the corner of my eye, pretty sick of cryptic conversations. "What do you mean? What do you know about Grace? Have you heard the stories here?"

"What stories are those?"

"About Grace," I repeated, fighting to maintain patience. "The desert tribes united because of her, because they believed her killed. Now, there are other stories, based on some longstanding legends, I am told. I imagine at this point we all have a part in those tales, because Ren said—"

"Who is Ren?"

"Guy with the yellow hair," I said, reminding him, pointing at my own head. "Chip on his shoulder. Sort of like Grace, although Grace doesn't let it get in the way of how her mind and mouth function."

He made that weird, muttering laugh. I smiled, despite myself, and went on.

"I'd never heard of The Crone until a few days ago. Before we reached the City of All Dwellers, a girl gave Grace a small talisman that looks something like this figure. Made of stone, though. Not as pretty."

His silver-gray brows lifted. "I believe the Crone is a symbol to the desert dwellers of the momentous journey that is life, that is universal life. The beginning and the end. To us, she is a symbol of harmony and balance—the Giver. We do our best to live as one with the land. But those who have been calling themselves Wildron these past hundred years and more have no such icons, no structured belief systems, about anything. Their minds are chaos. They are in constant battle within themselves. But you say one among them gave this talisman as you've called it to your friend?"

"Yes."

"For what reason?"

I shrugged. "She didn't say. Only that she wanted Grace to keep it safe."

Kerrick walked away from me, toward a log laid across two others. I followed him over. We both sat. I shoved my hands between my knees.

"I want you to think hard," he said. "Your desert friend and the other two in the city, if they were to be named by, say, rumor only, could they be given the titles of warrior, thrice-gifted child, witch?"

A chill wind rushed through the leaves overhead, precursor to the storm they'd talked about earlier. I shivered at its touch. "Yes," I admitted with reluctance. "Grace, as you already know, is a warrior. Carina, a mystic. I'd had my doubts about that back on the Emerald, but she's proved herself more times than I can count. And my sister…well, that's a bit too complicated to explain. But yeah, those titles are pretty accurate. And I've heard something of what people are saying about legends and the like. Ren and a companion of his, Joy-Li, told me."

Kerrick spent a long time in silence, his gaze on the Giver as though lost in thought. I began to think he planned to keep his mouth shut about the particulars, just like everybody else. I stood, hoping he'd stop me, tell me something. Even though I didn't know where I was going, I'd placed a half dozen strides between us before he spoke.

"Duncan."

I stopped. The breeze blew again, rattling through the branches. I resisted the urge to smooth the prickling skin on my arms, my neck. Kerrick pivoted on the bench to face me.

"It has always been beyond me to allow myself

to believe the prophecy refers to children," he said.

I winced at the term. I hadn't considered myself a child in more years than I cared to count. Gran had been good at reminding me of my tender age, but other than her occasional reference, I never felt it. Not that this prophecy, this foretelling, referenced me. But Grace was my age, Carina only about a year shy of it, and Resa the one amongst us I considered a child. She was only twelve and my sister, after all. Besides, she had that air about her I didn't expect would ever go away.

"It doesn't refer to children," I said, "because they aren't. None of us are. I don't think anyone in this world has the right to call us children. Not anymore. Because not one of us can be called a kid in the present circumstances. Years are no longer the defining factor."

He nodded at me, half smiling. "Well said, Duncan."

"Tell it to me now, this prophecy or legend or whatever the heck it is," I said, "so I know what we're up against. All I've heard is something about the 'darkness'. Sounds like crap to me, but you know what? A lot of what I would have viewed as crap has come to pass. I've lived it. We've lived it. And you know what else? Grace and Carina and Resa will not be alone in whatever it is that's coming. Mika and I will be there with them. I don't care what we have to do."

He stared at me for several long seconds. "You are brave."

"The Lyoness called me that, too." I barely refrained from spitting on the ground, faltering just short, the intent obvious on my face.

"I think I need to hear your story," Kerrick said. "Yours and what you know of the others. Sit down. We have time."

I would have said we didn't have time at all, but here in the grove with the Giver standing by, it seemed the time existed. I sat beside Kerrick again, hands between my knees, and started speaking from the shaming place in my past where it had all begun. I couldn't stop myself. I didn't want to.

*　　*　　*

Halfway through the night, everything had been decided. The storm never materialized where we were, likely wreaking havoc closer to the shore. I slept for a few hours. I needed it. In the morning, I addressed all the escapees, told them Mika and I would be returning to All Dwellers, as Kerrick called it. The shorter name was so much easier to say. Kerrick spoke as well, told them they would be embraced into the ways of his people, would become part of them, if they wanted. He advised them the life wasn't an easy one, but that it was fair. Explained, too, that the Kanon's neutrality was being tested, what with the Lyoness on one side of the Perimeter, and Tiran pushing into Ogdo beyond The Wilds. War might yet come to them and this, too, must be accepted and dealt with.

I felt compelled to remind those who would accompany me and Mika that we held to one plan: to rescue our friends. If they didn't want to be part of it, they were on their own. I hated saying it, yet I couldn't do otherwise. Perhaps, had they been without alternatives, we might have considered something different. But they had a chance now to survive in a life with the Kanon as opposed to death in the mines, and we had to save Resa and Carina and Grace. Mika and I had no other options.

This was it. Nothing else. Prophecy be damned. Even if I hadn't heard it, the plan would be the same. I wouldn't be ruled by something beyond me. I acted on what was within me.

Kerrick arranged to lead us through the Perimeter, away from the glass fields and possible recapture. We'd come a long way from the city. Kerrick said we'd be traveling for at least two days. I asked Mika just once more if he had the strength for it.

"Stop. Asking. Duncan."

"Ouch. Got it. Won't ask again."

Outfitted in more substantial clothing than what we'd been wearing, as well as the cutters and a glass knife each, and carrying packs containing as much food and water as we could reasonably carry, we headed away from Kerrick's village prior to midday. Although the storm hadn't been a direct hit, the air had cooled considerably and continued to do so with each passing minute. Leaves fluttered down from far above, littering the ground with color. I could see my breath. I could see everyone's breath smoking in the air. I'd never experienced this on Riley. The moon didn't rotate. We had one season. Period.

"At this elevation and caught as we are between the ocean and the desert, the seasons change abruptly," Kerrick said, spotting me watching the falling foliage. "Where you're eventually headed, it's going to get colder still."

I nodded. Mika and I bore blankets and extra clothing for my sister, Carina and Grace. Ren and his two carried what they would need. I knew they didn't plan to linger anywhere near All Dwellers. Once we succeeded in our rescue—I wouldn't dwell on failing—they would likely accompany us when we headed into the mountains.

And I was okay with this because a time would come when we'd need their help. What Kerrick had shared with me had scared me silly. The spread of war. Whatever this darkness might be. The hardships to come were inevitable. Knowing them made me resolute. Not fearless. Not fearless at all. Determined. I'd make sure Ren and Hugo and Joy-Li knew exactly what they were getting into, though, when the time came. They deserved the truth, even if they hadn't been entirely honest with us.

Mika strode on my one side, Ren on the other. Kerrick and the two with him, one a younger man, the second maybe about my sister's age, but quite a bit taller, stronger, walked ahead. They shared a profile, the younger and Kerrick. I figured they might be father and son. I watched them for a few moments, wondering what it would have been like had my father not taken off, had my mother not rejected him.

"They're not what we were taught," Ren said, following my gaze. "The Kanon."

"No," I said, "I guess they aren't. Nobody threw you in a stew pot."

"Yeah, well, I wouldn't have let them, now, would I?"

I grunted. Dream on, pretty boy. He'd have been vastly outnumbered, if that had been their intent. But I knew I would have fought them on his behalf. Of course, I would have. I would never tell him, though.

"I mean," Ren went on, "they're like...I don't know. Calm. Kind."

"Something you're not used to, eh?"

"No," he said, "it's not."

Mika leaned forward, eyebrows arching as he looked at Ren before straightening back up. "Wow," he whispered.

I made no comment. Sometimes we caught these soft-cuddly-Ren glimpses. They were always surprising. I wasn't sure I liked this Ren any better. This vulnerable, open Ren made me uncomfortable. I found it easier to relate to the one I wanted to pummel on occasion.

We marched on through the remaining daylight, stopping for a brief rest and a quick meal. Kerrick had a destination in mind he wanted to reach before nightfall, somewhere to camp that wouldn't be exposed. In the end, no one but Ren and his cohorts had opted for a return with us to All Dwellers. The rest had stayed behind. I couldn't blame them. Considering the circumstances in which we'd all found ourselves among the Wildron, they had no reason to go back. The risks were too great.

Toward evening, we came to a path, a visible one, leading upward along the stony mountainside without break. Once we were on it, we wouldn't likely be stopping. There didn't appear to be any safe place to pause, to sit, to rest. We all shirked our packs free for a few minutes, stretched aching muscles, talked quietly, drank, gathered the mental and physical commitment to make it to the top.

Beside me, Mika sucked in a breath. I glanced at him, finding his wide eyes focused on something off to our left. Ren whistled. I looked, too. We'd been climbing for some time beneath the low-slung branches, but the trees had suddenly opened up.

"That's beautiful," Joy-Li said in an awed, hushed voice.

I took in the vista spread before us, endless mountains touched with so many colors, too numerous to pick out and name. Faces and hands, the glass blades in our belts, glittered with the deep orange reflection from the lowering sun. Far below, a watercourse meandered through the valley like a gold ribbon. Mist curled out from the shadowed trees. I wondered if it was smoke. I asked Kerrick if he knew.

"There are settlements down there," he said. "But it could be fog drifting off the damp ground. Perhaps both."

I didn't want to leave. I only wanted to hold my breath, stay dead still, do nothing to shatter the moment. I felt several tears track down my cheeks. I nearly dropped to the ground, to my knees, to watch until the mountains, the valley disappeared into the coming darkness.

I couldn't help thinking of it that way. Not the night. The darkness.

"We cannot tarry here," Kerrick said, reading all our faces clearly.

"What lands are those?" I asked him, tilting my chin up toward the rising smoke.

"They are settled by different folk with one thing in common. They wish to be left alone."

I knew what remained unsaid. They wouldn't be left alone for very much longer.

Chapter Twenty-One

My bones ached. Every day had become a fight for survival. Doctor Symick's cautious procedures were being overridden by those designed for quicker results. At times, it seemed the Lyoness and her associates delighted at throwing us into danger, forcing Resa to lose control in order to determine how very powerful she might be. What they didn't know, what they could never know, was how we undermined them, Carina and I. The more time we were together, the more we learned, and the greater the ability to pretend. We were becoming accomplished liars, the three of us. Yes, even Resa.

Duncan wouldn't be happy. Silly, for me to be worrying about him now. He'd gone beyond caring.

Every day Carina and I still grieved, because a thought would occur to one of us, something we'd comment on, something to remind us they weren't coming back. Resa knew, now, too. I thought that would be the worst, but her emotions hadn't exploded, she'd taken them in and shut them away. I worried about the day she'd let them loose.

Resa had kept the glass mine image, folded it and shoved it away inside the cloth enveloping her pillow. Neither Carina nor I wanted to take the picture from her. She seemed comforted by it, although I couldn't imagine why. I knew only I had no desire to see it again.

Yes, because I'd turned into a coward as well as a liar.

I rolled on the thin mattress and bit back a groan. Our exercises had been completed for the night. We'd been fed, allowed to bathe, care for our wounds. The latter were minimal. Looked nasty enough to satisfy those who watched the experiments, but Resa was acquiring an ability to maintain some control, to limit trajectory, and behaving as though only Carina possessed the necessary attributes to keep her in line. We played a dangerous game, one that seemed to be leading us in the exact direction the Lyoness, her counselors, the technicians wanted. We attempted through our actions to gain what we needed most: time. The right time.

We'd pushed our beds together that first night to be close to each other. For Carina and I, the position also allowed cautious conversation after the lights went out. My bed had been damaged in the most recent episode tonight. Carina had helped me prop up the end with the remains from the desk chair. Lying as still as possible, trying to get my muscles to relax, I studied the glass walls. They showed stress cracks in various places not yet strategic enough to cause the whole front to give. We'd get there. Sooner, I hoped, than later.

"Did you see?" Carina whispered. "They've put on extra guards."

"I saw. They're overlapping shift change."

We were silent a moment.

"Do you think they suspect—"

"No," I said. "I think as they witness more of what Resa can manage, they're more afraid. That's all."

"They should be afraid," Carina grumbled, rolling onto her side. She grimaced and shifted back around off her bruised hip. "How much longer?"

"I don't know."

Her released breath sang into the dark. On her other side, Resa had already fallen asleep. She lay very still. Always. I wondered if Duncan's sister dreamed or if her mind's random exercise remained reserved for waking hours.

"I'm glad we're together," Carina said.

"Me, too."

I reached out and grabbed her hand. In turn, she slipped her fingers around Resa's. Exhausted, we fell asleep that way, clutching each other for solace.

In what seemed the wee hours of morning, someone pounded on the glass. I rolled over, saw the face pressed close to it, a hand pointing at me. I sat upright, wiping moisture from around my lips. I'd been sleeping with my mouth open, exhausted and careless. My tongue felt dry.

Carina had awakened too. She peered out from beneath the blanket, asked me what was going on.

"Someone wants me," I said. "I think we know who."

"Should I—"

"Stay there," I said. "It's still dark out."

With a gesture at the guard as to my intent, I headed into the toilet area. While in there, I rinsed my mouth, scrubbed my eyes, ran a hand through my hair and got dressed. I eyeballed the pillow case propped in the corner, bulging with whatever non-perishable items we could set aside each day from our meals. Preparation.

When I came back out, the door stood wide, the guard still on the outside, arms folded in impatience. I grabbed my boots and walked out beside him, bending quickly to yank them on. I hopped along, my left foot not quite inside. Finally, I dropped down onto the floor to pull the footgear on properly. The guard made a threatening lunge in my direction. I lifted my head and met his eye.

"Go ahead," I said. "You try it."

Defensive moves existed for even such a vulnerable position as mine right then. He may have known that, or he might only have recognized the determination in my gaze. He stepped back, waited while I latched the boot. Pretending to fumble with the buckles, I glanced around from beneath my lashes, studying my surroundings. There appeared to be no increase in guards here, only in the immediate area around the chamber where Carina, Resa and I were being held. Good. Things might be easier than expected, when the time came.

Standing, I brought my hands together, slapping them clean. The man's eyes shot to my whipping fingers, easily distracted. No wonder he was so jumpy. He truly had no clue from where an attack might come. He'd been forewarned, I supposed, by someone who knew little about the desert warrior's methods.

We continued on our way, headed once again toward Nimue's private quarters. I couldn't imagine what she wanted now. She already had my cooperation and yet she insisted I appear for an audience. To remind me as often as possible, perhaps, who had the upper hand.

Before the turnoff, however, the guard went left, one imperious glance telling me to follow.

I did unwillingly, but knowing better than to argue. A tall, translucent timepiece stood beside a double door flanked by two guards. I glanced at the hour. Not as late as I thought. The middle hour had barely come.

The guards pulled open both doors upon our approach. I had no idea where we were, but present and waiting several strides inside the long chamber beyond stood Nimue. She supported herself on a walking stick, something I'd not seen her use before, not even in the long trek from the underground to the city. No, not a walking stick. She used my *lathesa* for this purpose. Even though the weapon was not the one which had been presented to me upon completion of my training, and therefore not disrespectful to be used in such fashion, it was still irksome and ill-mannered and, I realized, a quite deliberate affront.

"Come in," she said. "So glad you could make it."

I said nothing. Sarcasm would serve no purpose. Not now. Not here. My skin shifted over muscle and flesh. I couldn't imagine what the next few minutes might bring.

She signaled for me to come near. "Walk with me."

I did, falling in beside her, tempering my stride

to her staggered one. Thump, thump, the stick sounding hollow on the wooden floor, the crystal at that end gone. The other still winked in the dimly lighted area. I walked with my hands behind my back, attempting to appear unperturbed. But this treatment was altogether new. I didn't trust it, not at all.

We continued the corridor's length to another paired door. No one guarded this one.

"If you wouldn't mind," Nimue said, nodding at it. I stepped forward, yanked the lefthand door wide. She swept a hand out for me to proceed her. I refused, pretending courtesy, holding the door until she gave in and entered first. Perhaps detecting her movement, lights came on. I followed behind and halted.

On plinths and hanging from the walls, the wider hall displayed animals in many poses, hunted, killed, preserved. I didn't recognize many, but one I did. Over and over again, *conjures* of monstrous proportion had been posed within, full in body, or only heads mounted on the walls, their long, corkscrew horns pointing ceilingward. I caught my breath and held it, lest she hear the sob fighting to escape my lips. She continued on, aware of my reaction, I felt sure, but making no mention of it. Her steps were deliberately slower, allowing me a more protracted view. I eyed every *conjure* we passed, looking for one with a white ring around its eye. Slowly, I let my breath out when we reached the hall's far end without sight of Chauncy among them.

"And this door, please," she said.

I obliged, wanting to slam her with it. We walked through into the next hall. I couldn't tell what hung from these walls. Armament of some sort, it seemed; vests like I suspected Ren had worn beneath his cloak, full garments padded within to display detail, here and there helmets and the like. We strode in silence the length of this hall as well, not lingering, as if reaching the far end was her only intent.

At the next pair of doors, she stopped me. "Have you no questions?"

I knew she wanted me to ask after Chauncy. I hadn't seen him among the dead ones, and as long as I hadn't spotted him, I would believe him still alive and not provide her with the satisfaction of my asking after him.

"No, Lyoness," I said. "No questions."

"You do not wish to know what these halls are called?"

I didn't. I really didn't. "Very well," I said after a few seconds, however, barely holding onto civility. "What are these halls called?"

"They are called the Walk of Memory."

I pressed my lips together, saying nothing more.

Her scarred face twisted in what I assumed to be annoyance. "Grace."

"Yes?"

"Ask me why."

I released a discreet breath. "Why?"

"Due to those things exhibited within. For example, the beasts of our forests, including the fiercest *conjures*. Warriors who have lost their lives in the hunt are remembered by the animal's head hanging on display. If the beast has been particularly deadly, the entirety of the creature stands in the hall in memory of its valor."

I attempted to keep my face composed. "And here, in this section?" I asked, knowing I must, and not caring to be prompted. "The accoutrements worn by those warriors?"

"Not quite," she said. Limping forward, she paused before an ornately constructed, full-face helmet hanging on the expansive wall to the door's right. Alone, as though in a place of particular honor. After taking a moment to adjust her stance, Nimue lifted the *lathesa* toward the faceplate, wedged the tip against the edge and pushed up. The plate, well-oiled, opened without noise. The only noise came from me.

A gasp, a stifled cry, the sounds co-mingled. I bit my lip to keep from giving voice to my revulsion.

Nimue gazed up with obvious satisfaction at the treated face inside the helmet. The skin looked odd, dried but lubricated to keep its suppleness, the mouth open, as if in shock. I frowned, wondering why they had kept her that way. If one were going to go to the trouble to preserve the woman's head, then close the mouth. I glimpsed bits of auburn hair peeking out around the face, not as easily cared for, dry and stiff-looking. A pair of green eyes surveyed the room blankly. I didn't know if they were real. I doubted it, after a moment's consideration. Still, why green, unless she had possessed green eyes in life?

Like me.

My frown deepened.

"Who is she?" I asked.

"My predecessor," Nimue said. "Morag. And my enemy. Don't become my enemy, Grace."

Again, I stayed mute. What could I say? Too late? I wasn't quite so foolish. Nor would I beg or lie. I reached for the door handle. "Are we continuing on?" I had no desire to speculate what might be in the next hall. I only wanted Nimue to reach the point in her exercise.

She did not speak, but stepped through. I trailed after, closing the door behind. We were now in what appeared to be the library, filled with disks and some ancient, published volumes on shelves. Liquid monitors were stationed every few feet on pedestals. We didn't tarry here. With her uneven step, Nimue marched straight to the other side and out, without waiting for me to tend to the door. I considered turning around, demanding the guard return me to the chamber with Resa and Carina, but some curiosity made me follow.

Startled, I stopped just within. The room appeared to be perhaps a private office, a place similar in design and accessory to the Lyoness' personal chambers. The only illumination came from a glass wall on our left. I went toward it, not waiting for any instruction from her.

At a level beneath, underground actually, a vast room stood open to view, filled with mechanical devices and people working. I placed my hand against the glass, felt the hum vibrating the surface beneath my fingertips. The voice of machinery. I wanted to know, almost asked the purpose of the work below.

While I watched, others appeared, literally appeared, and moved about, passing like ghosts through those who operated the machines.

"The replicants," said Nimue, coming up somehow silently beside me. "We are trying to perfect them. Right now, they work well enough as an illusion. After all, if you came upon an army of three thousand as opposed to one, you'd be more inclined to fear, wouldn't you? Even you wouldn't fight, Grace, if you believed yourself so vastly outnumbered. Not when you had something to lose besides your own life."

I didn't care for the reminder of how we'd been fooled by Ren in the forest. I held my tongue, though.

"My great-grandson betrayed me," she said, following her thoughts, rather than mine.

"Where is he?" I asked. "Ren, and the others."

"Gone," she said. "Died in the mine collapse, with your friends."

I recalled, then, Ren's casual reference masking his deep-seated fears as to punishment. I stared at the back of Nimue's head, her hood down, her thick, gray hair braided. I fought to keep my hands at my side.

She turned away, heading across the room. She waved with my confiscated weapon toward an ornate chair. "Well, sit down then. We'll talk."

How carelessly she dismissed the deaths. I refused to rise to the bait, however, because I had concluded the Lyoness meant to anger me for some reason I couldn't yet fathom. I sat, perched on a cushion every bit as uncomfortable as those in the chambers where we'd previously been meeting.

Lowering herself behind a desk carved with intricate design, she looked, as ever, totally out of keeping with the environment. When first we'd met, I'd thought her fierce and energetic, a warrior, like me. I didn't understand why she surrounded herself with the extravagant and non-utilitarian. I supposed some might say the same about many tribal homes, but even there everything had a purpose. Here, a lot of what I saw were just…things. Baubles and decoration, as though she'd moved into somebody else's life.

Which she had. Yes, I understood that now. She'd taken on the previous Lyoness' possessions as her own. A statement of her ambitions. "May I ask a question?"

She nodded, not exactly welcoming. Her gaze grew suspicious at my expression.

"Is Lyoness a lifelong title? Is it inherited, or does some august body vote you in?" I suspected I knew the answer. Nimue had killed the prior Lyoness, if her fascination with her things, her head, could be an indication. Nimue's demeanor changed. She shifted in her chair.

"It is a title hard won," she said. "In battle."

"So, there have been recent wars within The Wilds? Because, I know the people in The Wilds do not interact with the outside world. Not in any manner commonly known." I persisted, pretending innocence, curiosity, when I all I really wanted was one hard, cold fact.

"No," Nimue answered, her tone flat. "Not in recent memory."

I acted as though I digested her answer before speaking again, looking puzzled, pensive. Oh, Nimue, I thought, see what you have made me. "Are you telling me then," I said, "that you battled the prior Lyoness to obtain the title?"

She pressed her hands flat on the desk surface. "Yes, that is what I am saying. I took her title and her leadership and her head."

I smiled, actually smiled, having wrangled the truth from her. Nimue hadn't anticipated my reaction. She wriggled again on her chair, glanced around, likely remembering we were alone.

I leaned forward, clutching the engraved chair arm so hard my knuckles popped. "We take no trophies, from war or otherwise," I said. "It is not what we do, as a people."

"Which is exactly why, as a people, you will lose this war. You don't possess the ruthlessness needed to win."

Slowly, I loosened my grip, straightened, clutched my hands together against my abdomen. I watched Nimue watching me. I drew several deep, silent breaths, letting them out slowly. We didn't need to be ruthless, we warriors. Quite obviously, we didn't. If Stone Tiran and Nimue and whoever else involved themselves in this uprising were so sure of the outcome, the Lyoness would not be striving so hard to gain the advantage by training Resa and others like her—who had apparently failed at the task—to use as weapons in battle. I realized all those mage-blood Wildron who had failed her goals were still a worry to her, or she would not have them locked up. Why she hadn't had them killed, I didn't know. I expected she hoped to still find some use for them.

I wouldn't leave them behind. When we made our escape, I'd find a way to at least free them, if not take them with us. Nimue could not be trusted to treat them fairly. She had already sent Duncan and Mika, Ren and his friends to their deaths in the glass mines. She'd tried to act as though the deaths were accidental, and perhaps they were, but the point remained that she'd sent many prisoners, juvenile prisoners, to serve as labor in the mines. According to what I'd overheard, no one was ever expected to return from the term and no one ever did.

Yes, the young, those who hadn't learned to alter their disobedience, to hide their gifts, were all at risk here in the City of All Dwellers. What I didn't quite understand was why I still lived. Yes, she needed me to help with Carina and Resa, but I'd quickly proven myself expendable. Carina and Resa acted now as one unit, as far as Nimue could see. It was a sham, all of it, but the Lyoness didn't know that.

"Why am I still here?" I asked. Foolish, to challenge the Lyoness, but I needed the answer. I pushed my hands onto my thighs, feeling the talisman Hannah had given me deep in my pocket.

"You'll stay until I give you permission to leave," Nimue snapped.

"I don't mean that. I mean why do I continue to live, when you clearly don't need me."

She tossed her hand in a sideways gesture, certain she had me under control once more. "Who has told you such a thing? I'm not through with you yet, Grace. I value you. You know that."

I didn't respond.

"The rumor I spoke of links the three of you. I don't yet understand how, but I will find out. Soon, I hope, because time is running short. All those useless little children have been putting their faith in a story that is merely that. A story. Why is it always the children?"

I refrained from answering. She was unwise to ignore the obvious. The adults probably believed as strongly, but they'd learned silence. She wasn't safe among them. Not by a longshot.

"The ridiculous old legend has gained new life in recent months," she went on. "They don't quite understand as I do."

"And what is it you understand?" I managed to ask without breaking my teeth.

"I understand that, somehow, the three of you will serve me, my purpose. This, I have been advised by my trusted counselors and after what I have witnessed, I have no doubt it is true."

*Oh Grace…*

Skelly had been silent for so long now I nearly jumped.

*You will let me out soon. You must.*

I shook my head. Without the means to control what Skelly had become, I would never risk it. I'd hoped to find the answers here, but all I'd found was betrayal and loss and fear.

"Why do you shake your head? Do you not

believe me?"

"No," I said. "I believe you."

"Good. It's time I tell you why I summoned you."

I folded my hands together once again in my lap, holding held myself the way I had when I'd been so much younger, beginning my warrior's training in a class full of others. They were all hopeful, excited. I'd tried my best to look obedient while seething inside. I'd never been one for being told what to do.

*Me, either.*

My jaw tightened again.

*None of us are. Probably a good thing.*

Skelly had never referred to Duncan, Carina, Mika and me as "us", allying himself in his mind. Did his doing so indicate a shift in his thinking? I wondered what that might mean and waited for him to answer my thought, but he said nothing.

The Lyoness lifted a hand, recalling me. I looked up. A man, hidden until now, had obviously been awaiting the signal. He came forward from somewhere, perhaps a small alcove I couldn't see in the shadows, and held out a steaming cup to her. Taking it, she drank thirstily and loudly. No offer as to refreshment was made to me. I had not expected any. It also occurred to me the liquid might contain a medication. Old wounds were often the most painful, the damage to nerve and flesh and bone lingering. Her face was bad enough. I couldn't imagine what lay beneath her heavy garments.

She handed the cup back to him, returned her attention to me. "I have bad news, I'm afraid."

I thought of Carina, Resa, left alone in the chamber. Had she ordered something done to them in the time I'd been gone? I pulled myself forward on the cushioned seat, readying to fly up from it.

"I wanted you to know," she said, steepling her fingers beneath her ragged chin, "that Tiran has pressed his soldiers, his ships, into Ogdo. The Neutrality Treaty is no longer honored. He will be here soon, at my door, seeking further means of escalation in the world beyond. Looking," she added, "for the three of you."

I froze a little, midbreath, staring at her. Waiting. Beneath all the scarring her face contorted, seeking an expression, trying them on, settling on one. Not sympathy. A mockery of such charitable emotion.

"I cannot protect you, Grace, when that happens. You must push your friends harder, before he gets here. Do you understand?"

My eyelids moved in a protracted downward motion as the air in my lungs rushed out. When they lifted again, I realized I was standing. Nimue gaped at me. The man rushing to her aid had paused with a leg lifted from the ground, like in the child's game of sculpture. Slowly, he set it down, spun, tried to run. I saw this all through a spinning black cloud, my anger, my righteous, long-held anger, coloring my vision. Yes, for the briefest instant this is what I convinced myself. Until I recognized where my hand had gone. Into the bag around my neck. Right down into it.

*Good girl, Grace,* said Skelly. *Time for some fun.*

Chapter Twenty-Two

I crossed the room surrounded by the dire miasma, wondering if Resa felt this way in chaos' center. Wondered, too, if she felt connected to the uncanny, frightening power that came from her. Not that Skelly came from me. He was *other*, surrounding my body only, his screaming echoing over and over through the darkness within my mind. He had words, but they weren't mine and I didn't understand them.

With each step, furniture slid away from me as if pushed by a solid wall, although I did not touch it. With a start and an unnerving gratification, I realized I had no need to do so. Nimue and her servant had leapt up, attempted to stagger across the floor, fell. The desk shot after them, crashed against the wall. I reached through Skelly's spiraling entity and snatched my *lathesa* from the floor where it had fallen. The single crystal shone in the darkness whipping around me. I saw it and was not afraid. Why not?

Struggling upright, the Lyoness managed to cling to the doorjamb. Her braids had come unpinned, her cloak ripped from her shoulders. "This is what we've been waiting for!" she shouted. "For you to show what you truly are!"

Her words should have angered me, but my voice sounded strangely calm when I spoke, as though a rift existed between voice and emotion. "This is not who I am, and I don't care what you've been waiting for."

I swung my arm at her in dismissal, the one not clutching my weapon. Something lashed out from my fingertips, long and dark and whip-like, knocking Nimue to the floor. Shocked, I slammed my arm down to my side, fingers clenched.

*Skelly,* I thought at him, *enough.*

*That's not me, sweetheart. Wake up.*

Lying, I knew he was lying. Trying to make me afraid, too.

Turning on my heel, I stormed out the door without looking back. Out? Through. The wood shattered before me, rose up in the air, sprinkled down like heavy rain behind. I hurried through the halls, the Walk of Memory, without sensing the boards beneath my feet. The whole structure creaked and groaned and warped. Objects fell, cast away from me. I felt powerful, unstoppable.

It's not me, I told myself.

*But it is. It is you, Grace. It's us, together.*

I stopped caring how inaccurate his statements. Stopped caring about anything but the one realization, the only one that mattered.

Our time had come.

People fled in fear, or cowered to the ground. I heard Skelly laughing, heard the noise from my own mouth and clamped my lips shut. He stayed with me, though, every single step of the way. When the guards tried to stop me, I tossed them aside. Their weapons, too, before they could fire them. I heard shouting behind me, increased my pace, running now, faster and faster to the place where Carina and Resa were held. Before word reached the guard there, before they might seize them, keep them from me. My heart pounded; my head felt like it would explode; stars danced before my eyes—no, not stars, the brilliant flare of impulse guns. Deflected. Not by me.

*Yes, by you.*

*Stop lying to me, Skelly. Stop lying. You won't make me believe.*

I slowed in the corridor to our chamber, frowning, squinting, puzzling out what I saw through the ache in my head. The scene made no sense to me. Where once the treed corridor stood wide it now lay blocked. Blocked by…a sphere, a suspended sphere.

Bits and pieces formed it, clung together. Wood, metal, glass, other things I didn't recognize, didn't want to recognize, circling, swirling, expanding outward.

"Resa," I whispered. The sphere exploded. I felt the blast, saw the effect, every piece flying with lightning speed, crashing, cracking, falling in deafening sound, Doctor Symick in the middle of it all. His was the face I hadn't wanted to recognize, pressed and spinning in the debris field. He lay sprawled across the floor now. I thought him dead until he moved, moaned, pushed himself up from the ground. Only then did his gaze find me, did it find us.

I have never seen a man look so afraid.

I reveled in his fear.

"Enough!" I cried aloud.

Yet I knew no matter what I did, I could never remake what had come undone. I'd let him out, let Skelly out. I couldn't go back. The warrior, the witch, the thrice-gifted child.

*Who can stop us now?* Skelly whispered.

This was what the Lyoness wanted, exactly what they all wanted. Spurred by legend, rumors, they desired to weaponize us, to use us in their war, to use Resa, not only for what she could see and hear in far-off places, but to make a killer of her, a twelve-year-old girl.

I ground my teeth together, forced my jaws apart. "No," I said, but the word spun away into nothing.

Carina and Resa stepped out from the shattered room. Carina held Resa's hand, and in the other the pillow case from the bathroom. Her eyes widened when she saw me, her transmutable eyes, shocked, saddened, and I thought, Carina, can't you stop us? I lowered my lids, felt Skelly fighting me, pulling away, to freedom. *No,* I said, calling him back.

"We're leaving," I managed to say to Carina. She heard me, nodded. I held out my hand and they both walked toward me, straight into the raging cyclone, and stood at my side. Symick rose from the floor. His whole body shook, clothes flapping. He wiped the blood smeared across his face from his cut lip, stared down at the crimson stain on his hand as if confused as to its origin. Other than that, he appeared astoundingly unharmed.

His eyes lifted, took us all in. He opened his mouth, struggling for speech, finally managed a question. "Where will you go?"

"Away," I said. "Away from here." Beyond that, I didn't know, didn't have an answer. But we wouldn't be used. Especially Resa, possibly the most powerful of all. Resa, the thrice-gifted child.

"Will you take me with you?"

I cocked my head in confusion. Skelly's cyclone entity shimmered, strained, wanting to hurt him.

"I have to find my daughter. I want to take her home. Back to my people."

I understood that longing. Home. We all did. I nodded, forced my mouth to make words, and did. "Can you walk?"

"I can."

"Then keep up."

I didn't wait.

*Isn't it a joy to be heartless?*

"You're not heartless," said Carina.

"You can hear him?"

"I did just now," she said. "Don't listen to

him."

I felt him, then, trying to push them out, Carina and Resa and the doctor, who had slipped in smelling of fear. Armed guards were coming, so I redirected his intent toward them. With glee, he tossed them aside.

*Your glee.*

*Shut up, Skelly.*

I tried to recall the way to the cells where I'd been kept before my agreement to help with Carina and Resa. The corridors emptied as we advanced, although in the distance I heard shouted orders. Symick began directing, pointing out the way. I realized his daughter must be in those cells. We turned and turned again, my thoughts growing more closed and lightless, my body becoming less my own. We arrived at the cells aligned along the walkway so suddenly, it was as though I'd already forgotten the steps we'd taken to get there. I recognized horror, though, in the eyes of those inside when they spotted us, and it seemed only then was I reminded of Skelly's surrounding presence. How could I have forgotten that, too?

"I need to get my daughter free," Symick hissed, whipping a device from his pocket.

"Get them all out of there," I said, struggling with the words.

Grunting, he broke through and raced along the row, passing the apparatus in his hand over each door, causing them to slide open. Frightened, the inmates wouldn't come out. Afraid of me, of Skelly. I understood I couldn't hold him much longer without losing myself. Not outside the crystal, where he felt his freedom, his power.

*Let me go, then.*

"No," I said out loud. Carina looked at me, her eyes dark. So did Resa, as if she'd heard me. I knew she hadn't. I think she was gauging me, somehow, taking my measure, trying to understand what was happening. And yet she wasn't afraid. Good. I don't know what damage would have taken place had she let loose again, here within.

Turning my gaze from theirs, I struggled to follow movement as the captives fled their cells, fled me. "Doctor Symick," Carina shouted after him when I failed to say the words struggling to free themselves from my head, "please, tell them we'll take them with us. Tell them they'll be safe."

There are no guarantees of that, I thought, but couldn't say. I felt broken, but whole. Alive, but dead.

"Carina," I finally whispered.

Clutching Resa's hand almost desperately, Carina shook her head. "I can't help you, Grace. I'm so sorry."

*See? Even your friends fail you.*

*NOT TRUE!*

I felt him falter at my denial and I fumbled my free hand into the bag around my neck. I clutched the crystal, the edges cutting into my fingers, warm blood running along my flesh. Closing my eyes, I ordered him back inside and heard his distant laughter, feared he'd left me. Hoped he'd left me. My skin burned as though fire danced across it, as though it had been laid open and every nerve ending knew the flame. Knees buckling, I hit the ground, nearing unconsciousness. A hand touched mine where it lay against the crystal, and another on my back. Two more, on my face. Small hands. Tiny hands. Carina and Resa, together. I had been the one to fail. Failed them. Failed Duncan and Mika. My friends. Me. Pain struck deep in my heart, and was gone along with everything else in the world.

*Duncan*

Chapter Twenty-Three

I whistled between pursed lips. A long, low, tuneless note. Of surprise. From our position on a rocky ridge, I saw the City of All Dwellers spread out and glowing in the blackness below. Kerrick had been right. Two days. Two days of hard travel. Now all we had to do was get inside unnoticed. We'd have to hurry, what with dawn only a few hours away.

I rolled over on the rough surface, looked at Mika beside me. On his other side Kerrick and Kerrick's son lay sprawled across the stone. Beyond them, Bris, the hugely muscled nineteen-year-old. I had three more years to make myself look like that. I doubted I'd get there. Compulsive workouts in the prison gym hadn't done it for me. I figured nothing would.

The original plan had been for Kerrick and his company to leave us once they'd shown us the proper direction. Somewhere along the way it had been decided otherwise. Ren, Hugo and Joy-Li had been happy to hear it. So were Mika and I, to be honest. We truly didn't know how we were going to manage this. No one wanted to admit to that out loud.

Suddenly Kerrick shouted. "Back into the trees!"

We scrambled into the tree line, bent low to the ground, packs bouncing against spines. I heard it then, what Kerrick's better hearing had picked out sooner. Ships in the air. Multiple ships, coming this way.

Hidden beneath the trees, we watched a dozen of them pass overhead in a long, triangular formation toward the city. The insignia beneath was hard to distinguish. I didn't really need to see it to know whose it was. They came from the general direction of Tiran's compound in Duhm and the Ogdonian border. Blood surged into my head, blinding me. I squeezed my eyes shut, trying to clear my brain of the knowledge we might be too late.

At a noise, I turned and looked in Kerrick's direction. He stood, removed the cylinder with its telescopic lens from his pack. He held it up to his eye, squinted with the other as he focused the glass in. I sidled over and he handed it to me.

"It is him, isn't it," I muttered.

He nodded.

"We have to get in there now."

Stupid thing to say. We were still the better part of an hour away on foot. My stomach twisted in a cold, violent roil. I handed Kerrick back the telescope, jerked my pack up onto my shoulder. "Come on, let's get moving."

Mika fell in immediately beside me. We

weren't waiting. Not at all. Time had run out. All the way out. Nothing remained in that clichéd hourglass.

We raced down the mountainside, careless, disregarding safety. Several falls that could have gone bad didn't, but only through dumb luck. Kerrick lost his temper. I understood why. I got it. But when Ren repeated Kerrick's words, I nearly took his yellow head from his shoulders.

"Enough," Mika said. I stared at him in surprise. Hugo, silent, sullen Hugo, stood behind him, glaring agreement, Joy-Li at his side. "You're not helping anyone if you break your neck, or if you break his."

Ren made an 'as-if' face, but remained mum.

We took more care after, discussing possible strategies in breathless, abbreviated sentences as we clambered down the steep incline. We had no idea where the girls were being held. We had no idea if they were together. We didn't reference the other possibility, that they might not be alive at all. It seemed most likely they were, due to what Nimue expected to gain from them.

I fought nausea and deep panic the whole way down to the barren plain encircling All Dwellers. A cloud cover had formed in the sky, filling the air with rain-scent. I couldn't remember the last time I'd seen rain. I hoped we'd be able to take advantage when it came. Lessened visibility could only favor us, as long as we kept our own eyes wide. I started to pick up my pace. Kerrick lunged and reached for my arm. "Wait."

He pointed toward the place the ships had

landed. Lights surrounded them, casting their weird shadows across the city's structures. I spied movement, too, although I couldn't make out what I saw at that distance. I assumed Tiran's soldiers, perhaps mingling with Nimue's own warriors. Kerrick broke out his telescope once again, raised it to his eye. He shielded the end with bent fingers to keep the magnifying surface from reflecting any light from the ships.

I followed with my eyes the line the instrument took. Frowning into the dark, I extended my neck forward, straining to see. A sudden blue bolt shot up from the ground near the ships, causing me to jerk back. This was followed by several more. They met, made a shape like some sort of energy field around a more solid shape beneath. A word tore from Kerrick's throat, a native word I couldn't understand. He handed me the glass.

"What do you make of that?"

I fixed the telescope to my eye, jerking it up and down in my impatience to find the target. "Cages?" I suggested. "Transport cells?" Many barred containers lined the ground, all generating the strange blue light, although only a few displayed the full energy field. They appeared empty, black inside, but I couldn't tell for certain. The blue light dazzled and confused me. I understood only one reason for them, though. Prisoners. That meant Resa, Grace and Carina, and whoever else they decided to grab, considering the number. My lungs deflated in a rushing whoosh, as though brutally punched.

If Tiran had them, if he got to them, they wouldn't survive. Those cages would only be temporary. We'd taken my sister from him, his prize. We'd escaped the planet where we were meant to die. He had it in for Grace for whatever psycho reason. If he got me and Mika, too, well, we were bonus deaths. He could sleep easier knowing we were gone.

I shoved the telescope at Kerrick and started to run. Footsteps pounded behind me on the unyielding earth. I ran faster, harder, on fire with dread. Suddenly I hit the ground. My lungs emptied again as I skidded across the soil and grass with a heavy body sprawled across mine.

Bris. It had to be. I could barely breathe from the weight of him.

"Stay down."

The rest joined us, crouched low, moving awkwardly across the landscape. Mika shoved at Bris's bull shoulder. "Get off him. He's turning blue."

"He's going to get us all killed," Bris hissed back at him. He, too, knew our tongue.

"Never," Mika answered. He meant it. I knew he did. This time, though, he might be wrong.

"Something doesn't seem right in there." This,

from Ren.

Freed from Bris, I pushed up onto my knees, sucking in air. "What do you mean?"

"Listen."

Shouting. Lots of it. Not jubilant. Angered. Possibly even fearful. I tried to make out words.

"Maybe the Lyoness wasn't expecting guests," Mika said.

I snorted at his tone. Mika could be truly funny. Sometimes it was hard to tell. He possessed a sarcasm that made you wonder.

"We need to get in there now," I said.

"I know," said Kerrick. "Just take a few deep breaths first."

I was sick of listening to him, listening to any of them. Kerrick had no stake in who came out of the city alive. No one did but me and Mika. We didn't need him. We didn't need any of them.

But we did. Ren and his cronies to show us the way in through the same route they'd exited the city to find us, undetected—at least for a time. I couldn't forget the fact their little coup had been discovered. We also needed Kerrick and Bris for some extra muscle. I worried about the kid, though, Kerrick's son, Kai. Kerrick should never have brought him. Not here.

At a commotion near the transport cells to our right, all heads swung back toward the ships. I reached my arm toward Kerrick without looking at him, waved it around, wriggled my fingers. I wanted the telescope. Now. Wanted it more than words right then.

He slapped the cylinder into my hand. I

rammed it against my eye, grunted, switched to the other. For the third time in as many minutes I found myself impeded by rapid air loss. My mouth dropped open, vacuuming oxygen back in. I turned to Mika.

"You want to know what's in those cages?"

He shook his head, not to say he didn't know, but because I believe he already did.

I whipped around to the others. "We have to get away from here, as fast as we can. We've got to get the girls and go now. Ren, how do we get in?"

"What is it?" he asked, not answering me. "What's in the cages?" He stretched his hand toward me for the telescope.

I gave it back to Kerrick instead. "They're creatures from Emerald. None of us stands a chance. Not armed as we are. Believe me. *Believe me.*"

"Then how did you escape them when you were up there?" Ren persisted, not moving. I grabbed his arm, Mika's, too, and began hurrying us all across the plain, parallel to the city, away from the ships, the transport cells.

"Grace," I said, and pushed them faster.

*   *   *

"Fool!" Mika cried, when we paused for breath, to reconnoiter, to figure out how we were going to get into the city and out again with our friends and all still alive, intact. "Does he think those things won't tear him and his soldiers apart as easily as they will anyone else?" He added a few choice expletives in addendum.

293

"What are they?" Kerrick asked.

I explained to him as best I could the manner of beast they appeared to be, the way they hunted, the mind control, their ability to rend flesh from bone. I told him how I'd lost Skelly Shane. I'd never liked the guy, but I wouldn't have wished him dead, not in that manner especially. I could still hear him screaming sometimes.

"Fool," Kerrick said, echoing Mika, but softly. Like he meant something far worse. "I've heard tales—"

"About those?" I interrupted, jerking my thumb over my shoulder.

He nodded. "About what I think they are, from what you're saying. About where they came from, how they were made."

"Made?" The saliva in my mouth instantly dried.

"Created. If they are what's been rumored, then I fear for all of us. Have you ever heard of genetic manipulation?"

"Yes," Mika said. "My father is a doctor." He didn't speak those words with pride. I knew what his dad had done.

"Then imagine experiments in that regard going far beyond intended," Kerrick went on. "Bringing those creatures back to this planet is not going to end well, for anyone. Bringing them here for purposes of war is suicide."

I swallowed, hard, nearly choked. "Are they— were they once—like us?"

My recent nightmare reared up in my mind's eye. *We are all the same. We are all monsters.*

Kerrick met my gaze, held it. "In part, yes. They were spliced with the genetic pool of others, beasts that already existed. I don't know the particulars. Suffice it to say, the end results were more horrible than imagined."

Behind me, Joy-Li started to cry. Everyone else went dead silent. Kerrick turned, placed an arm around his son. He murmured to Kai in his native tongue. After, he explained.

"I told him I am glad he is with me."

I thought that odd, until I realized why. Here, Kerrick could at least protect his son, or share their last moments together. Beyond All Dwellers and us, no one else possessed any knowledge about the horror coming their way. I pictured Kerrick's woman, mother, I presumed, to Kai. She wouldn't know. None would.

"Go now," I said to him. "You and Bris and Kai, go. Get the heck back to your village and prepare. We can handle this."

Ren opened his mouth, snapped it shut. He nodded, at me, at them.

"And pass on the warning to all you can, okay?" I added to Kerrick.

He grasped my wrist, avoiding the mangled fingers in the bandage on my hand, and shook it. "I will. Get word to me someday if you can. I would like to know of your success."

I threw my other arm around him and hugged him, fiercely. "Thank you," I said, rushing the words before my voice broke.

The three Kanon left, silent, disappearing into the dark pre-dawn hours. As one, we five turned to face the hated city. Off to the right, angry shouting continued. I thought I heard the sharp retort of impulse fire. To our benefit. With all the upheaval going on over there, we surely could find our way inside unmolested.

Yes, this I hoped as we made our way forward. I knew getting out would be the bigger problem. I tried not to think about it. That was always my way.

*Grace*

Chapter Twenty-Four

An arm supported me, dragged me forward. My heart hammered as if I'd been running. I supposed I had been, my body had been, and my mind was just now catching up. I glanced aside at spiked red hair, pale, silver-gray eyes, set close together, so familiar.

"Hannah," I gasped.

"That's me."

"Where's your father?"

"So, you know?"

"You look very much alike," I said, pulling myself upright, away. "He said he was looking for his daughter."

She released me, looked back over her shoulder. "He's herding the rest along. Most didn't come, Grace. They were scared."

"Of me."

"Well, yeah."

I grimaced. "Where will they go?"

"They'll try to make it back to their families, I guess."

Abruptly, I looked around, relieved to find

Carina and Resa close behind me. A bit further back, mere shadows beneath the dark, clouded sky, Symick followed with his arms spread like he was shooing a flock of egg-laying hens up the hillside. Too few. I saw several carried blankets with them, but nothing else. We were going to be in dire straits for food and water before long.

Far below, the city rose up within its forested boundaries. I scanned the lightless pathways coming out from it. They appeared to be empty. No warriors had yet exited the city in pursuit. I told myself they were afraid, but I knew better. They were probably marshalling a force big enough to assure anything we did wouldn't matter. They couldn't let us walk away. Not after what they'd witnessed. They'd received a full, unplanned demonstration of a power that made me breathless in memory.

"Wait," I said, realizing we'd passed the paddock. "I have to go back."

"Chauncy isn't there," Carina said.

I stopped, visualizing the Hall as Nimue had described it, heads mounted like trophies on the wall. My lips quivered, grieving over an animal when we'd lost so much more. Yet, precisely because we'd lost so much more. I'd thought he at least… Well, I don't know what I thought.

"Grace," said Carina, "it looked like he escaped the field. The gate was bashed to pieces. Don't you remember saying that?"

I shoved fingers through my cropped hair. "No," I said, "I don't."

Hannah and Carina exchanged a look, as if

they'd dealt with this absence of recall in me more than once in the brief distance we'd been running. I spun on my heel.

"Let's keep going. We need to get under cover."

"That's the plan," said Hannah. "Already discussed."

I swore and Hannah grinned.

"Welcome back, Grace," she said.

Snorting, I turned and caught hands belonging to two younger Wildron in my own. Hannah did the same. Together with Carina and Resa, Symick shepherding the rest to our rear, we ran toward the thick woods ahead.

Once inside, everyone halted for a brief rest. I noted the looks sent my way, the distance kept between me and the other escapees. "Will someone tell them they don't have to worry?" I snapped, not really caring who I addressed. I sat on the ground, put my head in my hands for a moment, squeezing my eyes shut against the lingering pain.

"Where is he now?" Carina asked, kneeling beside me.

I probed around inside my mind, into the crystal, calling his name. Nothing. I was about to say as much when I felt a stirring, a sulky, angered presence.

"He's in there," I said. "In the crystal."

"And it is Skelly, isn't it?"

"Yes. Whatever he's become."

"How?"

"I don't really know. It happened back at Tiran's compound. You knew he followed me from the planet, didn't you?" In another tone, the question might have been accusatory, but all I could muster was a weak whine.

"I saw something," she said. "I only recently knew it was…whatever Skelly is now."

I turned my head against my palms wearily one more time before lifting it. "I thought you called him a portent."

"He is, and he isn't."

I let out a long, slow breath. "Okay," I said, unable to gather my thoughts enough to understand. I probably wouldn't have understood clear-headed. Carina would have to explain it to me at some point. Right now, it didn't matter. "Okay."

Resa stood behind Carina, head turned, her gaze on Symick. I couldn't read her expression. I seldom could. I wondered if she hated him for what he'd been putting her through. I suddenly thought not. In the shattering of the spherical debris field, he had remained unharmed. That had to be her doing.

Carina had been watching her too. She turned back to me. "There's something else you need to know."

I breathed, nodded, closed my eyes, opened them. "Go ahead."

"Ships landed while we were fleeing toward the hills. We don't know whose, but…"

I understood. Nimue had indicated he was on his way. "Then we need to get moving," I said.

"Where do we go from here?"

I shook my head from side to side until it slowed to a stop. "I don't know."

"To the mountains," Hannah said, having not

left my side.

"The mountains," I echoed. "Why? You need to tell us why."

"Not these," she said. "There's a range beyond."

"That doesn't answer my question."

"Hannah," said Symick, who'd come close enough to overhear, "it's too dangerous. I want you to return with me to my home. With your mother gone, you should be with me." Clearly, by his words, he did not mean to accompany us. Despite his help to get the others freed from their cells, that was fine by me. I didn't want him with us. I both trusted and didn't trust him and the clash in my head in that regard worried me.

"I don't run from danger," Hannah said to him, then looked at me. "Do I, Grace?"

"Not so far," I admitted.

"Hannah."

"Dad." I could tell by the word's form, the inflection, that it meant little to her. I supposed he'd been gone from her life for some time. Why and when he'd come to take her home, I couldn't imagine, nor for how long he'd been trying to convince her to leave with him. Having her thrown into a cell with the other mage-bloods had likely not helped him in his plans.

"When did you start working for the Lyoness?" I asked, interrupting their staring competition. Symick looked at me, his gaze troubled, perhaps sad.

"When she threatened Hannah. Completing the job was supposed to be the guarantee I could take her away. I didn't want to perform the testing," he said. "Not on any of them. It's what I was trained in, though. I tried to do it gently."

I nodded. I knew he had. I could tell when he returned with all the pictures his intent had been to act without harm. But he'd persisted. Why hadn't he just taken advantage of his cell access to escape with her at the first opportunity? Perhaps this had been the first opportunity. I couldn't judge him. Planning didn't always work. Sometimes, one had to rely on luck, on a chance occurrence.

"Besides," he said to Hannah, as if he'd been continuing his conversation with her in his head, "you don't know this place exists. Nobody does."

Huh. The last statement struck me as a falsehood. At this point, having disturbingly uttered so many of my own, I knew how to recognize one.

"Legend says it's there and I believe it. I told you that. And," she added, her brows now lowering into a scowl, "you've seen what they can do, Grace and Carina and…"

"Resa," I prompted.

"Resa, yes. It's where they're meant to be."

I looked at the ground between my boots. No, where I was meant to be was sitting around the table with my parents, my brothers, discussing the day's news during the evening meal. Spending cool desert evenings beneath the stars. Helping my mother get the garden weeds under control. Walking out with Mara to visit friends. Maybe teaching the young ones their first steps in concentration. Yet even as I thought it, I pictured Duncan's face instead, and Mika's. I bit my lip. Loss spiraled through my soul.

"Heading anywhere away from here is good enough, for now," I said, rising. "We can't delay."

Getting them all up off the ground didn't prove an easy task. Everyone suffered the debilitating effects of incarceration without exercise or proper nutrition and they'd just run a long distance. Some of those who'd been confined were quite young. Looking at them, my hands clenched into fists at my sides. Did their families not know what had become of them? Or had they opted for caution, to avoid being taken in for their own gifts, biding, I could only hope, for the proper moment to rescue their children? I didn't understand it. I couldn't understand it.

My thoughts shifted to the latter possibility. If these detainees had families to return to, what right did I have to take them away?

"I don't know what to do." I didn't realize I'd spoken aloud until I noted both Carina and Hannah turning my way.

"About what?" Carina asked.

"Them," I said. "They probably have families they should return to."

"Let's ask," Hannah announced, like we were all sitting in a park somewhere and she wanted to find out who was up for a game of *stropi*. She clapped lightly for attention. "Who's not from the city? Raise your hand."

Many more than half did so, hard to glean in the dark. One by one, Hannah asked them where'd they been taken from, what village. Only three were named, one of which happened to be the settlement we'd passed through on our way to the City of All

Dwellers.

"Do you still have family there?" I asked. All but two said yes.

"Did they know where you'd gone? Do they want you back?" Hannah again. All but those same two answered in the affirmative. But even those without families or who were from the city itself, looked longingly at their neighbors, announcing that they were known to each other. A tall boy, whose age I could not determine, stood.

"I'll take them," he said. "We can go to my home and from there, get them all back where they belong."

I stared at him. He reminded me of Duncan a bit, with his unkempt dark hair, his gangly appearance, not yet grown into his height. Adorable, sure, yeah. Brave. Breaking my heart. "Are you certain?"

"They're really after you now, aren't they? And you're going into the mountains. I heard her say," he said, jerking his chin at Hannah. "This lot won't survive that. Chelain is not far. I know ways that will keep us from sight. We should be there by sunrise."

My lips twisted. I strode forward and hugged him. Awkwardly, maybe a little alarmed, he patted my back. Of course. He'd witnessed what I'd been for a time. I stepped away.

"There's a stream about an hour on," he said. "We'll drink and then carry some water with us." He yanked a deep cylinder from his pocket, the same we'd been given to drink from in the cells. "A few of us brought these. We'll work it out."

I wanted to hug him again, but I knew he wouldn't tolerate the demonstration. "Thank you," I said.

"No," he responded, "thank you."

They left immediately, all the remainder going with them. No one really wanted to escape into the unknown. I couldn't blame them. I hadn't mentioned nor offered any supplies from the pillowcase Carina had brought. Trying to think practically, I expected they would reach safety, sustenance, before too much longer. Whereas I didn't know when we'd attain either. I had to think about those still under my protection.

"Well, then," said Symick, after they'd gone. "Why didn't you go with them?"

I looked at him. "As he pointed out, we're the ones they want. Our path is not with theirs, anyway."

He nodded, contemplated the area where up until a few minutes ago they'd been standing. "Since Hannah is so insistent about accompanying you, I'll be going with you, too."

At his elbow, Hannah scowled, but I believe secretly she felt relieved, if not exactly pleased.

Me? I'd gotten used to relying on my friends. I didn't require the supervision or the help of an adult. Still, he could come in handy, as long as he didn't start questioning every decision we made.

With Hannah's assistance, we brushed away all evidence left behind by our short respite. The moment we'd finished, we gathered the little we'd brought with us and started heading higher into the forest. I hefted the pillowslip I now carried. We were five and had barely enough for three.

Using the strategy Duncan had always employed, I tried not to think about it. Whether he'd realized it or not, he'd acted a lot on instinct. He'd been good with instinct. He said I was, too. I hoped so, because I was trusting it to help us now. I had no real plan.

*   *   *

The more we walked, the more my mind cleared. With a clearer mind came increased trepidation. Stone Tiran was here, in The Wilds, in the City of All Dwellers. Even if his arrival had inadvertently saved us in terms of the Wildron's delay, it wouldn't be long before his troops scoured the area, and likely not alone. Nimue would have warriors out in force as well. They knew the land better, after all. I could only hope those who had separated from us would escape to safety and find their ways home.

No clear paths existed in the upper elevations. The terrain would abruptly become strewn with gigantic boulders, forcing us around or along narrow, rocky trails, and then would open up again. The trees up here had grown crooked from lifetime exposure to the winds. The air was so much colder than below, too. We all stood shivering whenever we halted for a short rest. And they were frequent. I doubted we could go much longer without food and some sleep. When we finally reached a vantage point over the valley below, we all paused to stare back down on the city.

"It looks…beautiful," Hannah said, sounding

surprised, disgusted.

It did, with its lights glimmering here and there like diamonds in the dark. Had their color been different, the scene would have resembled firemites flittering up from the foliage in our garden at home. To one side, however, many lights shone, blue strokes flashing in their midst.

"Is that where the ships landed?"

"I think so," she said.

"They look very far away. As long as we remain undercover, we might be able to take turns sleeping for a bit."

Symick moved to stand beside his daughter. "They could be pursuing us on foot."

"They could," I agreed, "and probably are, but when they come, it's not going to be a handful of soldiers. It'll be a whole squad. We'll hear them long before they get close."

He eyed me askance, grunted and shrugged. "We need to get out of this wind."

"Agreed. There should be at least one blanket in the pillowslip. We'll have to share somehow."

We made camp in the lee between two very large rocks. Gnarled and bent over the opening, trees blocked most of the wind. Carina had brought two blankets, a cylinder filled with water, some fruit, nuts, edible vegetation, bread going stale. A few sweets, too. I'd tasted one, back there in the chamber when they'd first been provided. Like Carina's birthday cake on the Emerald, I hadn't liked the taste much. Still, they'd be good for energy.

I took first watch. That had always been the

call of it. Me first, then Duncan, or sometimes with. Hannah volunteered to take second.

"All right," I said, but didn't plan on waking her. In order to move quickly, they all needed to be rested. I could manage.

Carina distributed equal portions of food between everyone, setting aside a smaller amount to be divided sometime tomorrow. She'd brought enough water that we could all take a few swallows from the container. Hopefully we'd find a clear stream soon for refills.

"You seem to be used to rationing," Symick said to me.

"We've been doing it since we escaped the prison," I answered. The Ogdonians had given us numerous supplies before we entered The Wilds which would have kept us for a while, but Nimue and her people took them."

"Under guise of helping," Hannah said, her voice heavy with sarcasm. "Relieving Grace and her companions of excess burden."

Symick scratched his forehead. "I see. We'll need more."

"I know," I said.

"And water."

"I know."

"And more blankets or—"

"I know," I said, finally losing my patience. "I'll be outside on watch. Everyone, get some rest."

I squirmed out from our small shelter and lowered myself, cross-legged, onto the ground. I'd been given one blanket, and Carina and Resa, Hannah and her father had agreed to jam together inside under the other. I wrapped the woven cover around my shoulders, settled my *lathesa* across my knees. With the one crystal missing, the balance was off, but I wouldn't remove the lone remainder. Wielded properly, the thing would still do its job.

Symick's head and shoulders, his left arm, appeared in the opening. "I'm sorry."

I glanced back, away. "Don't worry about it."

"I've offended you."

"No," I said, "I just..." I paused, counted carefully backward from five. "We've managed since we escaped the prison. We've had help, sometimes, but for the most part we've been on our own. I understand, given your age, you feel you should be the one in charge, but it's not going to work that way. Okay?"

I heard him draw a short breath through his nose. "Understood."

He disappeared back inside.

I listened to the small noises from within the shelter as everyone rearranged themselves for comfort. In time, the rustling, the whispered voices stopped, became silence and then the steady, repetitive exhalations of sleep. I kept listening, knowing which was Carina, which Resa. Once, I'd listened to Duncan and Mika in the same manner, assuring myself they were safe, nearby, defended.

I nearly wept at the memory. A desultory rain began to fall almost in response, pattering the dry ground but not reaching me through the interwoven conifer branches above my head. I gave in then, allowing the tears to fall in silence, my fist crammed into my mouth to keep any noise I might make from reaching the sleepers inside. My stomach cramped with weeping, my jaw ached, my heart split and raged, burned to ash, blew away. Hollowed out and empty, I sat on, keeping watching over the others in the night.

I missed Duncan. I missed him so very much.

Chapter Twenty-Five

"These corridors are impassable."

I had to agree with Ren, whether I wanted to or not. Some destructive force beyond imagining had brought down trees and walls, shattered glass, torn up metal and twisted it into unidentifiable shapes. I wondered briefly if Resa had a hand in this, but somehow, I didn't think she had. The damage seemed beyond her capabilities. These things weren't just thrown around, they'd been viciously transformed into ruin.

One benefit: whatever was taking place in the city beyond, no one could reach us here. The bad thing? We couldn't move further in our search. I swore.

"You know, that sounds so much better when Grace says it," Ren rumbled at my ear.

"Shut up."

Unwilling to admit defeat, Mika and I tried to shift the nearest debris. Distant shouting continued. I reckoned Nimue didn't want Tiran here either, especially with the captive creatures in the transport cells. It wouldn't surprise me if combat broke out over it. I could only hope. It would certainly keep that lot distracted. If they set those beasts loose, however, we were all finished.

"Hugo?"

I whipped around at the unknown voice. Dirty and bleeding from a cut on her scalp, a young Wildron knelt behind us, nearly lost in the shadows. We must have walked right past her. She stared up at Hugo with wide, surprised eyes. "Hugo?" she repeated. Suddenly, he rushed over to her, scooped her off the floor, started checking her head wound.

"Who is that?" I asked. "Anyone know?"

"His cousin," Ren answered for him, clearly bewildered.

"Let me have a look," said Mika, and abandoned the debris for a more immediate concern. I continued pushing at the broken metal, resisting the urge to shout out Grace and Carina's names. After a minute or two, Mika returned.

"It's just superficial. Hugo's leaving, taking her somewhere safe. We're leaving, too."

I straightened. "No, we're not," I growled.

"Duncan, they're not here, Carina, your sister, Grace. They've gone. That's what she said." He nodded toward Hugo and the girl. "Gone. Escaped. This mess?" He waved his hand. "It was them."

"What?" I exploded. "Resa?"

"I don't know. Sure. Likely. But they're not here. That's the point. And we shouldn't be either."

I didn't argue. We hurried back the way we'd come. Outside, I questioned Hugo's cousin further, but she didn't have much to add to the story she'd hastily told Mika and the others. All we knew in the end was that they'd escaped and taken many with them. Yeah, that would be Grace. Leave no one behind.

She wouldn't have left Skelly either, if she could have managed it. But by the time she got to me back there on Emerald, he was already dead.

I shuddered in memory, at the nearness again of the very beasts who had killed him.

Hugo removed his jacket, threw it around his young cousin's shoulders in protection against the chill rain beginning to fall. He looked at us and shook his head. "I can't stay with you," he said. "I'm going home, get my family, get away from here."

I nodded, wished him luck, wished, in a small part of me, we were going with him. Turning without another word, he strode away into the darkness with the girl. Joy-Li watched after him for all of five seconds before shirking her pack from her shoulders and shoving it at me. "He's carrying enough to keep us fed, if we're careful. You're all going to need what's in there more than we will." She hurried after him, all three soon disappearing into the rain-driven gloom.

I turned to face Ren, tipped my head in the direction they'd gone. "Well? Aren't you going, too?"

His lips twisted. He held my gaze for an uncomfortably long moment before turning his head toward the hills. "No," he said, "I'm not. Which way do you think they've gone, your friends?"

"Anywhere but here," I said, not meaning to be flippant, but realizing it came off that way. "I don't know. Any ideas?"

"What about that place Joy-Li talked about? The Sleeping Myth place," Mika said. "Do you think they might have gotten wind of it and headed there?"

"Maybe," Ren said, his tone thoughtful. He raised a hand. "It's rumored to be in that direction somewhere."

I followed where he pointed, making out the black hills through the rain "How far?" I asked.

"On foot? Many days beyond the nearest ridge."

"That direction might not be right at all. We could easily miss them."

Ren shot me an impatient glare. "Yeah, we could, but like you said, I'm pretty sure they didn't stick around here. Higher ground would be their best bet."

"You're right," I admitted. "Okay. That way, then."

Behind us, the rainy sky bloomed in blue. With a loud crack, the energy field lights vanished.

"That can't be good," Mika said.

"No," I agreed, "it can't. Run."

*　　*　　*

Joy-Li's unwieldy pack in my arms, we lifted our knees and raced across the open plain. The ground had begun its rise into the foothills before we stopped for breath, turned, looked back. I set the extra pack on my feet to keep it off the damp ground, bent over my knees, sucked in air. The other two did likewise.

"I can see them," Ren said.

I jerked upright. "See what?"

"Sorry. The blue lights around the cages. They're back on."

I closed my eyes in gratitude. Hopefully nothing had escaped in the time they were off. I heard no screams carrying through the air, though. A good sign.

"Let's keep moving," I said. "I won't feel safe until we can't see the city anymore."

And not even then. I didn't say the last out loud. They didn't need to hear it.

We spent the next two hours climbing through the dull rain. We didn't call out for the girls. Not yet. Our voices would be heard below. We looked back toward the city often, until it became blocked by the trees, and then I started checking the sky for any sign the sun would be rising soon. I had no idea what time it was.

The higher we climbed, the chillier the air. Fortunately, we were dressed warmly in the clothes Kerrick had given us. I doubted the girls possessed anything but the loaner garb provided by Nimue. I'd often wondered why she'd done that. The whole can't-eat-dinner-with-the-Lyoness in our dirty condition hadn't really rung true then. I mistrusted it even more now. We'd been dressed for travel. Perhaps, she wanted to assure exactly what had happened in the event we escaped. A promise we'd suffer from exposure to the elements.

I almost wished a caged creature would reach through the bars and drag her inside. Almost, because I couldn't really bring myself to wish that agony on anyone.

We reached a point in our ascent where cliffs and gigantic boulders forced us to seek other paths up to the peak. I scanned the ground while we went, hoping to spot some sign the girls had passed the same way. Pointless, really. In the dark and the wet I could have been treading in my own sister's footsteps and I wouldn't have been aware.

Mika stopped, swiveled his head from side to side. "Do you hear that?"

"Ren's grunting, you mean?"

"Ha, ha." Ren passed me, slamming my shoulder with his as he went. He halted beside Mika, listened. "Yeah, I do. What is that?"

I hustled over, clamping my arms around Joy-Li's pack to stop the items jostling about inside. I listened, too, holding my breath. "Something big," I whispered. Slowly, I settled Joy-Li's pack on the ground, opened it, rummaged inside for the glass-cutting tool. We all carried our makeshift knife blades, but they required a certain skill and an assurance a body getting close enough to a thing to use them wouldn't mean you were going down first. Seeing what I was doing, Mika and Ren followed suit, removing the lasers, yanking their packs back in place. No reason to risk leaving them behind.

Even though we tried to be quiet, we couldn't help the noise we made. Whatever followed us must have heard, because the steady steps ceased, as though suddenly cautious. I thought I heard heavy breathing, but it might have been me. Or Ren, standing at my elbow.

"Do you think that's water dripping, echoing

off the rocks?" Ren suggested in a whisper.

"I don't think so," I said. I looked to Mika. "Those creatures hunt in packs. This sounds like only one."

"Maybe only one escaped the cages when the shields went down," Ren said.

Not helping, pretty-boy. One could be quite as deadly as a dozen.

We moved on, stepping carefully, ears pricked for the sound coming up from below us. Other beasts existed in the wooded Wilds, yeah. We all knew that. But the proximity of the cages, the temporary power loss, all added up to one beast in my head. A skilled shadow hunter with a canny, deadly telepathy and a means to kill that I had no desire to witness again.

I began to sweat. Not due to exertion. That's a different kind. This stunk like fear. I could smell it, even in the rain. Smelled it from Mika and Ren as well, through our clothes. Fear. Surely the thing tracking us could smell it, too.

"I can still hear it," Mika hissed through his teeth.

"We should run," Ren said, and bunched himself together as if ready to do just that. I grabbed his sleeve.

"Let's find a spot we can defend. Or at least see what's after us, before we start running."

Wordlessly we agreed. To my relief. All I needed was to lose Ren in a fall down the hillside. It was dark, the ground was slick, and he hadn't proved himself the most sure-footed among us. We started looking right away for higher ground among the rocks, a vantage point for a better view, where we could see the thing making its way closer. Managing to clamber up a pile of tumbled boulders, we stood a moment on top surveying the narrow trail below.

"Gods, you two stink," Ren griped.

"We all do," I said.

"Duncan," Mika whispered, "did those creatures have a smell? Do you recall?"

I tried to remember. It seemed to me they had. Something foul and unsettling. Something like what we all smelled right now.

I whipped around, scanned the trees above, reached back and pushed the hair down on my nape before returning my gaze to the rocky trail beneath. Jumpy. We were all jumpy. Soon enough, we would know what hunted us. If it was really only one creature, I hoped the mind hack would be limited, that we could fight it. Grace had managed to resist a pack, battled them, won. I had to hold onto that. We could do it, too.

In barely two minutes the beast showed itself, a lumbering shadow reflecting no light from the overcast sky above. I couldn't yet see its gruesome, humanoid face. I didn't want to, didn't need to, because it remained all too clear in my memory. I wouldn't let it get me, wouldn't let it get my friends. Gods, had I just included Ren in that statement? Flicking on the laser cutter, I opened my mouth in a silent cry and leaped from stone to stone down the rockfall, determined to destroy it before it did us.

*Grace*

Chapter Twenty-Six

Hannah woke up on her own, crawled outside and sat beside me. She scratched her head, ruffling her already disheveled hair, and looked around.

"It's stopped raining."

I nodded at her, yawned, straightened my legs and stretched my arms out until I touched the tips of my boots with my fingertips. My back cracked, like an old warrior. Old before my time.

Hannah laughed a little at the sound, shook her head at me. "You should go inside and get some sleep."

"I'll close my eyes out here," I said. "We can share the blanket."

She hadn't yet asked where Duncan and Mika were, nor Ren and her other two friends. It wasn't up to me to tell her they were dead. I couldn't have anyway. I didn't want to talk about it. After last night, I was holding tight to the emptiness. I refused to do anything to risk it.

I supposed she knew, after a fashion. Not the way Carina knew things, but the way Hannah would be able to figure things out, considering she'd been living beneath the Lyoness' cruel leadership for who knew how long. The fact I'd said nothing about any of them likely provided its own clue.

She grabbed the blanket from my shoulders, slid closer, wrapped it around us both. "It's quiet out here. My dad snores."

"Yes," I said, "I heard him. Probably the reason small animals are staying far away."

She giggled. The sound made my lips curve, pushing up the chilled flesh around them.

"The sky's clearing."

"A bit," I said, without looking.

"Are you okay?"

I didn't answer. Not even to lie.

"It's weird," she said after a few minutes. "I don't really know my dad. Not well. Him wanting to protect me is…I don't know. Never had that before. I mean, my mom was okay at it until…until she wasn't. She joined the Lyoness' warriors. Before that, she made blankets and things. She liked working with textiles. Tried to teach me. I sucked at it."

I made a sympathetic noise. "I've always been a warrior, even before I started my official training. It was my destiny, my gift. I haven't known anything else."

"Do you have a mom and dad?"

"Yes," I said, "and three brothers."

"There's just me."

"I'm sorry."

"It's all right. I enjoyed being the only one for a while."

We sat in silence again. I started to hear birdsong, lower down the mountainside. To me, that meant morning was not far off. We would see it here first, being higher up, and yet despite the gradually clearing sky the world remained filled with shadow, the sun still absent.

"I wish I knew what time it is," I muttered.

"Time for you to get some sleep," Hannah answered.

I nodded, leaned my head back against the stone behind me, lowered my lids. "Not for long," I said. "We need to get moving again."

I don't know if I slept. It's possible I did. A dreamless slumber, a sleep marked by exhaustion. It ended as if I hadn't, though, when something fell across me, a smothering weight on my face. I flailed out, reached for my *lathesa*, found it gone. I leaped to my feet, spinning blindly, weaponless. The blanket tumbled from my head to the ground.

Hannah stood before me, facing the valley below. I saw her silhouette, my *lathesa* held by her in two hands, the length of it along her side, roughly parallel to the ground, like a jabbing spear. Stepping forward, I reached out, took the weapon from her.

"What do you see?" I whispered.

"Nothing. I can't see anything. But I hear it. Them." Hannah raised her hand. A small flicker appeared above her cupped palm. Quickly, I covered it with my own.

"Don't do that. You'll give away our exact position. Go wake the others. But keep them quiet."

Standing facing the dark, I spun the *lathesa* slowly, getting a feel for its canted weight. Below, in the shadows, deeper shadows moved. A fizzing chill worked its way up my spine. I glanced to the crystal gracing the weapon's tip, expecting to find it glowing and surprised when I did not. I shouldn't have been surprised, though. We'd left those beasts behind on the Emerald. Yet, still oddly relieved, I continued observing the slow, careful progress. I couldn't make out shapes, only movement. Animals? I waited, listening to the quiet noises in the shelter as the others awakened, shifted about. I heard only a mumbled word or two, barely audible. Down below, the shadows made their way up the incline, getting closer.

Abruptly, like a flaring blue flame in the blackness, the *lathesa's* crystal point began to gleam.

I swore as confusion started to take me. A voice, Duncan's remembered voice, spiraled through my head. I fought it, the muddling mind, spun my weapon, the blue glow whirling, my thoughts following it, the heaviness of heart, the doubt, threatening to pull me down. I tried to remember battling to save Duncan, the determination, the focus, but he was gone now, gone, and I didn't care anymore…

Something slammed into me, knocking me to the ground. Skelly, poor Skelly, remembering his own demise began to scream. My throat felt raw with it even though I was silent, fighting, fighting now for my life. Because the others, the others needed me. I couldn't forget them. I mustn't forget them.

The ground beneath my head vibrated. Out of

nowhere, a hand latched onto my arm, yanking me sideways. Human fingers, narrow, not clawed. A scream followed. Still not mine. Something otherworldly, terrifying, and cut short. I jerked away from whoever held me back, the *lathesa* whistling, the crystal shard lightless now, my mind suddenly clear. Clear enough to see what lay before me.

I stepped forward, looked down. Motionless, a beast from the Emerald. Here on Talia? How? Dead, though, and not by my hand. While I stood there, gaping, gasping for returning breath, a long, corkscrew horn withdrew from the beast's chest, a huge head lifted, a white-ringed eye turned my way. With a cry, I threw myself at Chauncy, burying my arms, my face into his stinking fur.

"What about us? Don't we deserve a little of that?"

I froze. My mind reeled once more, this time from shock. Releasing my grip on the *conjure*, I swung slowly around. In an instant I found myself wrapped around Duncan, around Mika, reaching out for Ren. I couldn't stop crying. Again, with the crying. My stunned, re-formed, dust-particle heart burst anew, this time from the joy it couldn't contain.

I stepped back, patted all three down, making sure they weren't a wicked deception. A body rushed past mine, threw itself into Mika's arms, right up off the ground. Tears ran freely. Could I not stop? Could none of us stop? Even Ren received an affectionate greeting from Hannah. Her father watched at a short distance. I could see the questions in his face.

With an arm wrapped around Resa, Duncan came back over to me. He slipped his hand around mine.

"We were told you died," I said, voice cracking. More tears. I wanted to kick myself.

"I'm sorry. We almost did but, you know, we don't go down easily."

I laughed, actually laughed. I wiped my eyes, my nose with my fingers, my sleeve.

"I didn't think we'd find you," he said. "At least, I thought the chances were slim."

I pushed my hand down along my thigh to dry it, realized it was empty. My *lathesa*. Where had I left it? I looked around, spotted it on the ground. I let it lie. For now. "How did you find us, then?"

He dipped his head at Chauncy. "He came. Scared the crap out of us all. Started herding us along. I figured out what he was trying to do before we got skewered. I…I did almost stab him, though. I thought he was one of them." His chin swiveled toward the creature lying dead on the ground.

I tightened my grip on Duncan's fingers. "How did they get here, Duncan? How?"

He squeezed, let go, ruffled my short hair with a crooked smile. "Tiran brought them. Cages full of them. Did you know he was here?"

I nodded. "Nimue said he was on his way. And then the ships landed." I didn't explain to him I hadn't seen them. An explanation would have required a why.

"The cages are shielded. The power went down briefly. I don't know how many might have gotten out.”

"At least one,” I said.

"Yeah,” he agreed, “at least one. Good thing Chauncy was here.”

I grinned at the *conjure*, marveled anew at his integration, not just with me, but with our group. Breg would be disbelieving. I realized how much I'd give to see his face again, to tell him. It didn't seem likely. I had to accept the mounting losses.

We both turned at the same time, Duncan and I, looked down the hillside. Light grew, dawning over the far hills, not yet sunrise, not yet illuminating the valley of the City of All Dwellers in the distance.

"We have to go,” I said. "We can't stay here. Damnable man, bringing those creatures down from the Emerald. It's like unleashing disease on your enemies. It's not only them that are going to die.”

He let out a long breath. I felt it rumple my unkempt locks.

"Where are we going now, Grace? You, the witch, the thrice-gifted child." He spoke the last statement lightly, like he might be teasing, but I sensed the weight beneath all his words.

"Into the mountains,” I said. "A place Hannah talked about.”

"The Cavern of Sleeping Myth?” he asked. I frowned at him. "Joy-Li mentioned it. She's gone now. Not dead,” he added hastily at my expression. "She and Hugo are gathering up family and fleeing.”

Family. All our families needed us, and yet we couldn't go to them. Not yet.

"With a name like that? Has to be the place,” I

said.

"Who's the guy?"

I followed his frowning gaze to where Hannah and Symick stood. "Hannah's father."

"Really?"

I laughed again, at Duncan's tone this time. The sound seemed overloud in the morning air. Behind me, Chauncy made a rumbling noise in his chest.

"I think I need to talk with him," said Duncan. He took Resa with him and wandered over. I noticed a pack at my feet. The three of them, him, Mika and Ren, all possessed one on their backs. I made a face at the filled bag, shoved it with my boot.

"What do we do with that thing?"

I glanced up at Hannah, thinking she meant the pack, but I saw she grimaced at the beast lying dead in a growing pool of very black blood. I shrugged, feeling oddly indifferent.

"Shove it over the rocks?" she suggested.

I shook my head. "I don't even want to touch it."

"Where'd it come from?"

"The prison planet," I said. "There may be more."

She looked at me, the sunlight now touching her hair, turning it to flame. "And you're afraid of them."

"With good reason," I said, hearing an impatient note in my response. An apprehensive one, too.

"Then I suppose we all should be," she said,

"because you're not afraid of anything."

Together, Hannah and I covered the beast with branches in case any ships left the ground, searching. Not for the creature, of course, but for us. If they came across the beast dead, it might lead them to check the area more closely. I wanted to proceed undetected for as long as possible. I held half a hope they might give up then, if we weren't easily found. I knew better. We all knew better.

The fourth pack had belonged to Joy-Li. She'd parted with it for our sakes. I didn't anticipate getting the chance to thank her, so I sent the thought out into the world believing, somehow, it would find its way into her ear. We were all grateful for the warmer clothes. Even Hannah now had a set she slipped over her thin attire, since she and Joy-Li were close enough in size. We had more food now, too. Even so, we'd need additional supplies long before this journey ended.

Symick left, heading to the Perimeter. His quarrel with Hannah about leaving her with us had been short-lived and futile. His people needed him, though. Needed every capable man and woman. To flee or to fight, to keep the children safe. By strange—or maybe not so strange—coincidence, it had been Symick's brother who had helped Duncan and the others after Duncan and Mika led the escapees from the mine. I'd asked Symick upon his departure to extend to Kerrick my eternal gratitude, and I meant it. If I could ever help him, repay him, I would.

I stuck my hand in Duncan's again. Maybe for the tenth time since he and Mika and Ren had appeared. He kept saying everything would be all right. I didn't think he really felt that way. How could he? How could any of us? Standing beside him, watching Symick disappear over the ridge, Joy-Li's pack on his back with the supplies we could spare, felt final somehow. Like the next steps would change all of us.

I suspected it just might.

But we were together. That meant something.

Something? It meant everything.

Chapter Twenty-Seven

So, this is who we are now, is it? An intrepid band of morons and freaks. Off to see the world. Or at least that part of it they're hoping can save them. So selfish. So…them.

The yellow-haired idiot has come in handy, at least. He recognizes this white stuff falling from the sky. Calls it snow. And he's right. Unlike the rest of them, I've seen snow, too. I could be explaining it, though. I could be the one to state the obvious. But I'm in here. And she won't let me out. Not ever again, or so she keeps saying. To me, when she deigns to honor me with acknowledgment, and to that pale little oddity, Ka-reeeen-aaah. Otherwise, she's still keeping me secret. Not good, Grace. Don't you ever learn?

Sometimes I like Grace. I remember that from when I was alive. Sure, yes, alive, but what does that make me now? It makes me not-dead. I'm not sure what it means, but there's a difference. I know there is.

I do remember those moments, though. From before. Sometimes she shone, and I would think, yeah, I could be that if I wanted to. Turned my stomach, it did. Like a bad meal. Because I knew I only lied to myself. It wasn't that I couldn't be like that. It was that I didn't want to. Seeing her shine reminded me of another me. So long ago. A kid I hated. Weak. Afraid. I thought I'd grow out of it. And I did. But not the way I'd expected.

The part about liking her confuses me. I don't want it. Especially now. I'd been ready to kill her to keep from going back inside this place she's keeping me. She made me, though. Somehow, she made me. I think it might be the liking her that weakens me. The weak kid. The afraid kid. What I need is more hate. I could be stronger then.

Strong and unafraid.

I rub my hands together, ignoring the fact I don't really have them anymore.

Hating Grace will be so much better.

I'll work on it.

Until we meet again, cupcake.

Hopefully before the Darkness. Because, yeah, that's coming, too.

Other books by Jo Allen Ash

Book One in the Shadow Journey Series – *The Shadows We Make*

and
coming July 2023

Book Three in the Shadow Journey Series - *The Sleeping Myth*

Also coming soon:

Anna Avery: Automatons in the Attic
a magical, suspenseful adventure for the middle grade reader

For more about the author and her works, please visit:

https://www.joallenash.com

or:

https://facebook.com/JoAllenAsh